Penguin Books
Arigato

KT-452-727

Richard Condon was born in New York in 1915
and educated there. In 1938 he became a
professional publicist and has spent twenty-two
years working with the American and British
film industry. His first novel, *The Oldest
Confession* (a Penguin book), was published in
1957 and since then Richard Condon has been a
professional novelist. His publications include
The Manchurian Candidate, *The Vertical Smile*,
The Ecstasy Business, *Mile High*, *Any God Will
Do* and *A Talent for Loving* (all published by
Penguins). His books have been translated into
nineteen languages and five have been made
into films.

Since 1953 he has moved with his family and
their intrepid dachshund 'Pepper' to a new
country every two years and has lived in Paris,
Madrid, New York, Mexico City and Geneva,
where he now lives. Richard Condon is married
and has two daughters.

Arigato

Richard Condon

Penguin Books

Penguin Books Ltd, Harmondsworth,
Middlesex, England
Penguin Books Australia Ltd, Ringwood,
Victoria, Australia

First published by Weidenfeld & Nicolson 1972
Published in Penguin Books 1974

Made and printed in Great Britain by
Hunt Barnard Printing Ltd, Aylesbury, Bucks
Set in Monotype Plantin

For Margaret Stephens

I

The errand was out of his way and he was afraid he was running terribly late but he had the airport taxi take him to Asprey's to be able to bring along a small surprise for Bitsy. He was able to find an alligator glove case, a remarkable little contraption really, which could carry one dozen pairs of gloves or three pairs of ski mittens. He had almost chosen a stunning, green, portable backgammon set but he had realized its probable significance to Bitsy just in time and had pushed it away from himself on the display case.

The second taxi was difficult to get, then it drove through the maddening traffic which choked Bond Street, across Grafton Street then down Hay Hill to Berkeley Square, beating its way through and around the rigid steel boxes to Farm Street like a guerrilla moving across a swamp.

The Farm Street house was five storeys tall. It had a fat bow window at street level which displayed four bottles of wine which offered an attractive special from Cruse et Fils, Frères, Bordeaux, behind a gold-lettered legend which said:

HUNTINGTON
Fine Wines (London)

He paid the cab then stopped in the doorway to compose himself. His hand trembled badly as he tried to get the scrolled, engraved key Bitsy had given him into the lock. At last the door opened.

He went in through the deserted shop so he could reach his

office at the back of the building. His solicitor, A. Edward Masters, was waiting, seated, wearing a bowler hat and holding a most unseemly (under the circumstances) blond ostrich skin attaché case on his lap.

'Good evening, Captain,' Masters said, not rising.

'I take it to be a mark of special disrespect that you choose to greet me from a sitting position,' the Captain said, instantly chagrined that he could have uttered such terrified words.

'Sorry about that,' Masters said. 'My Achilles tendon. Quite painful.' In pain or otherwise, the Captain decided, Masters always had the pleased look of any member of that closed fraternity of Irish bookmakers; that band of forty-odd gleeful men who travelled like an excursion across Ireland, from race meeting to race meeting, boasting to each other of the grand day they had just had.

'Sorry I'm late,' the Captain said. 'Any news?'

'Only a greeting.'

'I must say they are most insensitive in the way they can deny a man access to his own living room,' the Captain replied. Wearing his own bowler hat, he sat down morosely behind his desk and faced the elegant office whose walls had been designed to hold a two-hundred-and-forty volume library of books about wine, all exquisitely rebound by Sangorski & Sutcliffe; at carefully placed objects such as a fighting bull sculpted from thirty-one yards of twisted brass wire and four magnums of wine which were much, much older than any sensible person should have ever allowed them to become, flabby wine for the sort of people who would drink it only from between the lines of a newspaper someday, he thought.

'Did they all arrive?'

'I really don't know. I was greeted by your wife through the intercom at the front door and told to sit in here.'

'You know – ' the Captain said with some exasperation, 'considering all that one would assume that they had to do and the distances they have travelled for this – well!' He shrugged nervously.

The telephone rang. The Captain picked it up at once and listened intently. 'Thank you,' he said into it. He stood up and lifted the remembrance from Asprey's from the glistening desk.

Mr Masters got to his feet clutching a heavy, malacca wood cane which had a rubber tip like a tiny elephant's foot. The Captain led the way. They crossed the large, square room to a staircase where they hung their bowler hats on the sterling silver clothes tree which the officers of the squadron had given to the Captain when he had retired as the youngest Captain in the Royal Navy.

Captain Huntington insisted on helping Masters up the stairs which made the way uncomfortable for both of them because it was a fairly narrow way. When they were five steps from the top he went onward and upward alone because it was a theatrical sort of stairway which pulled the climber up quite a steep rake and in profile to those waiting in the enormous salon. As he climbed he felt like Essex coming up from the dungeons to see Elizabeth for the last time, which made him feel so rotten that he had to mock the thought by pretending he was Errol Flynn climbing the stairs for the sixth 'take' as it was called to see some actress for the last time and, amazingly, that helped.

They were all there. It was absolutely not to be believed but they were all there.

'Good evening, Colin,' Bitsy said gravely.

'Good evening, Bitsy.' He bowed. He turned to face a florid, white haired man who was as tall and as slender as himself but the oldest man in the room. 'Good evening, sir,' the Captain said. He could not call this man Daddy and yet he could not believe his first (or for that matter, second) name existed when he read it two and three times a week in *The Times*, because Bitsy said Daddy, six times a day.

Daddy was joviality itself, but in the manner that good surgeons are jocular with the patient before they introduce the anaesthetist. 'I must say you are looking fit, Colin,' Daddy said with his reedlike voice which had layers and layers of the most occluded sort of Massachusetts accent, pumping Colin's hand with a grip which suggested too much knowledge of judo.

'Good evening, sir,' the Captain said. Then, disengaging his hand from the vice, turned to the first uncle in line.

'Good evening, Jim,' he said, moving along shaking hands. Uncle Jim (who was to the White House what Daddy was to the executive suite of the CIA) would surely be the anaesthetist because Uncle Jim was not smiling and, professionally, Uncle Jim was a smiler. They smiled in the White House or they got out, Bitsy had told him. It was one of the strictest of the Attorney-General's rules.

The Captain shook hands with Uncle Pete who was the bridge between the American military establishment and the producers of all the amazing new weapons systems and other reassurances of additional defense spending such as the anti-ballistic missile, the Moon Shot program, the Main battle tank, the Navy's F–14 jet aircraft program, the Navy's submarine program and the entire Defense Department research and development program. Uncle Pete also headed 'operation Wide-Eyes', a civilian organization made up of suppliers to the Pentagon, in which he was assisted by two former chairmen of the Joint Chiefs of Staff. Uncle Pete was a bluff, hearty, lovable kind of man who was famous (in Washington) for his quote, 'You *can* fool all the people all the time.'

When he shook hands with Bitsy's cousins, Harry and Larry, who were Undersecretaries of Defense and Treasury respectively, they were charming. For a moment, the Captain thought that perhaps this meeting was not what he had imagined was going to happen because Uncle Pete and Bitsy's cousins were absolutely agreeable.

10

Bitsy was a handsome dark woman whose perpetual expression was puzzlement. She sat on a large sofa between Daddy and Uncle Jim. She wore a sea-green dress. The sofa had a linen loose cover which had a bold yellow and blue Jacobean pattern which rather thrust the three of them at the Captain. The room itself was large enough to be able to wear Italian furniture which is built larger than any other. The effect of the huge, bold sofa and the enormous wing chairs which had been arranged to flank the sofa, was to make quite large people appear normal-sized, even small when seated, and to make normal-sized people to appear on the tiny side.

Bitsy was a quite large woman; a quite large, very beautiful woman with large intelligent grey eyes and a foaming, deep bosom which tapered down into a slim waist. She had a sweet, thoroughbred filly's behind and thrilling long legs. She wore many diamonds quietly; an inherited knack. Her shoes had special glamour. Her hair, so deeply blue black, rested upon her with ineffable perfection and had not the Captain been beside himself with dread he would have noticed how long and how carefully his wife had prepared her attractiveness for the meeting.

When he had met her, nine years before, she was just out of her teens and had tried to deprecate her height and size by affecting a dismaying, slouched posture which her parents had done nothing to correct. Improving that posture had been chosen by the Captain to be one of his first duties to her. Now, seated on soft cushions, her posture was almost the equal of the Captain's.

Bitsy's puzzled eyes had watched him intently as he ascended the stairs but, as he turned to face her, she dropped a veil of indifference across them. This was the fourth time in two weeks she had called this meeting, only to cancel it, herself, three times. If Daddy had not insisted, if Uncle Jim had not been so uncharacteristically stern, if all the men in her wonderful family had not rearranged the complexities of two days in their incredibly busy lives she might be putting the meeting off still.

She had refused to see Colin alone for five weeks and had changed all the exterior locks at Rossenarra, in the country, because she could not bear to let him set foot there again. She felt such pain and such shame. She had believed that love could never be extinguished but she had had no idea that a man of his breeding could have brought himself to behave this way about money. She had loved him more each day for year after year after year, and she still loved him more each day, but he must have always been secretly anti-American or something to have turned on all of them, his dearest friends, as he had and to strike at her so savagely at the one place which he *knew* was the most inviolate part of what these wonderful men around her, and herself, of course, had always shown that they had believed in most. The pain and the shame had outweighed the love. She had to do what she was going to do or give up her self-respect. If she were to relinquish that, then everything except Colin would go; when all that was all gone, he would go too. She had to act. She had to force herself to act.

'Please sit down, Colin,' she said. 'We haven't bothered with the mockery of tea.' Everyone had carefully ignored A. Edward Masters in the sense that he was an enemy mercenary. Bitsy was embarrassed that she had done such a thing to an old friend but rules were rules. Masters started at Daddy's end of the line and introduced himself with courtly ease all along the way. 'How do you do,' he said. 'I am Edward Masters, Captain Huntington's solicitor.' They all shook hands with him briskly. Uncle Jim managed a frosty smile which frightened the Captain considerably.

Daddy said, 'Good evening, Edward.' Daddy knew everybody.

The Captain extended the Asprey package to Bitsy.

'What is it?' Bitsy asked, not moving to accept it.

'A small remembrance.'

'Isn't it from Asprey's?'

'Yes.'

'Did you charge it?'

'Why – yes.'

'Then I would have to pay for it. Take it back to them, please, Colin.' The Captain sat down abruptly and put the package on the floor beside him.

'Now,' Daddy said.

'Allow me, Vincent,' Uncle Jim said. He turned to the Captain, changing his light, amber-framed bi-focals slowly for a pair of light, amber-framed close-up glasses. 'I think you know how we work, Colin,' he said.

'Indeed, yes.'

'I think you will agree that we are a unit – all for one, one for all.'

'Precisely, Jim.'

'Will you tell your lawyer that we did our best, from our hearts, no-holds-barred, to make you an integral member of that unit during the past nine years?'

'A member surely, Jim. But not integral. I wouldn't say integral.'

'You wouldn't say integral?' Bitsy asked shrilly.

'Factually, darling, I shouldn't have wanted to be integral, if you see what I mean. You have your investment pools and your special information and at no time did I feel that, not being a blood relation as it were, I should have become integral.'

'We were not talking about that kind of integral,' Bitsy said sharply. 'Uncle Jim didn't mean that and you know it.'

'I'm frightfully sorry,' the Captain said.

'Jim, lemme say this,' Uncle Pete said. Pete was the only member of the family who switched diction at will and he had been spending a lot of time in Texas and Seattle – and even more with the Rolls Royce teams, so he spoke with a sort of southwestern, northwestern, City of London drawl which was very appealing. No one knew that he had been studying the voice of the late Gary Cooper who had come from Montana after being educated in British public schools. 'I reckon Colin and I have been good friends so I'd like to be the one to break the bad news.'

'The bad news?'

'Yep, deah boy, it is presently my jooty to tell y'all that our Bitsy has decided she wants a dee-vorce.'

'No! It is out of the question,' the Captain said, his voice rising, in a flat break, one full octave.

'I want a divorce,' Bitsy said, 'and I want you to sign over to me this building, one-half of the wine company, and the house at Rossenarra.' She ticked off the items by tapping the ends of her beautiful fingers so bright with diamonds. She no longer seemed to be a large woman, in charge, but smaller and helpless.

'Bitsy, darling. Of course. Please. Anything. You can have anything but a divorce.'

She began to sob gently.

'Each of you has always been so proud that there has never been a divorce in your family. Bitsy, darling, what will Cardinal Hanly say?'

'What has that got to do with anything? We have never had a rotten-sick compulsive gambler in our family either.'

'It isn't as bad as that.'

'We actually, factually believe it is as bad as that, Colin,' Uncle Jim said grimly.

The Captain ignored Uncle Jim and talked softly to Bitsy. 'You don't mean it, darling. You can't mean you want a divorce.'

'More than anything else I must have a divorce!' She glared at him. 'I finally took myself and shook myself and made

14

myself see that something has to be done or you will gamble away everything I own.'

Cousin Larry shuddered delicately. Daddy looked very bleak. Cousin Harry, a physical fitness nut, seemed to be deciding to punch Colin on the nose.

'Let me reason with Colin,' Uncle Jim said soothingly to Bitsy. 'As you know because we've never made it a secret in any way, shape, or form, we are fed a series of reports on you, Colin, because we have felt it to be necessary for your own protection. We have never complained, for example, about your keeping a mistress. That was your own business and even Bitsy acknowledges that all work and no play makes Jack dull. We have, and we have openly shown that we have, taken much pride in your development of your wonderful cook, Juan Francohogar, to internationally seeded rank and it has helped your wine business no end, so we have never considered your personal chef an extravagance. Have we ever complained to you about your gambling? Never. You know gosh darned right well we have never complained about your gambling. But this is different. I mean, Bitsy has complained about your gambling. The reports show that Bitsy's check stubs show that you have thrown away over two hundred thousand pounds of her money on the gambling tables and we say that is shocking, Colin. Not your own money – your wife's money.'

'Still,' Colin said stoutly, 'hardly all of my wife's money.'

'I didn't say that, Colin.'

'In fact, not even a fraction of my wife's money.'

'You just try investing in straight E treasury bonds,' Larry said, 'and see how much of a lump sum you'll need to earn two hundred thousand pounds plus.'

Bitsy's eyes were closed. She was trying not to remember when they had found him in the basement of the Central Hotel in Macao where he was a shrieking part of a mob of eighty or ninety Chinese coolies who were shouting around games of fan-tan, games where he was betting for pennies against the pennies of coolies while wearing the uniform of a captain in Her Majesty's Navy after he had lost twenty-seven thousand pounds in the elegant, wood-panelled hushly-carpeted gambling rooms of the same Central Hotel, just three floors above. She opened her eyes. 'I will not go on this way.'

The Captain was perspiring lightly because he was appalled to remember that he had a very important appointment in just about a half hour yet if he looked at his watch to check that it would arouse Harry into some sort of physical violence. 'If I could say it and make it mean anything,' he said quietly, 'I would swear to you that I would never gamble again. But I cannot say that. But I do swear to you that I will never again gamble with your money.'

'But you will gamble, dear boy,' Uncle Pete said.

'Yes,' Uncle Jim said nastily, drawling it out. 'Therefore there will be gambling debts to be paid. The most elegant sort of threats will be passed until the debts are paid or Bitsy will be disgraced again.'

'When Bitsy is hurt, we are all hurt the same way,' Harry snarled.

The Captain was appalled that they should reject his offer, the first voluntary pledge he had made in the nine years of their marriage. It was as though what he had said had no meaning whatever. He ignored the men and concentrated directly on Bitsy. He had to get this thing disposed of or the meeting adjourned so that he could get out of here and be waiting where he was expected to be waiting in about a half hour. Somehow he stole a look at the grandfather clock by pretending to look across to Masters in dismay. He had exactly twenty-six minutes.

'Haven't I done whatever I said I would do when you needed me to do it?' he asked Bitsy sharply, trying a bit of mastery. Then he made a gross error. 'Didn't I leave the navy and go into the wine trade because you wanted it that way?'

16

Daddy stared at him with unconcealed contempt for the first time in their long and pleasant relationship. Harry gagged on a sob. Bitsy just stared at her husband while Uncle Jim cleared his throat with a noise like a snow shovel moving across a city pavement. 'You left the navy, Colin,' Uncle Jim said, 'because you are a compulsive gambler. Your gambling had become such an obsession that you were found to be a command risk and a security risk and not even our connections, not even Harry's intimate relationship with the Joint Chiefs and theirs with the Admiralty was able to save you from yourself.'

'You know why you are in the wine trade now, don't you, Colin?' Bitsy asked.

The Captain stood up as though the tea time chat had become a courts martial. 'At no time was I ever considered a security risk,' he said with a shaking voice. 'I may have been classified as a command risk for carriers, yes. But nothing such as your insinuations was in any way specified in my entirely honourable discharge.'

'We were able to do that much for Bitsy, buster,' Harry snarled. 'We were able to get the Joint Chiefs to lean hard enough to get you an honourable discharge.'

'My dear fellow,' the Captain drawled, 'how would you like to have your arse booted right out of my house?' Harry started out of the chair but Uncle Pete's heavy hand held him firmly where he was.

The Captain concentrated on utter control, to keep his emotions from flying off in all directions. He refused to think about what these extremely vulgar people had just said to him and concentrated on examining, for the first time since they all had met, the undeniable fact that they were extremely vulgar people. 'I think, perhaps,' he said calmly, 'that anything beyond the facts which are a matter of Royal Naval records should be regarded as hearsay.'

'What does it matter who did what? You had to resign your commission because of your gambling. That is that,' Bitsy said.

The Captain's eyes looked like a shattered windscreen. Memories of his cherished command, the greatest years, the highest moments of his life, poured over him like caustic. He had been born for everything he was privileged to do each day of his life as part of the squadron, in command of the *Henty*. Now Bitsy had spoken what they had agreed never to recognize. He stared beyond Bitsy and her militant family. He was sitting in his gig being taken from the *Henty* to the flagship for the last meeting with the Admiral before he would be called before the board. He sat in the sunny cabin wearing his white tropicals with all his decorations pinned on his chest. Admiral Sir Francis Heller stared at him sadly for an eternity from behind the mask of his white beard. He said, at last: 'They don't understand your sickness, Colin; that is not their job so they don't wish to. But they are Englishmen who have had a navy for five hundred years and, in the course of that time, they learned certain things about their commanders. They learned that when a man must gamble – when a man, however excellent in every other single way, can no more stop gambling than he can stop breathing – it must follow that he is a terrible risk. He cannot win most of the time. When he loses, because he cannot stop, he loses more. Then – nothing is left. He has to have money to gamble and – out of somewhere – strangers appear and are friendly. They offer money. When he can't pay it back they ask for certain information or say that they will turn the fellow in. Is that what happened to you?'

'Yes, sir,' Colin answered smartly.

'Well, they have turned you in. And the Board won't have it because it has happened before in a navy which is five hundred years old. Or if the fellow is rich – or his wife is rich he broods. He can no longer concentrate on his duties to ship and men and, in due time, the ship has an accident. Is that how it happened to you, Colin?'

'Yes, sir.'

'You are finished in the navy, my boy.'

The Captain looked at Bitsy again. He strolled to the long table and made himself a drink. 'Whiskey, anyone?' he asked. No one answered until Masters said. 'Yes, thank you Colin.' As Colin came back with the glasses in hand Bitsy said, 'Now do you remember that, because there was no other single way to save you – Daddy put you into the wine trade?'

'Bitsy, that is preposterous. That is simply pure twit thinking. Your father – and you I might add – made a very, very good thing out of my knowledge of the wine trade and let us not allow any of us here in this Star Chamber to forget that.'

'It did keep you going, Colin,' Uncle Pete said reproachfully. 'It paid for your mistress and your personal, private world-famous chef.'

'Balls,' the Captain said. 'You have so much money invested in business and industry on the special information which your lives permit you to obtain that the pittance of the loan to me to start a one man wine business meant absolutely nothing.'

Bitsy blurted at him savagely because he was trying to make it sound as if he were right and they were wrong. 'Is it better for me to stay with you so that you can pretend I love you when I cannot respect you?'

'Love and respect are entirely different things,' the Captain said loftily.

'Respect is what changes lust into love,' Bitsy said bitterly. 'Respect means you know you won't be let down at every turn.'

'I'm sorry, Bitsy. And I am also *very* sorry. But I must point out that a divorce will destroy both our lives.' He was trembling. He would be late. He would be late for the one engagement where to be late would mean the loss of honour – the greater loss for his caller than even to himself; a barbarity committed.

'The papers are ready,' Uncle Jim said.

Edward Masters said mildly, 'I think we must be allowed time to read those papers.'

'They are merely simple instruments of assignment, Mr Masters,' Uncle Jim said cheerfully.

'Nonetheless, I must insist – '

Daddy spoke. Every head turned to face him. His deeply pink face, so well-boned, so aristocratic, was benign but he could not keep habitual firmness out of his voice any more than he could have sung the role of Carmen. 'Edward is right. More than right. He is correct.'

Bitsy began to remonstrate but her father gazed at her until she had quieted down. 'Although we may not stay over until tomorrow,' he said, 'you may have twenty-four hours to study the papers. Colin will sign them here at this time tomorrow afternoon.'

The Captain made himself move. He patted Masters on the shoulder as he passed and went directly to Daddy to shake his hand with grave expressions of appreciation. Bitsy stood. He kissed her and, for a moment, looked deeply into her eyes. He shook hands with everyone but Harry then he crossed the room and disappeared down the flight of stairs.

As he hurried with long, rapid strides down Chesterfield Hill he knew he was in bad trouble but he would have to think about that later.

2

Some years before, Captain Huntington had been invited to
work as map man on a hurtle across Spain over execrable roads
en route to Clermont-Ferrand, because he was one of the two
honorary members of the British Racing Drivers Club. Like
Bentley owners, he was diffident about this and wore his
BRDC blazer buttons on his pajamas. He had been made one
of the two honorary members because after Todham's pilot
had been killed and no one else had been available to sit beside
the rather terribly disturbed Todham, the Captain had volun-
teered and, in twenty-two hours, had charted every turn, bump,
straightaway, street light and sign post on a long roll of complex
roadmap and had been able to call out each driving problem
so accurately and so far ahead that Todham had beaten Alfredo
Nasheri to win the Mille Miglia.

He made the Spanish run, not a race at all, just a journey
from one country to another, with Francis Homer driving a
ferocious sounding Ferrari, from Cuarton, near Cadiz to the
French frontier, a distance of about five hundred and seventy
miles, in six hours, four minutes, averaging just under a hundred
miles an hour on comparatively open but really dreadful
roads. They had done no more damage than killing one small
burro, from which Homer recovered control of the car with
mastery, and had frightened several hundred farmers and
pedestrians. The Guardia Civil shot at them twice but Homer
had been moving the car too fast for hope of anything but a
lucky hit. Still they were quite happy to cross the frontier,

needing to choose a remote point used by Andorran smugglers and priests on errands of mercy, and to find themselves having enormous hunger just as they reached a small inn-restaurant at the foot of the Pyrenees called *Ammej* on a wooden sign. Food was only fuel to Francis Homer who seemed to live on ketchup so Juan Francohogar's soufflé Ecrevisse (and Francohogar was only twenty-nine years old at this time) made no impression, but the Captain had almost slid under the table in an insensibility of admiration. He concentrated his every resource upon the Faisan Souvaroff and well into the *bombe* whose exterior beauty could have been designed by Fabergé while the blended taste factors, echelon upon echelon, were as intricate as a watch by Abraham Breguet. When he had finished he explained to Homer that he would be unable to accompany him further, admired Homer's driving art, thanked him for the marvellous ride, then bolted to the kitchen to confront the master who had orchestrated the carnival of the senses with which he had just been blessed.

In the kitchen, over an old-fashioned coal stove, amid a *batterie* of kitchen implements which were most certainly pre-Carême, in his precise pompidoulan French, Captain Huntington had negotiated a fifteen-year contract with Francohogar to remove to London within a fortnight, to cook solely for Huntington Fine Wines (London), knowing as he signed the contract that Bitsy would be thrilled to pay Francohogar's salary of £9800 a year, plus travel and living expenses, to be paid into an account in Geneva.

As it turned out, when he uncovered this surprise at the Farm Street flat after an amazing dinner which had caused Bitsy to grunt, squeal, burble, and gong – he had been quite right. Bitsy had admired the *shrewdness* of the deal. La! he thought, but he did not question what she said because he knew all would shortly be demonstrated, which it was: Daddy, Uncle Jim and Uncle Pete, Harry and Larry began to triple the number of their trips from Washington to London after the installation of Francohogar in Farm Street where each gave a series of dinner parties which had to do with the objectives of their public work and their private investment plans. It had even helped the Captain, indirectly, because the guests were the sort of people who bought a lot of wine and Daddy, Uncle Jim, Uncle Pete, and at least Larry saw to it that they equated the quality of Huntington's Fine Wines (London) with Huntington's fine food.

But the Captain had greater recognitions planned for his great cook. Day after day he told Francohogar that he deserved to stand as a peer among the great cooks of France and assiduously he attracted the most distinguished cadre of feeders of France to his dining room in London. He sought out and cultivated the most authoritative French writers on food; a category which does not, in any serious degree, exist anywhere else in the world with the possible exception of Belgium, and in an earnest but hopeless way, in Switzerland, in hard-nosed commercial and industrial food reportage. These men who wrote about food in France were much more like critics of poetry and music than the food writers of Australia or the United States. For one thing their literary standing at home was higher than that of French playwrights and poets. As these men came to London to scoff and stayed to plead to be allowed to remain longer, as the trumpetings of their intensely felt regard for the art of Juan Francohogar were heard across the Channel, French citizens began to respond. Millions of French feeders were constantly salivating without really understanding the cause.

Within three years such enormous curiosity had been aroused that pressure was generated which the Captain had decided he must recognize and, building a staircase for his cook into the French Panthéon of cooks, saw to it that Francohogar was invited to pincer, réduire, dépouiller, saucer and farcir with the Ten Great Cooks of France at their annual celebration of their culinary gifts, in Bordeaux. These Ten Great Cooks of France were claimed by the motherland as Picasso is claimed by Spain, and as Shaw was claimed by Ireland until he died and left a legacy to establish a commission for the improvement of Irish manners and speech.

The great gastronomic fair had happened at Chez Otardi, Bordeaux, a mere twenty-one hours before the evening the Captain had faced Bitsy and her family and, as a result of the acclaim and immeasurable recognition he had worked so long to arrange for his cook, certain other events had taken place which had gravely compromised each demand Bitsy had made, just as her demands cross-ruffed retroactively the invidious thing he had done.

3

Everything had begun so auspiciously. He was in Bordeaux so he did a rather large amount of business with Cruse et Fils, Frères, his principal wine suppliers for Huntington's Fine Wines (London). He had installed Francohogar in a suite at the Hotel Splendide and had ordered him to sleep for two hours. It was two o'clock in the afternoon. He would conduct business then he would return to drive Francohogar to Chez Otardi.

He moved the chocolate-coloured, drophead Rolls with its Hong Kong licence plates along the Quai des Chartrons thinking with such pleasure that another important ambition had been realized, that his cook was about to be invested with the French equivalent of the rank of prince or cardinal, that he had played an important part in this and that Francohogar's contract with him still had twelve years to run.

As he drove he mused that he should not have sold the Watteau, of course. But he most certainly had never dreamed that anyone other than an art dealer, and most especially not Bitsy, would have shown all that interest in a Watteau at this part of the century. Bitsy was behaving badly because property was involved, not that she placed any other value on the thing. It was indubitably her property but they were man and wife and he was facing an emergency. A gentleman could not go to his wife and ask for money. He had only taken the Watteau temporarily for heaven's sake. And further, how could a woman conduct these endless long distance, trans-Atlantic

25

telephone calls, work with that stock ticker he knew was installed in her powder room, and handle that extraordinary family's extraordinary business (which must never be referred to as a business but as 'government service') to find the time to notice that a small Watteau was no longer on the wall of an obscure room in a country house?

He made a turn on the Quai des Chartrons and parked directly in front of the Cruse building. Inside the building he was greeted warmly by three of the people he passed. On the first floor he spoke to the receptionist by her first name and asked for Monsieur Chezfrance.

He and Chezfrance strolled along the labyrinth of corridors to the rear stairway leading to the warehouse then across the reception cellars of the great wine firms making small talk about the intensely felt hope of magnificent food that night. Chezfrance inquired about the health of Francohogar the way the deeply committed would ask about a great racehorse or a ranking matador. They walked along the rows of high cement vats, eighteen of them at either end of the bulk wine storage area, separated by two storeys of smaller vats, all of them connected by pipes and automated pumps which would take the wine through seven pipe lines which stretched over four hundred and twenty yards to the series of endless belts of the bottling area. These wine cellars were the greatest in France. Their surface area was almost three hundred thousand square feet which stored one million, two hundred and ten thousand gallons of wine in four hundred and fifty-six vats and forty-four hundred barrels; in all, four hundred and forty thousand gallons of wine in two million, seven hundred thousand bottles; wines of enormous diversity from the most classic vintage wines to the most abundant ordinary wines.

The Captain worked with Chezfrance amiably for almost an hour and a half. He placed an order for four thousand two hundred and ninety pounds' worth of winestocks to be shipped to London. He paid with a check in full amount as the French government required so that it could be sure it would collect all taxes due without delay. At the front door to the building the Captain and the sales director for Great Britain agreed to meet at eight o'clock that evening at the bar at the Hotel Splendide. Chezfrance looked forward to the evening and not only because of the magnificent food in store but because he thought of Captain Huntington as a man who did not have a care in the world and was therefore the best of company.

4

Juan Francohogar was waiting just inside the door at the Splendide as the chocolate-coloured Rolls drove up. He stowed his small satchel behind the seat and got into the car.

'Did you rest?' the Captain asked.

'Yes,' the assured, bass voice said. 'I bathed with a free product which is provided by the hotel. I thought the patron before me had left it behind but when I telephoned the concierge he said it was a service of the hotel. It softens the water, the box says. It was all right.'

'I am very interested to see the wines they have chosen for tonight.'

'You may not agree, sir, but the wines will be right. A little showmanly but precisely right.'

'I hope there's none of that damned pink champagne like last year.'

'Oh, one mustn't think about champagne. There will be serious wines.'

'It is a very important night for me, Juan. More for me than for you, perhaps, because you are an artist and you know you belong here. I am a spectator.'

Francohogar chuckled. 'You are the greatest taster a cook ever had, sir. You made tonight possible. I did it, but you made it possible.' He polished a red apple with a large handkerchief. They stared at the road leading west out of Bordeaux toward the manifestation of the soul of a nation, even if that soul happened to be gluttonous, which was as solemn as the trooping of the colours on the Queen's birthday, the merger of two gigantic conglomerates by the Mafia in North America, or the wedding anniversary of Princess Grace in Monaco: the soul, that which from, or, as in this case, into which, all blessings flowed.

The French television crews which would cover the event would number more than thirty. The French press would deploy photographers by the dozen, reporters, researchers, experts, fashion writers, fixers and beyond all else, the food critics. The national radio would find new unctions of language. Thirteen hundred vintners would sob themselves to sleep that night because only six French wines, one cognac and one liqueur had been chosen.

Although he greeted Otardi with warmth, asked for his wife, Emilie, and his daughters, Hortense, Denise, and Françoise, the Captain did not get out of the car to enter the restaurant where the other great cooks were assembling and preparing. He drove back to the hotel and bathed, leaving Francohogar in Otardi's kitchens to conjugate their joint glory.

While he was bathing the telephone rang. The telephone was in the bedroom thirty feet away. Mumbling about the unfairness of a system which could insist that it be answered at once, into a darkness of purpose or identity, he stumbled across the vast space to the phone, dripping.

Wrapped in a huge towel he said, into the telephone, 'Hello?'

'Colin?'

'Yes. Who is this?'

'Uncle Jim.'

'Uncle Jim? Are you here for the cook-out?'

'I'm in Washington. At the White House.'

'Ah. Yes. Of course. My best to the President.'

'He's on the road. Say, this is a fine connection. You sound as if you are in the same room.' Uncle Jim always said that.

'How's – uh – Daddy? Uncle Pete? The boys?'

'Fine. All fine, Colin. Colin – we're all flying to London in the morning.'

'Marvellous.'

'It's not really so gosh darned marvellous. We're sort of a lynch mob, I guess.'

'Who're you lynching?'

'Well – as a matter of fact – you. Can you be at Farm Street by six o'clock tomorrow evening?'

'Me? Why me?'

'We'll explain everything at the meeting. Can you be there?'

'This is most unusual, Jim. I mean – it is only fair that you give me some *inkling* – '

'Can you be there, Colin?'

'Of course I can be there, but – '

'See you at six. Don't take any wooden chewing gum.' Uncle Jim disconnected.

The Captain suddenly began to feel his head coming to a point. This was the most pressure they had ever applied. The five men had not been in the same room at the same time, in London, since he and Bitsy had been married. He began to need to gamble to lessen the tension. It was the only way he could get out of the vice. He couldn't stand it if he had to wait until six o'clock the next evening to find out what was so serious for Jim to refer to a lynch mob and to refuse to say what or why. He began to put calls through to Bitsy but she was either out or she was not answering the telephone.

Captain Huntington did not show the face tics he had earned, or the pain and weakness of the duodenal ulcers his endlessly conflicted life had him deserving. He stared at the wall as he sat on the edge of the bed in the towel. His handsome face seemed to have been composed of angular blocks which, had they been alphabet blocks, might have spelled out words which he would dread to read. He stood up slowly; a tall man with the ecstatic carriage naval officers have been taught. He swanned into rooms regardless of all shocks, chin properly cocked, shoulders level, backline at true vertical. He wondered how long his watery legs would support him, whether he could make it back to the tub. His wife was getting ready to tell him that life was over. Life without her was nothing he really wanted. He would have achieved a unique suicide using roulette wheels, some dice, and many hundreds of decks of cards.

He was relieved that he and Chezfrance would be dining with John Bryson, a vastly-game periodical gambler, the Captain's sort of company. Bryson should be vastly game, the Captain thought ruefully. He was always winning.

5

They had decided it would be too uncomfortable to try to jam into the bar at Otardi so they met for an aperitif in the bar in the Splendide. The Captain had not seen Bryson since the banker's last summer holiday. He was looking very fit. He was brash, sardonic and about twenty years older than Chezfrance or Captain Huntington. He was an art patron who had been married four times. He was a Pittsburgh banker who was very, very rich and who was an amused rather than an anguished gambler perhaps because of having so much money it didn't matter a damn whether he won or lost. He loved to gamble for high stakes but, being a good banker, would not gamble in his home country: not at bridge, not at Vegas, not anyhere but in the stock market or during his six weeks annual holiday in Europe where he would gamble on anything including fondling the bottoms of newly-introduced wives while he stared into the eyes of their husbands and grated on about Renoir or the Common Market, stating each or any topic wrong because he didn't feel he was on holiday to educate.

He was a tall, almost white-haired man who wore heavy hornrimmed glasses. Chezfrance was a small, blond man who had overlarge teeth which gave him the impression of a small boy walking around with a mouthful of water. Everyone was glad to see each other again and Bryson stood them to a bottle of Dom Perignon '61 and got on with the business of conversation.

'Nixon's a short-term plunger,' Bryson said in answer to the

Captain's question of 'how is everything?' 'We'll be able to buy the goddam country for ten cents on the dollar again, just like in '32, if that little son-of-a-bitch gets reelected. I'm all for him.'

'I understand – there is a rumour,' Chezfrance said, 'that someone will cook the fish with a red wine sauce tonight. Had you heard this?'

'I only know what Francohogar will cook,' the Captain said.

'What the hell is wrong with cooking fish in red wine?' Bryson asked. 'If cooks as good as these guys tonight say cook red wine with fish then where's a better authority?'

'I did not say it would happen,' Chezfrance replied. 'I only said I heard it would happen.'

'As John says – why not?' the Captain agreed mildly.

'Like to bet on that? Like to bet me a thousand pounds that not only will they serve fish in red wine but that the press will flip?'

'You're on.'

'Which side of the bet am I taking?'

'You are betting me one thousand pounds that there will be no fish in red wine tonight and therefore the press will not flip.'

'Got it.' Bryson made a note with a gold pencil in a cheque book, but on the back of a cheque.

'I think we should be on our way, gentlemen,' Chezfrance said. 'This is not a dinner we would want to be late for.' They finished the wine and got to their feet. The Captain felt relief from the pressure which Bitsy had only begun to apply for the first time since he knew that she had discovered the disappearance of the Watteau.

It took them only twenty minutes to get within fifty yards of Otardi's then twenty minutes more to make it to the door through the excitement of crowds, lights, cars and police. The

3

French became inordinately excited at the sight of a Rolls Royce adding together its probable cost with the probable income tax it would require that its owner pay, under the French system. International events were rated by the number of Rolls journalists had been able to spot at such galas. The fact that this Rolls was chocolate, had its top down to reveal extremely rich looking men in black ties and boiled shirts, and wore Hong Kong licence plates brought burst after burst of genuinely admiring applause from the crowds on either side as the car inched through.

Inside the restaurant it seemed as if le Tout Paris, le Tout Bordeaux, le Tout Cannes and le Tout St Moritz had come spinning in out of a giant centrifuge of couturiers, coiffeures, masseuses, parfumeurs, joailliers and les tailleurs du mode Anglais. The three men kissed cheeks, pressed hands, admired, appreciated, were in turn admired and appreciated and were conducted by Otardi himself (because Captain Huntington was the only individual sponsor of one of the Ten Master Cooks of France since perhaps Monsieur le Prince or a few Rothschilds) to an elegantly placed table for three where they could see the beautiful ladies and the hungry gentlemen and yet be able to look through the long, wide plate glass screen into the kitchen itself where the great men were even then at work.

'Jesus,' Bryson said, 'I came all the way from Pittsburgh for this and I thought I was going to meet some new French broads.'

'Comment?' Chezfrance said.

'Always the same broads. They travel in a pack and only at night.'

The Captain had opened the menu and was staring with no little awe at what he had wrought. The billing was cold and clear. Between Paul Bocuse, Collonges au Mont d'Or and Jean-Pierre et Paul Haeberlin, Illhaeusern, stood Juan Francohogar, Huntington Fine Wines (London).

'You really have the knack, don't you, Captain?' Bryson said.

'The impossible dream,' the Captain murmured, still staring.

'Your boy must be a pretty good cook.'

'I assure you, Monsieur Bryson – ' Chezfrance began but Bryson was intent on building a bet.

'Francohogar is a great artist,' Chezfrance persisted to say.

'You think so, too, Captain?'

The Captain smiled at him dreamily. 'You've been saying that yourself, John, for the past three years.'

'Bet your ass,' Bryson said. 'I would know this particular cook's work blindfolded in the bottom of a coal mine sniffling with a head cold.'

'No.'

'Why no?'

'You have no palate and he's only making one dish out of eleven and each other dish will be fit for the gods.'

'Will you give me ten to one?'

'Eight to one.'

'Should be ten. Make it nine.'

'Eight.'

'What are you betting, gentlemen?' Chezfrance asked.

'I am betting that I can tell which one of the dishes we'll eat tonight will be cooked by Francohogar,' said Bryson.

'Formidable!'

'One thousand pounds,' Bryson said. 'Eight to one.'

'Done.' The Captain marked the wager down inside the elaborate four page menu.

The large room, overpacked with shrillness, seemed to have bales of smoke like so much organdy floating in mid-air over the heads of the diners, enraging 23·7 percent to whom a Kubeb smoked in a parking lot behind the restaurant could endanger the enjoyment of the food.

Otardi, his face contorted with outrage, ran through the diners snatching cigarettes and cigars from the hands and mouths of Philistines and flinging them into a container a small *commis* carried. He stood on a chair. He announced, 'The windows will now be opened to clear the filthy smoke from this room. Anyone who dishonours me by smoking before the cognac is served will be escorted from my restaurant.' He stood down to tumultuous applause.

There was a feeling of excitement, of movement. Sommeliers burst into the room carrying magnums of wine. Simultaneously the diners who had already memorized the menu looked down at it and read again, showing intense interest. The wine was listed:

> Dom Perignon Rosé 1959
> Puligny-Blagny 1961
> Château Canon 1955
> Taittinger 1964
> Cognac Pellison 1929
> China-China

'Looks like I won me a thousand pounds, Captain,' Bryson said, trying not to grin.

'You did?'

'No fish in red wine on this menu.'

The Captain glanced down at the listing of the food to be offered. 'Indeed, you have, John. But look at this balance. It is flawless! Did Otardi compose this? It is so elegant and refined, it has such exquisite counterpoint of texture and flavour and scent and sight!' The three men stared downward reverentially. Otardi, working as Beethoven, had written a score for the great artists beyond that glass wall to bring to vibrant harmonies: Beluga caviar – 'If I know Otardi it will be sterlet,' Chezfrance breathed; Dieppe turbot in golden mustard sauce! a saddle of veal with a daring onion sauce, it had to be delicate for such flesh, it had to *pique*, it had to marry and never to dominate; there would be Basque rice and a courgettes au gratin – simplicity throughout, genius throughout, always *balance*, the Captain marvelled. After that came a sorbet Dom Perignon to clear the mouth for some quail in aspic then les fromages somptueux followed by small cakes, glazed fruit, petits fours.

Bryson lost by choosing the *Selle de Veau* as the dish Francohogar had cooked. Wrong. He had cooked the fish. 'Who the hell ever hearda letting a Basque cook fish, for Christ's sake?' Bryson said. The Captain picked up a thousand pounds when he doubted that the Dom Perignon Rosé was 1959. Otardi was summoned and admitted that a freight problem had delayed things but that the menus had been printed and Moët had been gracious enough to fly in the '61. 'Anyone could tell the difference,' he added, 'but so far yours is the first complaint, Captain Huntington.'

'I detest champagne rosé,' the Captain said. 'I should have preferred Raspberry Soda '72.'

The Captain picked up a surprise two thousand pounds when Bryson doubled his bet to recover and bet that China-China would have an apricot brandy base blended with armagnac because he had had it at the French Embassy in '34 when that son-of-a-bitch Roosevelt had been in the White House. When the dinner was over the Captain was feeling wondrously relieved, felt little apprehension about what Bitsy might be planning for him the next afternoon, and wondrously lucky. After they had congratulated Francohogar and his colleagues and the Captain had posed for a few pictures with his cook and had said a few felicitous words concerning *la belle France*, acme of civilization, into the television cameras, thus also making the front pages of *Le Monde*, *Le Figaro* and *France-Soir* (. . . 'for my ladies and my gentlemen of France, all over France, it is as your great President Pompidou said on the last day of the year 1971 – ' in French the Captain's voice was stridently Gallic, 'you are among the most respected and happy people in the world and why hide it.' The Captain's voice was strong. 'Your President's reasons proving that you were the happiest and most respected people were to the point – but incomplete. He told you that it was because of the visits paid to France by the Peking government, by the Soviet chief, Leonid Brezhnev, the summit meeting with President Nixon and France's settlement of the monetary crisis – and he is right! But I say to you that France is what France is, whatever France is, because of the greatest of great arts which we have witnessed here tonight') they departed for the casino at Arcachon, some forty miles to the west, where the Captain lost thirty-two thousand pounds; a sum which he did not have.

His clothes were damp with the sweat of fear; any hound would have veered away from him to avoid the stench of hopelessness he emanated. He arose from his seat at the chemmy table with all surface correctness and good cheer and carelessly tossed five hundred francs to the croupier who bowed low to him and continued the play.

The Captain wandered off across the high stakes room. He remained cheerfully correct until he reached an alcove which was the backgammon corner where so few people played that it would not be there the following season. He dropped into a chair and lowered his face into his hands. He felt rather than heard the chair being moved across the table from him. He looked up, composing himself. It was John Bryson.

'Feeling down, Captain?'

'Beastly headache,' the Captain explained.

'Hell, why not, the way you're losing.'

'Yes. Well, excuse me, John. I must pop off in search of an aspirin or two.' He did not move because he felt that the only courteous thing would be for Bryson to move because it had been made clear that he was presently intruding.

'How about a little backgammon?' Bryson said.

'No, thank you, John. The desperate fact is, I am flat broke.'

That should certainly not come as news to Bryson who had won most of it.

'Hell,' Bryson said, 'I don't want to play for money.'

'What else can one play with?'

'Thought you might like to play for your cook.'

'My *cook*?' The Captain was not only incredulous, he was offended.

'He sure is one helluva cook, Captain.'

'It would be barbaric for a man to wager his cook.'

'Maybe where you come from.' Bryson took out a wallet which was fat enough to be holding several dozen frankfurters. He began to toss large banknotes on the backgammon board. 'Suppose you just let me give you a credit of two thousand pounds against your cook.'

'Two thousand pounds? The man is my friend.'

'Jessa same I suppose you have a written contract with him?'

The Captain nodded. Then he stared down at the impossible sums of money; money which, if he could wager it well could stall the terrible confrontation with Bitsy and her family. He began to sweat. Chezfrance came up.

'Are you all right, Colin?' he asked.

The Captain nodded. 'I'm fine, I think. But I bet a little too heavily and I am a bit worried now that if the casino gets to the bank before you do the cheque I gave you for the order this afternoon won't be much good at all.'

'I will cancel the order, Colin.'

'Thank you.'

'How about it, Captain?'

'The bet you suggest would be utterly out of the question,' the Captain said hoarsely. 'However, for a credit of fifty thousand pounds I'll play you for my building in Farm Street.'

'What the hell would I ever want another building for?'

'Frankly, John, I don't intend that you shall win.' It was a pathetic line, delivered from behind sand-bags of self-delusion.

The Captain had never started any gambling play without knowing he would win while secretly hoping he would lose.

'We'll just see about that, Captain,' Bryson said, grinning. He picked up the dice cup and began to shake it.

6

By the time the gamblers got back to the Splendide at two forty-five, Juan Francohogar had checked out and had returned on the night plane to London. There would be no other planes out of Bordeaux, the concierge said, until ten minutes to ten the next morning.

'Hell, Captain,' Bryson said, 'I got the bank's Gulfstream II over here with me so's I don't have to get hung up on airports and baggage. Come on, we'll shake the crew outta bed and get on up to London right now. I just hate it when you're this depressed.'

'You are really very kind, John,' the Captain said.

The Grumman was almost ready when they got there and they passed the short waiting time by having a good breakfast in the cabin.

'Fine looking craft,' Captain Huntington said, chewing Irish bacon with French eggs.

'Yes, she is. She has a good old sixty-eight foot wingspan and two Rolls Royce Spey Mk511–8 jet engines that will cruise us along at five ninety.'

'What's the range?'

'Just about four thousand. We fly right outta Allegheny County Airport into Paris. I just step outta the bar at the Holiday Inn – they make a helluva hamburger – and into the old Gulfstream and there I am. How's about we have dinner tonight?'

'I have a very, very important meeting tonight.'

'Thought you had something heavy on your mind. How about lunch today then?'

'Lunch will be fine.'

'Where?'

'If you can let's make it at Tiberio in Queen Street. It's so nearby to Bitsy's and to Yvonne's.'

'One-fifteen.'

The Captain nodded. He took a deep breath. 'Bitsy and her entire family have called a meeting at Farm Street at six o'clock this evening.'

Bryson was impressed. 'All of them?'

'Yes. They come over for a good meal every now and then. But tonight – at seven o'clock – I will come face-to-face with an old opponent, Commander Uto Fujikawa of the Imperial Japanese Navy.'

Bryson's eyebrows went up. 'I didn't know you were old enough to be in the Pearl Harbor war.'

'No, no, no! For the past eight years Commander Fujikawa and I have been re-fighting all the battles of the Pacific by mail. I keep this big tactical board at Yvonne's to work out all the manoeuvres. In all that time we've never met.'

'Everyone to his own taste, as the man said when he kissed the cow,' Bryson shrugged.

They had arranged to air freight the Captain's car in the morning. In London, Bryson's Rolls was at the airport to drive the Captain to Yvonne's house in Charles Street.

The Captain let himself into the hushed house silently then moved along the hall and went down the stairs to the kitchen to have a glass of milk and to try to get his terrible predicament sorted out. When he opened the heavy door to the large refrigerator the trick of light made it seem as if he were robbing a bank vault then the yehudi went on and revealed the inside of the fridge. As he removed a bottle of milk, the overhead lights in the kitchen went on. The Captain turned toward the click of the switch. Wearing a bulky bathrobe and looking more rugged than his countryman, Paolino Uzcudin, Francohogar stood in the doorway. He had a tall, *toque blanche* cook's hat on above his nightdress.

'Do you sleep in that hat?' the Captain asked reflexively.

'I am greatly excited,' Francohogar said, showing all the excitement of a sea turtle basking in the sun. 'I would not be able to sleep until you came home.'

'Mademoiselle is all right?' There was sudden panic in the Captain's voice.

'Oh, yes.'

'Then what happened?'

'I wanted to show my deep appreciation for all you have done for me. If I did not accomplish this I would never feel that you knew how grateful I am.'

'Accomplished what?'

'Do you recall mentions in histories of gourmandise of the exalted *Pâté de Banquier Henri Emmet*?'

'Well, yes. Of course.'

'Have you ever tasted it?'

'No. Of course not.'

'The *Pâté de Banquier Henri Emmet* in all the time since its discovery in 1868, in Marton, Department of Seine et Loire, has been capable of being made by only three cooks. The *Pâté de Banquier Henri Emmet* is such a *pâté* that it requires six and a quarter days to make and if the precise balance of its thirty-two ingredients is disturbed, everything is ruined.'

'I know. I know.'

'Tonight there are four cooks who have made it.'

'Juan!'

'I have not only made it but I have advanced it by two taste factors and have made it seven percent lighter and easier to digest.'

'*Juan!*'

'I did this before we left for the gala yesterday – for six days before – only that you could know the extent of the appreciation I feel for what you have done for me.' He moved stolidly to the kitchen counter. With three hand movements he pulled the cork out of a bottle of wine. 'Chateau Palmer '55,' he said. He lifted a white, porous cloth which covered a large *pâté en croûte*. He took up a sharp knife, cut three equal-size portions rapidly, hesitated, then cut a fourth.

Captain Huntington was seating himself at the kitchen table, tying a large white napkin around his neck. The great cook set a plate before him which held three slices of the *pâté*. 'Taste!' he commanded.

The Captain sipped the wine. He disregarded the silver beside the plate and picked up a slice of the *pâté* and bit into it. He chewed thoughtfully. Francohogar chewed abstractedly, leaning forward. The Captain swallowed then quickly sipped more wine. He took a larger bite of the *pâté*.

'Alors?'

Captain Huntington looked up at his cook with tears glistening in his eyes. 'You have done it,' he said.

'Did you sense the two additional taste factors?' he pressed.

The Captain nodded, deeply moved. Tears were now rolling down his cheeks. 'You have added one pasilla *chili*,' he said brokenly, 'and the juices of a Belgian gherkin.'

Francohogar's face became as a great searchlight, beaming all over the room.

With a choked voice the Captain said, 'On the day you bring me the greatest *pâté* the world will ever know, on the day after you reached the summit with the greatest cooks of France – a terrible thing has happened.'

'What has happened? Madame is all right?'

'Madame is all right, but I have lost you at backgammon to a man from Pittsburgh.'

'What is Pittsburgh?'

The Captain arose with the plate of *pâté* and the wine. He walked to the counter next to the shocked cook and set them down. He kissed Francohogar on both cheeks, ceremonially, but he was unable to speak. He wept as he picked up the food and wine and walked off into the darkened building.

On the second floor he opened the door into a totally lighted room in which the nude Yvonne rested her lovely bosom across the top of the ice-blue sheets of the enormous bed. She stared at him fixedly but did not speak. The Captain crossed the room to sit on the side of the bed nearest her sweet right breast. He extended the plate with the *pâté*, his eyes red-rimmed from weeping, and the wine. She sipped the wine then tasted the *pâté*. Her face became suffused with awe. 'Is it –? Can it possibly be –?'

He nodded. 'It is the *Pâté de Banquier Henri Emmet* – but more than that – Juan has succeeded in adding two perfectly balanced taste factors.'

'I sense the pasilla *chili* – but what is the second?'

'Gherkin juice.'

'Mon dieu!'

'Indeed.'

'Why were you weeping?'

'We went to Arcachon after the gala. I lost rather badly.'

'That made you weep? You?'

'Then John Bryson and I played backgammon and I lost the Farm Street building, Rossenarra, and the wine company.'

'You fool. You poor, helpless fool.'

'Not only that. The cream of the jest is that I have also lost our cook.'

'Comment?'

He nodded.

'You are telling me that you bet and you lost the great Francohogar?'

He nodded again. 'It is a new low.'

45

'Until now it is a new low, Colin.' She spoke in English but her voice was entirely and most unmistakably French. 'But when your wonderful wife is told what you have done with the Farm Street building and Rossenarra, and that you have lost the wine company, she will have you thrown into jail for thirty years. That, my friend, will be the new low. Eh?'

All at once he truly comprehended the trouble he was in. Not in isolated pieces, but in a grand, immovable, unavoidable whole. LORD GLANDORE'S BROTHER TO PRISON FOR FRAUD it would shout from the front pages of the Boise newspaper. That saddened him. It hadn't been a very old title. It had not been a title conferred in a noble cause. It wasn't a title which had been respected by the two men who held it, but it was his family's. Prison would shame it more than operating a bowling alley under it, like his brother, more than procuring young ladies for Prince Edward VII, which had obtained the title, like his father.

'That doesn't have to happen. I still have the chance to make it all good. You know how rich John is. He has agreed to give me sixty days to buy everything back. All he wanted was the cook anyway.'

She lifted his hand and put it on her left breast to comfort him. It was bread cast upon the waters because it comforted her as well. 'How are you going to buy them back?' she asked gently. Her eyes poured love on him while her words poured scorn. 'How could you buy back a pair of socks?'

'It can be done,' he said stolidly.

'She will put you in jail. That is certain. You can't spit on her money. Your wonderful wife will put you in jail because she only has about thirty million dollars left.'

'Oh, more than that. However, I must say, there is an unusual complication.'

'What complication?'

'Uncle Jim called me in Bordeaux from the White House.

The whole family will be in London tomorrow for a confrontation with me. About the Watteau, I thought.'

'The Watteau?'

'I sold a silly Watteau Bitsy had hanging at Rossenarra because I owed some money at the Denbigh Club and I certainly couldn't bring myself to ask Bitsy for money.'

'But she has already covered you for more than two hundred thousand pounds!'

'It doesn't matter really. It turned out not to have been about the Watteau after all.'

7

When the Captain left the meeting with Bitsy, Daddy, Uncle Jim, Uncle Pete, Harry and Larry he was cursing himself for not having had the tactical board moved out of the bedroom and downstairs to his study because then he would not have had to discomfort Yvonne. He positively flew from Farm Street to Charles Street, let himself in and rushed up the stairs.

'Yvonne!' he cried as he burst into the room.

'They are going to put you in jail,' she wailed from the bed where she lay nude under the ice-blue sheets, her soprano saxophone stretched out beside her.

'No, no. Darling, look here. With all these pressures I forgot to tell you that Commander Fujikama will be here in about forty-six seconds so there is –'

'Commander Fujikawa?'

'Yes. His first trip to London since the war. But, you see, there will be no time to move the tactical board down to the study so I am very much afraid that I will have to ask you to dress and tidy up this room a bit while I delay him with a drink downstairs.'

'But what did your wonderful wife and her family want to say to you?'

'I will tell you all about it, darling, the moment the Commander leaves.' They could hear the doorbell. The Captain rushed out of the room and Yvonne leaped out of bed.

The Captain was downstairs just as Michaels was opening

the door. He beamed upon the small, handsome man who was precisely his own age.

'How marvellous to meet you at last!' the Captain said.

'Oh! No! I assure you that I am so honoured to be allowed to come into your home that my legs are trembling.' The Commander had a Royal family British accent which was even fruitier than the Captain's.

'Do come in.' The Captain pulled him through the door and led him along the hall to the study. 'Whiskey?'

'Thanks most awfully.'

'Please sit down. How long will you be in England, what brings you here, did you have a good journey?'

'Only three days. Family business. Splendid journey.'

The Captain brought the two whiskies out and they clinked glasses. 'To the Imperial Navy,' the Captain said, at the very moment Commander Fujikawa said, 'To the Royal Navy.' They smiled at each other with great affection and tenderness.

After two drinks the Commander apologized that his London representatives had so tightly organized his visit to London that he hardly had twenty spare minutes to turn around, that it had been so tremendously delightful to see the Captain but he must think about leaving shortly for the next dreary appointment, this one about electronics. Could the Captain conceive of anything more dreary than a company dinner devoted to electronics.

The Captain could not.

'It's quite stimulating actually,' Commander Fujikawa said.

'Good heavens! You must see the tactical board before you go.'

'Tactical board?'

'Don't you use one? Frankly, it's the secret weapon. It's why I have won one more battle than you in our eight year series.'

'I say! I must see it!'

They went upstairs. The room was scrupulously tidy, the bed

was made and, at the centre of the room, the tactical board stretched out in all directions six feet by ten feet, not quite as large as a snooker table. On it had been painted, or was settled in bas-relief the entire Pacific Ocean with all islands indicated as well as the coastlines of North and South America, Australia and Asia. Commander Fujikawa gaped at it with admiration. He reached into the board and lifted out a light cruiser of the Obitsi class from its position in the line of battle with the Japanese main fleet. 'By jove,' he said with much happiness, 'I think this is my old ship.'

The Captain's happy nod confirmed that fact. 'I was frightfully sorry when I had to sink her in our last go at the Coral Sea.'

'You were brilliant in that battle. I fail to understand how there could have been any other actual consequences of the actual battle.'

'Of course, heavy seas make a difference.'

'Ah, yes, but the way you handled your aircraft!'

'Thank you. I would much rather have been the author of your brilliant manoeuvring at Wake.'

'I am most impressed with that tactical board and – I warn you, Captain Huntington – they shall have one ready for me when I reach Tokyo.' He glanced at his watch. 'What a pity. I must leave.'

The two men shook hands fondly at the front door. The Captain waved to the car from the doorway until it was out of sight.

Yvonne called out to him from the door to the study. Reluctantly, he closed the door and went to join her. 'Why stay here?' he asked.

'Of course. I wanted to be sure he had gone.'

'Splendid fellow.' He put his arm around her and they went upstairs. In the large bedroom they both began to undress.

'He was most awfully keen on my tactics at the Coral Sea.'

'Why are you talking like a Wodehouse character?'

'Oh? Am I?'

'What did your wonderful wife and her wonderful family say to you?' She was totally undressed and had crossed to help him unbutton his shirt and his trousers.

'She wants a divorce. They all do.'

'Colin! How terrible for you. You didn't agree, of course?'

'That was the least of it. They demand that I sign over all ownership in the Farm Street building, Rossenarra and half the wine company – which, as you may remember,' he stared at her, 'I have already signed over to Bryson.'

'Oh, my God.' She stripped his shorts off and led him to the large bed.

The Captain rolled off Yvonne. 'It's no use, darling,' he said.

'You could have *continuer* just a few moments encore before announcing to me that, Colin,' she said breathing heavily and appearing quite flushed. 'You leave me like six hundred kilometres of stretched piano wire.' She pulled herself up into a sitting position on the huge bed. She had utterably beautiful breasts; strawberries on firm, whipped cream pounces engineered and muscled to rise and point directly at what they wanted. She had a pronounced southern accent that is the accent of the Midi, probably downtown Marseilles.

The Captain stared at the ceiling. His face was haggard. He spoke hopelessly. 'I am not only about to lose my wife, my business, my houses, my honour and my freedom but that bloody family of Bitsy's seem to have impounded my last erection.'

'You were programmed to lose those things. Like a computer. You don't care. You don't give a damn.'

The Captain got out of bed and put on a white wool dressing gown which had French blue piping. He shuffled into slippers and crossed the room to the great tactics board and stared down at a sector problem in the Battle of the Coral Sea.

'I care about my wife,' he said morosely. 'I could lose all those other things but I can't lose my wife.'

'You are a liar.'

He wheeled on her. 'I worship her!'

'O.K. Keep up the good work. But worshipping and loving are two different things, n'est-ce-pas? You may say until you are blue in the face that you worship her but you love me. That is what counts – eh, chérie?'

He stared downward at the great board. 'This is a wonderful battle. The Coral Sea was the first naval battle fought by carriers between carriers. Commander Fujikawa says his side lost because the Americans had broken the Japanese code and knew every move in advance. Well – I told him to re-engage with any tactics he cared to use, that I would fight him with the Yorktown and Lexington and the three cruisers and no matter what he does I'll blow him out of the water.'

'Colin?'

'Yes, darling?'

'I don't mind it when you talk for an hour or so about your wife. I mean I understand her problems. I can sympathize with her. But you are out of your mind if you think you are going to talk to me about some horrible war that was fought before I was born.'

'It just happens to have been one of the most decisive battles of the world. It brought to an end the run of Japanese victories and it also showed that henceforth the carrier would be the key factor in sea warfare.'

'I will scream. I swear to Jesus I will scream so loud that everyone in Mayfair will think it is lunchtime.'

'Very well.' He turned away from the battle and went back to sit on the edge of the bed beside her. 'You are such a very good girl in every other way beyond naval battles that I must state the facts. The calm facts. I love my wife. You are my friend.'

'You love me!'

'Please, darling – '

'All of the time you could spend with your wife you spend only with me. And you never fool around with other women – eh?'

'You are sure of that.'

'I am sure of that. Women know these things, my friend.'

'How?'

'Because you were raised in France. Who but a Frenchman would be absolutely certain to never be with more than two women at once? What sensible man needs more than two women? When one is mad with him, the other is automatically glad with him. Who needs more?'

'I am not promiscuous, I will admit. But not for any pragmatic French reason.'

'Why then?'

'Because my father, small, rather liverish looking, somewhat elderly, fuzzy bit of a man had such an allurement for all sorts of women that he was knighted for having procured the most delectable of them for the late Edward VII. In short, he exploited women. I shall never do that.'

'You won't do that because you lack your father's confidence. You feel unworthy because your brother, Lord Glandore – '

'Never mind Glandore!' he snapped. His own brother, the second Lord Glandore who could have lived on serenely at Clearwater House ran a heinous bowling alley in Boise, Idaho. It brought actual physical pain to the Captain when, every Christmas, he received a garish *open* postcard of seasonal greetings which showed a one storey, plaster building holding up an enormous neon sign which said, in orange and violet: LORD GLANDORE'S BOWLING AND BILLIARDS then, in a vomitous yellow, WEINER CURB SERVICE. Whenever the Captain thought he had sunk to the bottom, he would think of his brother and that beggar had even sold Clearwater House and had left him, a bloody orphan, to wait at Mrs Good's until his Aunt Evans had come from Canada and had arranged to have him apprenticed to her sister's husband who was in the wine trade in Bordeaux.

'When did you last sleep with your wife – eh?'

'That is irrelevant. You know we have been having these damned misunderstandings about money. I've not slept with her because she refuses to sleep with me.'

'She is frigid!'

'Ho-ho-ho.'

'No? How is she compared with me?'

'You know very well I will not discuss that.'

'Of course not. You are always the perfect gentleman, n'est-ce pas? But you betray this great lady you love every day. And worse – you betray me and yourself when you try to say how much you love her.'

He stood up and walked back to the tactical board, leaving abruptly and stiffly saying, 'My entire life proves, I think, that it is not possible for me to betray anyone or anything. Do you understand that?'

'No. Please tell me about it, mon capitaine.'

'What sort of a man would I be if I gambled away my wife's fortune and I didn't love her more than life? What sort of a man would I be if I bought all this for you out of a wine business her father had handed to me on a silver platter, if I didn't love her?'

'You would be the man you are.'

'No!'

'What is wrong with that? I love you as you are. Do you know what you are?'

'What do you think I am?'

'You are a boy who plays with toy ships on a piece of painted board. You are still a boy who dreams that he would have been a high milord if it were not for his vulgar brother. You

54

are an infantile personality who believes in war and navies but you are also a wise, kind man whose gentleness prevents him from being ridiculous.'

'If I thought you really believed that, I should leave you.'

He turned away from her and began to move the toy ships tentatively. Yvonne, her eyes filled with tears, took up the long, silvered soprano saxophone and began to play the shreddingly mournful oboe passage which told of Lucifer's terrible loss from 'Night On Bald Mountain'.

8

If Bitsy had met Yvonne Bonnette face to face instead of relying on a budget-conscious CIA photographer who had therefore used black and white instead of colour film she would hardly have been as complacent about her husband's little fling, now in its third year. For one thing, the black and white film had given the mistaken impression that Yvonne was a blonde and secure women do not fear blondes the way they used to because, dimly, they had slowly come to understand that men are attracted to all women, not only blonde women, and because Bitsy believed that blonde women were essentially shallow women.

To testify about Yvonne's hair under the best of circumstances would have edged toward perjury. It was a changing red-into-blonde-into-copper-into-brick shade which can have fantastic beauty all by itself but when it was combined with everything else Yvonne had and the everything else was combined with Yvonne's mind and her tenacious loyalty, Bitsy might well have suffered deep shock and, in her frantic desire to protect her husband, might have ruined the loving masochistic relationship on whose bed their marriage lay.

Yvonne's mother had wanted her to be a school teacher. Yvonne's father, a direct man, had refused on the grounds that she would be the cause of creating thousands of tiny French sex maniacs before their time. Yvonne had an identical twin sister from whom she could not be told apart until well after the girls were sixteen. Claire had become Queen of the Bidets at fifteen and had reigned upon that effluent throne in Marseilles then across the Cote d'Azur against formidable claimants from the film industry, letters, and what often appeared to be the entire female population of Scandinavia under twenty-three, until she had lost her looks and her figure had sagged from downward pullings.

The twins looked alike until they looked like the lives each led. Each girl had reacted differently. Claire became hard; Yvonne resilient. Claire was self-indulgent; Yvonne stayed wary. Claire became a bully like their father; Yvonne a cherisher like their mother. Claire wanted quick, easy sensations to jump off the surface of her skin like body lice. Yvonne wanted something more or at least something else, she didn't know what.

Yvonne's mother was Charles Bonnette's second wife. Yvonne never knew what had happened to the first one. She had asked her father once and he had said she was killed in a bull fight. Unaccountably, Yvonne's mother was English. When the twins were fifteen and Claire had headed out into the night, her mother had sent Yvonne to Miss Jupp's Classes at Wonersh, Surrey and she had stayed there for five years.

Yvonne's mother had met her father when she had been a tourist in Turkey. She was still quite out of her bird-like, English, do-anything-to-please-a-man skull about Yvonne's father. When her mother died Yvonne was nineteen. She had won her teaching certificate to teach French or English. She returned to Marseilles for the funeral and became filial in that she decided to stay on in Marseilles to teach.

That is called Le Collision Course.

Her father loved her. He lavished any number of useless things on her. He still thought the girls looked identical but Yvonne thought Claire looked like a whore, the kind who would shriek like a foghorn that she was coming while she ate an apple in the customer's ear. Claire was on heroin. Claire sounded as if she had been kicked in the throat.

No matter how hard he tried to tell himself that he could not tell his daughters apart, which was a sound ruse to teach himself that he loved them equally, Charles Bonnette, with the chips down, preferred Claire because he did not trust Yvonne because he had been able to prove again and again that she always said what she meant and he found it impossible to believe that a daughter of his could be that stupid. Mistrust brings fear, fear brings dislike. He loved Yvonne so he would try to imagine that she meant something else than what she said and he would try to figure out what that could be so he ended up making himself a fool to himself. No one can stand having anyone around who makes him do that to himself.

He called the girls together, gave them each a copy of his will which said they were to share everything equally then told them what they were to do to get through to two separate safe deposit keys, one for Yvonne and one for Claire, which held a considerable amount of money for each, in Switzerland. It made him feel better. He had bought his way out. Then he suggested that Yvonne develop her English speech even further, as her mother would have wished it and that he thought she would be happier in England. And he handed her a plane ticket. Then he drove her to the airport in two hours. Yvonne, a happy girl, returned to London.

At the airport he tried to give her a thousand pounds but she said she had many friends in London and that it would be so much better if she could make it on her own but that she would most surely tell him if she needed money. In London she sold her mother's amethyst brooch which had six diamonds and the proceeds gave her enough for a classified ad in the *Evening Standard* and enough for six nights of bed and breakfast in a guest house in the Finborough Road, between the Fulham Road and the Brompton Road, which was run by a marvellous cook who had retired from stage management named Mrs Bennett. She stayed in the room for two days until the classified advertisement appeared. Looking for her own ad her eye was drawn to a large, bold-faced ad which said:

WANTED:
INTELLIGENT GIRL WITH
MASTERY OF FRENCH AND
ENGLISH TO ASSIST WINE
COMPANY DIRECTOR AND
LEARN WINE TRADE.
GOOD WAGES.

Yvonne went directly to the telephone box in the corridor and made an appointment for an interview at eleven forty-five the next morning.

Yvonne was not merely beautiful and achingly fetching. She was sensuously, provocatively, blindingly, eagerly beautiful and achingly fetching even if that is a fairly common sight in June on London streets. She had a heavy mouth of natural viscosity. She had heavy eyelids which somehow abetted a prismatic flaw within her eyes which absorbed light in a manner which made them seem perpetually glazed with lust and which suggested unimagined pleasures from her body which, standing still, seemed to be imploring to perform. This while the girl herself might be thinking about finding rye bread at the bread riots which happened around the clock at Selfridge's. Or wondering whether she should have her hair done on Tuesday or Friday. It was a prismatic flaw but it was a rich gift which combined ineffably with her high breasted body and her incomparably long legs.

She was dressed in Chinese red, a painter's colour, the first time Captain Huntington saw her. He was wearing a black suit with white piping showing at the waistcoat and cuffs; very much his managing director's suit. She wore no stockings, no panties, no brassiere. He wore Viyella socks because there had been a sock drawer supply problem that morning, but Viyella socks were much too warm for June. Londoners actually believe that June turns their city into Pernambuco. His underwear was sound, which is to say boxer shorts which give the organ and testicles a chance to breath; not clenching jockey shorts.

It was a hot day (for London). There had been a sock supply problem because Bitsy had gone to Hot Springs for a reunion with Daddy, Uncle Jim, Uncle Pete and the boys for the celebration of the twentieth anniversary of Harry's graduation from Groton. After the reunion Bitsy would need to go on to Fort Worth to look into the possibilities of a suede factory which (Uncle Pete said) could easily be converted to make sturdy leather garments for the Air Force. Further, his valet had been absent and drunk for three days making an acute sock drawer problem.

The warm day (always aphrodisiac in chilly countries) and one of those peculiar hangovers which follow drinking a Spanish absinthe called Ojen, had made the Captain horny enough to move lumber with his erection which he had thought was at optimum until he saw Yvonne Bonnette. He began to swell grotesquely under the force of that prismatic flaw and those fantastic charlies which stared at him blindly from under that Chinese red dress. He stood up, out of reflexive courtesy rather than from a need to brag, and Yvonne came to admire him – and not only for his posture and tailoring.

They spoke in French and they were greatly pleased with each other's French as only those who speak French out of some four thousand other languages in the world can be. People in Paris, even Montelimar, have sat for eternities discussing the correctness of Donald Duck's accent in the dubbed French version.

She thought he was the most beautiful man she had ever seen. No one could ever say he was old enough to be her father, even if he was, because he looked so young.

Captain Huntington continued the employment interview as they strolled across Green Park towards Buckingham Palace, where the flag was up, by telling her about his life in the navy, about how he re-fought naval engagements in the Pacific with a friend who lived in Tokyo, about how he maintained as his personal cook, the great Juan Francohogar and –

She stopped short in the path and grabbed his arm with urgency. 'You are *that* Captain Huntington? My God! You are the man who has Francohogar?'

'Awfully good food really,' the Captain said. 'Of course, if you come to work with us you'll be eating Francohogar's food every day.' He thought on that for a flash. 'Well, almost every day.'

'Mon Dieu – a man who owns a wine company and has one of the greatest cooks in the world.'

'Nature wants design,' he said fatuously. 'Nature insists upon completing perfect design wherever it can.'

They went into lunch at the Ritz at one-twenty but did not eat much. They were talking absorbedly, accidentally touching each other when the room was empty at three-fifteen. As they started out of the room they passed a piano.

'I think I will sing to you,' she said. She sat at the piano as he leaned across to her, his head quite close to her head. She sang to him softly in a husky voice unlike her speaking voice, '*L'important c'est la rose*'.

When she finished he said, 'I think it would be an awfully good idea if I were to book a suite of rooms here which would have a piano so that you might sing that several times again.'

'That would be good,' she answered gravely. They left the restaurant. He moved slightly ahead of her as they approached the reception desk and spoke to the receptionist who nodded solemnly. 'Bechstein or Knabe, sir,' he said.

'I think Bechstein,' the Captain answered decisively.

When the door closed behind the receptionist, they never made it to the piano. Indeed, for the time being they never made it to the bed. With vigour and deep appreciation they pleasured each other enormously upon the harsh hotel carpet in the foyer just beyond the entrance door. Later, when they had made it to the bed he was able to persuade her to permit him to maintain her at the Ritz until he was able to find a flat for her much closer to the wine company in Farm Street which was at least seven streets away. He forbade her to return to Finborough Road for her few clothes. 'This is a new life for both of us,' he said with a tremble and she held him closely once again. Then he became alarmed that the shops would be closed before they could get out of the hotel and they rushed out.

As a consequence of their compatibility, Yvonne seldom left the flat in Charles Street. The subject of the job never came up again. He would depart the Farm Street building early every morning when Bitsy was in residence, which was most of the time, and stride like a stork down Chesterfield Hill to let himself into her sweet house. She would be waiting for him. He gave Francohogar a rise in salary so that the cook would agree to stage a scene, insisting on a new arrangement of his job at Farm Street and to take his *batterie* to Charles Street because Bitsy was perpetually dieting and Yvonne was perpetually hungry. This 'new arrangement' was, considering the length of his contract, that Francohogar would have to make himself available at Farm Street whenever Daddy or Uncle Jim or Uncle Pete or the boys had important business or government entertaining to do. All in all, everyone was happier. Yvonne was one of the greatest cooking audiences ever to chew. She had knowledge of what Francohogar was doing and the problems he faced. She understood why greatness in a dish was achieved not just that it tasted good but because it must have the great lover's ability to woo all the five senses, not merely one or two. After most meals she would review each course sitting on a high stool in the kitchen, extolling his decisions to do what he had done to achieve what he had achieved and she knew wines and why they married with what he cooked.

They ate empyrean lunches but Yvonne almost always dined alone. She didn't mind. She wanted time to paint and to practise on her soprano saxophone to which she had aspired to master from the recordings of the late Sidney Bechet and which had a quality of wistful (and therefore safe) melancholy which made it evocatively romantic.

Bitsy was enormously relieved that Francohogar had departed because she could now really lay on with Swiss rye croustilades, beef consommé, and soda water to protect her line.

Bitsy was not a frigid woman: repeat, *not*. She was young, and fit and in love with her husband. Only the fact that the Captain was an ectomorph who rarely drank hard spirits and who, through an acquaintance with a Dominican diplomat, sipped tiny glasses of Japanese mushroom tea through the day enabled him to measure up to what each of the young women felt to be their daily due. The Captain planned to keep the unities of the ménage under perfect control; to have himself a flying fling at the moon without pain or trouble to anyone. But he and Yvonne and he and Bitsy had begun by being in love then, irreparably, they came to love. He not only did not want to change anything, he couldn't have changed anything.

9

As with all girls named Bitsy, her father had given her the name before anyone had had a clue as to the height and size she would attain. Fully-grown she was five feet, eleven inches tall. She had a firm thirty-eight-inch bust. She had a pillowy thirty-nine-inch behind. She had long heavy bones. She had muscle from much tennis, swimming, skiing, riding, archery and fancy diving, each begun the day she could walk out to the appropriate playing field. She was not lumpy or bulging, she was large. She could wear dresses – not ever slacks or shorts or suits – and look slight and girlish in them. The Captain had seated her in Italian furniture because it made her feel smaller. She rode in a Mercedes 600 SEL because it was bigger than any other car. Her hunters were enormous and she rode them with total command. The dogs at Rossenarra were Irish wolf-hounds almost big enough to take a saddle and do point-to-point racing. The doorways and ceilings of their houses were wide and exceptionally high. Not really because all these things very much mattered to her. It was because, of all things, when Daddy came to visit them he could still call her Bitsy and not gulp.

Her full name had been Elizabeth Blue Willmott which made her a Massachusetts girl by divine right; a descendant of the slavers, smugglers, and rum traders who had founded the American republic. Her mother, a strong woman, was a Ryan and Catholic, the daughter of another sort but just as great a figure as any on her father's side, but he had been an Irish immigrant not too long before so she had had to be strong to maintain the balance and had insisted successfully that Bitsy be raised as a Catholic and that Daddy (!!!) convert. After Mama had died they were not as militant about it. Daddy had taken her out of Radcliffe when he had headed the CIA unit in Great Britain and she had taken a degree in mathematics at Girton College, Cambridge, by the time she met Captain Huntington.

Daddy had held many high-higher-highest government posts, most of them invisible but all of them with maximum power and access to total information which came to be useful in investing the family's funds. However, no matter how far away from State his assignments seemed to take him for whoever was the incumbent President, Daddy's home always would be State. But they had all always been in interesting work. Uncle Jim had served six Presidents. Uncle Pete had been a governor and a two term senator but Mr Dulles had known he could really serve his country by bringing together the purchasing elements and the purveying elements of heavy industry, electronics, transportation, and aerospace, and he had served there ever since. All the men in the family served the nation in the sort of jobs where they could not hide from all sorts of interesting information if they tried. Something was always coming up, among the five of them, at least once a day, which offered thriving investment possibilities; the Sixties having offered them prodigious, even heroic opportunities. Service to one's country was both a noble and a profitable thing but, naturally busy men so high in government, surrounded by a radical Eastern establishment press who would have howled with delight at the misunderstandings which could have been created, could not stride into the marketplace directly so that Daddy, Uncle Jim, Uncle Pete, Harry and Larry channelled their information through to Bitsy in London and it was Bitsy who directed the Swiss company and the Panama

5

company to make the investments where they should be made.

Bitsy's own capital, which had not been inconsiderable to start with, had been increased many, many times. Bitsy's mother had owned department stores and an outboard motor company which Daddy had picked up for a song after the Depression and which he had pulled through to make it become a big winner. Even Daddy thought it was a big winner – and it was all Bitsy's and so were the stores. Bitsy's mother had died while Bitsy had been on an Antarctic cruise with the Girl Scouts of America. Cousin Harry had had the Secretary of the Navy send a bomber for her from the South Atlantic fleet which had flown her from McMurdo to B.A. then to Rio then to Kingston where an Army fighter flew her to Perfection, the family's lodge in Maine but it had been too late. 'She would have been pleased that it had cost over two hundred thousand dollars to get you here,' Daddy said mournfully, so even the taxpayers of America had mourned Mother's passing, unknown to themselves. Bitsy had loved her mother very, very much but when she was gone, Bitsy became the only female in the whole family.

When she was twenty, when she had married Colin, Daddy had settled even more money on her due to a fortunate shift in the small print of the tax laws which Uncle Jim had been able to slip through as an insignificant, prolix 'rider' clause to a bill for Alaskan Eskimo relief funds. Not that she needed it as a young bride, but it had brought a certain amount of relief to Daddy (as well as to the Alaskan natives) in the form of tax benefits. Even though Daddy was an able lawyer himself he always shifted legal counsel with each new President to the firm from which the President himself had come to the White House because he had found such firms always to be taken so much more seriously in the important things.

Bitsy was very keen at business things. She knew where her holdings (and those of the men in her family) stood at all times,

66

within four hundred thousand dollars, at the end of any given week. She never speculated. She only invested in 'sureties', in the 'positives', in the directions which were certified by the sort of information Daddy, Uncle Jim, Uncle Pete, Harry and Larry were able to get from the heads of business and industry who depended on all five of them so much for assured performance.

Three years after she and Colin had been married, Bitsy had been thrilled to get the letter on the heavy stationery with the deeply engraved crest from Lord Glandore. The envelope was really worth keeping, she thought, but the notepaper itself was as quaint as quaint could be. In four colours, using a process which made the printing look like neon, the notepaper said: LORD GLANDORE'S BOWLING AND BILLIARDS WEINER CURB SERVICE. The letter had wished her every happiness in marriage to the writer's brother then said that Lord Glandore was in a position to put Bitsy into chicken sexing about which he was prepared to send along highly confidential reports if she would care to invest twenty thousand dollars. On a hunch, and because the amount was so tiny, and of course for reasons of family solidarity, she had sent Lord Glandore the cheque (on a Calgary bank) and – for the only time in their marriage – Colin had flown into a towering rage until she actually thought he was going to knock her about the room. He had demanded that she call for a return of the investment immediately. She had told him she would do, of course. But she had not. First, because she did not want to until she could know the investment hadn't been a mistake. Secondly because the investment did repay itself to realize about a three hundred percent profit. Each year when Lord Glandore's Xmas (not Christmas) postal card arrived with its photograph of his bowling alley building front in Boise, she tore it up lest it upset or offend Colin.

But she had been curious about Glandore. 'What sort of a man is your brother?' she had asked Colin at the end of a wonderfully happy day at Rossenarra. She had flinched at his instant coldness, at the immeasurable distance the question had put between them.

'Lord Byron had a nanny,' he had finally replied, 'named May Gray who seduced him when he was nine years old and kept at it for three years evolving him into a confused and promiscuous man. My brother went to visit my Aunt Evans when she lived in the United States – every summer for three years. America was the nanny who seduced him evolving him into a petty, confused businessman. He was an Irish peer. His father had been the trusted friend of a great King of England. He had the family's estate at Clearwater, near Leap, towering above Glandore Bay. He had the respect of the district. He was a peer of the realm *and what did he do with it?*' Colin's voice twisted into riflings of sound which were close to a sob. 'He sold *everything*. He settled in *Peru, Indiana,* from whence he sent forth spectacularly tasteless notepaper proclaiming LORD GLANDORE'S GENUINE PERUVIAN CHINCHILLA FURS AT LESS THAN YOU WOULD THINK. A *hereditary* peer who, if he were to die tomorrow if he had that much grace, would automatically make me Lord Glandore and you *Lady* Glandore. I put it to you! If you were Lady Glandore would you rush to Boise, Idaho, to open a bowling alley with weiner curb service? Life, to my brother, is a petty transaction which is resolved in a blizzard of minimum profits. I should have had that title, I tell you. We should be living in West County Cork right now taking the salutes of our peasants as they touched the forelock. Oh, *God*!' He banged his forehead with his right fist. 'Oh, God, God, *God*! Don't you ever mention that man's name again!'

Bitsy had understood. Colin, she could sense, was so three-dimensionally, even wastefully, aristocratic, so precipitously noble, whereas she could hardly bring herself to feel empathy for a man who ran a weiner curb service (unless it should happen to grow into a national chain). Colin even gambled, she suspected in those days, as if he were only trying to amuse his friends; the highest act of aristocracy. And, of course, she would have adored having been Lady Glandore and, perhaps, quarterly taking her rubies and sapphires out of the vault at the bank to wear at some well-guarded dinner at Rossenarra. But beyond all that she loved Colin. Most of the time she loved him even more than she loved Daddy, Uncle Jim, Uncle Pete or Harry and Larry.

Bitsy met Colin because Daddy, being CIA chief for the United Kingdom, had to know, cultivate or proselytize all sorts of naval and military people. She had met Colin Huntington on the bridge of the aircraft carrier *Henty* of which he was Executive Officer. She had had to step from a gig into an elevator outside the hull of the enormous ship, then to be lifted up, up and up to the flight deck. She had been led through a labyrinth to another lift to take her to the bridge and the stupendousness of it all had made her feel small and so feminine for the first time since she had grown so lavishly into her teens. She had mastered her terrible disappointment at having been made so big for all of life that she was poignantly grateful to the Royal Navy and its carrier, *Henty*, for making her feel fragile and small.

At the very moment of that new realization of herself she had gone through a doorway and had faced Colin Huntington.

After nine years of marriage he was still the handsomest man she had ever seen. He was so perpetually scrubbed and immaculate. He could dance so well and he could beat her at tennis – something few men had ever been able to do, to her chagrin. He was so courteous, no more with her than anyone else, but no less either. He was blithe, he was vastly accomplished at his work and he had the disposition of an angel, Daddy said, because when Daddy learned how she felt about Colin he had had his agency pull a report on him.

The report had mentioned Colin's gambling, of course, but the gambling hadn't taken its deepest hold on him yet. The report also said that Colin was one of the biggest snobs in the British navy and that he had very, very slight ideas about the nature, meanings, or value of money, but Bitsy knew that all naval officers had to be terrible snobs and that they had no reason to have any clues about money because they all lived in, and were graciously supported by the world's biggest yacht club by virtue of being the elite of the yachtsmen of the world. Heavens, on the Pacific station she had been *expected* to bring the big Mercedes and all transport had been provided by the senior service just as Colin took along his Rolls, as all officers were allowed to do in peacetime. It had thrilled her. How else could they have racked up those two sets of chic, tax-free Hong Kong plates?

But Daddy's report had also said that Colin was a superb naval officer and that he could be expected to keep going up and up to the high reaches of the Royal Navy and that was what convinced Daddy. Colin was outstanding fleet admiral material. Bitsy could have told Daddy that without any report. You just had to look at Colin to know that. Also, she was absolutely certain that the nature of the CIA's mission had absolutely nothing to do with Daddy's admiration of Colin's potential.

After she had lived with him and had loved him even more, somehow all his colouration seemed to change, after the weird tattoos which seemed to have been inflicted upon his soul in such horrifying design began to move into visibility at the very surfaces of his actions, after his total helplessness seemed to be matched and balanced by his total indifference to whether the game would continue or not, whether he would rise or sink, succeed or fail she had loved him still more as she stared at the knowledge that the traditional outside of him seemed to be as incapable of change as his tragic inside.

Most of all she was twenty years old and he was a strong, demanding lover. Bitsy had had lovers before him. She was a Washington girl of high position so she was well courted by a rich assortment of the diplomats of the world because if a diplomat loves his work and lacks money he must have a wife with a fortune. She was healthy. She had been raised by Daddy, Uncle Jim and Uncle Pete to have no doubts and she had taken deep pleasure in sex until it became a hobby with almost slogan proportions: *Coitum plenum et optabilem*. Also, because she was a large girl, until she met Colin, she felt it was her duty to sleep with as many acceptable men as possible so that she could know and share with them the immutable proof of her extreme femininity. After she knew Colin, it never occurred to her again that her size would have anything to do with the intent of gender. In Washington, she had burst out the other side of what had only been a phase: from the frantic grapplings to a sort of opaqued indifference to sex. When Colin valued her as a woman she was ready.

Colin was transferred from the Caribbean station, on duty aboard the *Henty*, to Portsmouth, which she absolutely could not stand so, quite silently, Bitsy and Uncle Jim arranged to have Colin exposed to the British Embassy side of naval life in Paris where, in return for the favor, Bitsy had done such effective entertaining that she had won the gratitude of the Foreign Office. But Colin became terribly restless for being away from a command and he began to gamble rather badly. So (covertly) she had had a word with Uncle Pete who had chatted with a dear old friend of the Joint Chiefs who had immediately agreed to trade Colin off with Whitehall and the Admiralty in exchange for eight thousand tons of Freon gas for use in air-conditioning the tropical shoreside quarters of British commanders and diplomats in southeast Asia and the Pacific. This most certainly could not have been done, of course, had it not been for Colin's superb service record. Colin had been returned to the *Henty*, as its Captain, while his astonished predecessor had been booted upstairs with Admiral's stars. Uncle Pete was a marvel.

And, after all, the gambling hadn't always been such a terrible thing. The same people, she thought, who, of course, looked down on craps shooting in Harlem or that mysterious numbers game they play, thought it perfectly all right to win or lose on horse racing if you knew the trainer or the owner and bet because they thought it looked good. And the same people who considered a man something of a neurotic if he played three baccarat tables at the same time naturally were the same people who bet a million a year into a broker's computer in fat patches back and forth on half-point rises in the stock market.

The true fact, Bitsy knew then, was that if a gambler wagered his own money, even if he lost all of it, he should not be censured. And Colin's gambling, at the beginning, had only been relatively costly. That is, of course, it had cost more than Colin's pay as a naval officer and more than the income he had inherited from his Aunt Evans (who, to Bitsy's awe, had once been reported in Robert Ripley's 'Believe it Or Not' as the most appetant reader of mystery novels in history; reading, on an average, six crime novels a day: two thousand one hundred and sixty-four a year, actually exceeding the number of cowboy fiction titles read yearly by Dwight D. Eisenhower while in office). But Colin's losses were still not more than Bitsy found appropriate for a gentleman and were easily payable by her. It wasn't as if he drank.

Then, in the third year of his command, at the apex of his fulfilment as a naval commander, Colin had lost eighty-seven thousand pounds at poker to two mainland Chinese politicians who had enormous power in Hong Kong and Macao. It was infamous Macao that had tripped him and had sent him sprawling downhill, like an innocent, dumb-dumb Jack in the nursery rhyme, to break his crown, but this American Jill refused to come tumbling after.

The first time Colin had begun to become truly, obviously aberrant about gambling, he and Bitsy and about eight others from the squadron and their wives had all gone to the Central Hotel to watch the opium smoking on the top floor, then to peek through the knot holes at the whores working on the floor below, then down one more floor to the posh gambling rooms intending to have dinner on the first floor but Colin had begun to play baccarat and had won three thousand odd pounds in Mex dollars. It was as if he had been set afire. Although the rest of his life after that certainly proved that he gambled to lose he was, back there in the beginning, set aflame by winning and after a while she understood that all of his winning at everything had been so important to Colin – as a prelude to losing.

He went back to the Central Hotel again and again, sometimes with her but mostly alone, whenever he could get away from the ship – although he rarely won very much after that first time. Out of his magnified sense of courtesy he had not brought his eventual, inevitable problem to her. She could have paid his gambling debts to the two mainland Chinese or the CIA could have sent two of their colder-eyed 'solution men' out to deal with them. It would only have meant a telephone call and a short meeting to Daddy. But, because he did not go to her or her family, because he could not pay them, the two Chinese had gone to the squadron.

They were insupportably powerful local politicians from mainland China. Macao was nominally Portuguese but in every way it existed by the sufferance of the mainland. Of the two politicians, one was absolute dictator of Hong Kong, the other was the ruler of Macao. The English had nothing whatever to say in Hong Kong if it crossed the policies or wishes of the first. The Portuguese were helpless in Macao if it interfered with the purposes of the second. The two men entertained each other, alternating between Hong Kong and Macao and their greatest pleasure was winning at gambling. By their mission they controlled gold prices, the cost of food through the rate of its importation as well as the cost of water. They regulated shipping, docks, opium, prostitution and gambling industries, took orders only from Peking and transmitted all receipts which the Chinese government regarded as taxes to Peking. Among other things they controlled was the entire labour force, the harbour, all drydock facilities as well as all water, fuel and ship's stores, if needed. No squadron commander bearing the responsibility for the maintenance and safety of the vessels under his command would think of rippling the waters of his dependency on these two men. Captain Huntington had known who they were and all about them when he had sat down to play with them (an action which, in itself, could have brought about a courts martial) and as he had lost more and more, he had known he would be unable to pay them and that, as a direct result he was endangering his ship and the squadron and the Admiral who trusted him. The Chinese politicians went to the Admiral and demanded payment.

Admiral Sir Francis Heller, very old school, with a gorgeous white beard and the reputation of being a very, very keen embroidery worker, had sent a tactful intelligence officer to visit Bitsy while Colin was at sea. The Admiral did not choose to discuss the matter with Colin. Schute, in fact, had been Colin's Intelligence Officer but he was being invalided out of the service because of his loss of half an arm to a shark. He was a roundish man with snapping blue eyes, golden hair and a magnificent Full Set, Royal Navy personnel not being permitted to grow a moustache without a beard.

Commander Schute had spoken very considerately, even delicately. He had explained that his mission was most painful because Colin was his dearest friend who had once saved his life but there had been this almost sinister shoreside incident and that while it was altogether possible that Colin had been drugged or framed, the I.O.U.s signed by him were right there, weren't they? – and something demmed well had to be done, didn't it? – it could all develop into the most frightful mess and heaven knew that if there were any political repercussions they could well be sure the Chinese government would put full weight down on the old plunger detonators, wouldn't they – that, in fact, the entire thing was simply the most frightful mess.

Bitsy had paid the gambling debt in cash, of course, and Commander Schute had returned the Chinese receipt to her after delivering to her his own receipt. Everything had been returned to spotless order excepting that Colin had been asked to resign from the service.

Bitsy never mentioned the cause of Colin's resignation to Daddy or Uncle Jim or Uncle Pete (and she felt most disloyal about concealing such a thing) but she had thrown herself into an intense period of investing to get her composure back as well as the money and her work had really impressed the family because it was through that the idea evolved whereby Bitsy would do the investing for all of them, from overseas, proving that it is an ill wind which blows no good and every cloud has a silver lining. She never allowed herself to be diverted from her investment activities again, and if Colin complained about the gaps of time it put between them she merely told herself that he had no right to complain because he had caused it all.

Colin hadn't given her (or anyone else) as much as a clue that he had been in awful trouble and was now free of it. He allowed nothing to change; he remained the same as always. He did not know (as far as she knew) that the gambling debt had been paid at all and had not (for such a militant aristocrat) been concerned that it ever would be. He had never mentioned it and the fact was, if she had not earned back the eighty-seven thousand pounds through correct investment and gotten started as the investments officer for the whole family, she would have been really hurt and upset. As a wife she loved him for his aristocratic manners but as a democratic American she did love gratitude as well. *On the other hand,* he did not, therefore, as husbands will, blame her for having paid off the debt. Nor did either of them, at any time, admit or refer to the polished brass fact that he had been ordered to resign his commission. He had come home one afternoon and had asked her casually how she would feel about returning to London because he had decided to request permission to resign from the navy.

She hadn't known what to say. He had loved the navy so. The navy had been his reason for excelling in everything he did (except gambling). The navy was his substitute for his lost peerage and he had risen in it to the equivalent rank of earl. It was his reason for being in that odd male way. She had not known what to say so she had followed his lead.

'Resign?'

'We could be in Asia forever, darling. Asia isn't the place for us. We've had enough of Asia, haven't we?'

'Asia is a bit sticky.'

'I long for London, actually. The navy is all well and good for a man in his thirties but I'm forty-one now and, all things being equal, I shall soon be fifty.'

'What do you want to do in London?' Not how are you going to make a living. If he felt he must do something Uncle Pete could get him something selling aircraft to Harry at the Pentagon.

She was aware that he had to do something or be discourteous to himself. Colin cared very much about what he seemed to be – perhaps more than he cared about what he was, in that odd male way. Maleness was a far less predictable thing than femaleness, she knew, because men were romantics who fed on illusions which had no measurements except to themselves. Women treated realities and knew their cubic contents, their weight, and their accountability factors. She had no conception of how he would answer because she knew his answer would only be an evasion of the reality of having lost his illusion of the Royal Navy.

'I have a knack for wine,' he said: 'I am sound about wine.'

Colin had, it was true, put Daddy into a marvellous opportunity only two years before when he had passed along that information on Château Ambreaux. It was owned by the ancient, awesomely authoritative Henri Emmet, gourmet and oenologist, who was the banker one saw in France, if elegant banking were to be done. Daddy had acquired the entire vineyard, a *grand premier cru*, and had been able to take a tremendous tax-loss on the tip, and to send out hundreds of cases of the noble Ambreaux wine as Christmas cards and, in every way, had been entirely grateful to Colin. At Thanksgiving Dinner, Uncle Jim had arranged for the President to serve Château Ambreaux '49 with his turkey dinner, instead of bourbon. The French government had laid off pressure on the dollar for sixteen days due to this tribute to French wine and Daddy had moved sixteen thousand cases.

Therefore, she hadn't had to intercede with Daddy for Colin. They just adored each other and Daddy was in awe of all Colin knew about wine, so that when Colin said he wanted to set up a wine company in London and would like to swing a loan, Daddy had been delighted to advance the two hundred thousand pounds needed, and had cancelled the previous contract with some distributor who had handled Château Ambreaux for seventy-one years to make Colin's company the sole distributor of the wine for the United Kingdom.

The CIA bent over backwards to help the fledgling wine company with the Bank of England to speed up all necessary permits for exporting sterling without the delay of a lot of red tape. The embassy in France had leaned on the French government so that the sticky paperwork required for wine export could be expedited. No one was surprised when the wine company was an immediate, prodigious success (and Daddy's money was returned to him in record time) because the embassy, embassies of countries for whom The White House, the Pentagon, Treasury, State and the CIA were interesting factors, and over seventeen permanent missions, espionage units, presidential commissions and other departments of the American government in London, as well as one hundred and twelve American corporations and banks, had all been utterly delighted to order their wine and liquor for their London branch entertaining from Colin and even the volume of Château Ambreaux rose by 23·096 percent. If Colin had really cared about himself or the wine business and had devoted as much as half of his time to its development, instead of re-fighting the naval battles of the Pacific with some crazy Japanese in Tokyo, they could have lived quite well, quite independently of her income.

She knew he was re-fighting the naval battles with the Japanese because when Daddy had invested the two hundred thousand pounds with him he had, naturally, had the Agency put him under twenty-four hour surveillance and since they were as professional at their work as the best men of that group could be they had turned out a minute inventory of Colin's mistress's house in Charles Street so she knew he played with the six by ten feet tactical board and that he kept the board in the rear, large bedroom on the second floor of the house where he slept with the woman. She had looked at two of the tactical messages to the Japanese which the Agency had intercepted and copied. She didn't think of them as being boyish; just sad. They were very professional tactics and very sad because he would never engage them in any other, real way, again. They made her sad, too, because he had chosen to re-fight the battles of the Pacific under the roof of his mistress, rather than at home. But, in time, she understood that as well.

She knew about the mistress at first because Uncle Jim had

passed the word. The counter-intelligence unit of the Rural Electrification Commission's security wing in London had been the first to report on Colin's having acquired a mistress. The REC 'eyes only' report had gone through Larry at Treasury and he had cross-referred to Uncle Jim at the White House. Uncle Jim, very sweetly, had sent her a Xerox of the 'eyes only' with a large questionmark in the box for acting instructions in the margin. Bitsy had asked for photographs and tapes as a matter of course. She had been hurt at first but gradually it all came round right again. The young woman was banally French, and blonde with the usual breasts and legs mistresses have in cartoons. She was much too young for Colin and offered him absolutely nothing but sex (causing Bitsy grimly to press him for more as her shares) which was all right with Bitsy who immediately told herself she wasn't all that wild about it.

But, when she heard the tapes she wept. They were the saddest conversations she thought two people had ever had – all endless moanings by Colin about how much he loved and adored Bitsy and how he had this terrible feeling of inevitability about how he was driving himself to lose her. It was just too sad. She wanted to just bundle him up in her arms and carry him off to Rossenarra and keep him there because they had always been happy there so Bitsy shrugged the mistress thing off as being just a little adventure which was consistent with a man of his age in the precise measure, as she had studied it when she had first married, in Gesell's 'The Husband from Forty-Five to Fifty' published by the Yale University Press; an outstanding series.

IO

'What beautiful music,' the Captain said.

Yvonne finished a long phrase on the soprano saxophone then took it away from her mouth. 'Were you talking to me or to Fujikawa?'

'To you. The word beautiful used in any context always means you.'

'That's better.'

'You have no idea how phallic that instrument seems while you are playing it.'

She grinned. 'Let other girls study violin,' she said, 'but it is a long way from home. Symbolically, of course.'

He approached the bed. She patted it. He sat down beside her and leaned forward for a moment to kiss her right nipple. Then he said, 'That tactical board isn't the waste you think it is. It helps me to think clearly.'

'What have you thought?'

'Well – that I owe Bryson two hundred thousand pounds if I am to retrieve the buildings and the wine company which my wife insists that I sign over to her because I owe her two hundred thousand pounds.'

'I even admire you for the way you can get into trouble. It is such gigantic trouble that no one could possibly get out.'

'Working at that board for the past half hour, I think I have found a way to solve everything.'

She sat up and her lovely breasts boggled. 'No!'

'Yes.'

'How?'

'First I must give you a little background. It is in bad taste, to be sure, because it makes me appear such a noble creature, but I assure you that is not the intent.'

'Tell me.'

'I began to think of Clearwater House in Keamore right over the deep water at Glandore where it was said that the ghost of its first owner, Lady Jane Heller-Winikus, haunted and harangued any overnight guest who was in any way connected with the Irish building trades.'

'What has that got to do with –'

He held up his open hand. 'I began to see that people remember forever, perhaps beyond the grave, that which has affected them most deeply. That made me think of my old Intelligence officer, Gash Schute. We were testing some tactical cooperation with the Australians off the Great Barrier Reef a few years ago – what a beautiful place that is – and while we waited for a signal we decided to try some spear fishing. John Moodie, my Exec, and Gash Schute and I went off in the gig – no ratings – and when we got to the outer reef where one can look in and see the bloody fish as clearly as if they were on your plate, Schute showed us a golden sovereign which he had collected and, as those things do happen, it fell over the side. He was very quick. Particularly about money and reflexively his hand darted after the sovereign to retrieve it and it was taken by a Tiger shark, about twelve hundred pounds – maybe fourteen feet long – it just soared along from the far side and under the gig and took half of Gash's arm off.'

Yvonne gasped.

'And it took Gash out of the gig into the water – almost but John Moodie threw himself on Gash who was screaming like an Indian, I can tell you, and held him – but the shark still had Gash's arm and couldn't quite get it off so I went over the side' with an oar and jammed the oar into the old boy's belly until he got the point and ran away.'

'Colin!'

6

'Gash's arm had to be amputated, of course, but he's as fit as can be today.'

'Oh, my darling, you are wonderful.' She tried to grab him by the crotch, she was so moved, but he drew away.

'The point is: Gash was very grateful, you see. Now, to the point. Let me tell you about Gash Schute. I have never known anyone as wildly interested in money as he was. That is an odd thing for a naval person really. He had to leave the service because of the loss of his arm and he then founded The Cambridge Corporation which has become the most important Think Tank in the western world.'

'What is a Think Tank?'

'It is a forest of specialized brains which develop game plans and scenarios for elaborately committed governments. You have said I am infantile. Here are the Great Infants: the governments of men beating drums in what each believes to be the centre of the world but too immature to grasp their own problems much less their proliferating relationships with everything that lives. To be spared the pain of thinking they hire Think Tanks, the new condottieri, who plot the wars and the recessions and the economic carrots on sticks, for pay, and make the politicians seem to understand all that is going on beyond the yacht races, football games, musicales, and summits – and the big job, the management of upcoming elections. My friend, Gash Schute, does the thinking for seven governments. He doesn't know what he is doing either beyond each separate exercise he works out for them as a mercenary. All he does is supply logical solutions to temporary problems so that governments can have an answer, should anyone ask.'

'So you are going to ask him to *think* you out of this? It would be much better to ask him for the money.'

'No, no. I don't know what I am going to ask him – to direct him that is – toward a solution. He would never give up any of his money, it is the most important thing of his life. I understand that and in no way blame him. But deep in his mind is the vivid gratitude he feels toward me because of that fat shark. I will explain the problem and he will think it through.'

'But he must be paid hundreds of thousands of pounds just to think!'

'Of course.'

'So you would have to pay him his fees for his staff and his overheads and his costs. You would have to pay him the world. You would have to steal all the wine in France to pay a man like that.'

'If I could steal all the wine in France I wouldn't need him, would I?' and as he said it it crossed his mind that stealing wine wasn't like stealing money or jewelry or other shoddy things. If it were stolen they had merely to grow more of it.

'You would still need him.'

'Why?'

'To tell you how you could steal all the wine in France.'

'Yes,' the Captain said. 'I suppose I would.'

11

When A. Edward Masters and Captain Huntington returned to the Farm Street house, Bitsy's solicitor, Bartholomew Clogg and his assistant were fussing with heaps of papers at a refectory table. Bitsy was seated on a window seat staring at the entrance to a pub across the road. Her black hair was fixed with a ribbon at the nape of her ivory neck. She stared and wondered what she was going to do when Colin signed all those papers and consented to a divorce. She loved Colin so much.

As the two solicitors greeted each other and bumbled about the marching order of the documents, the Captain crossed the wide room to stand beside Bitsy.

'Must I sign these papers, darling?'

She didn't look at him but she nodded.

'Bitsy – listen to me with your heart and not with your pride and purse,' he demanded in a hoarse whisper. 'Things have shifted under us, but nothing has changed except money.'

She looked at him with horror. '*Except* money?'

He called across the room overloudly to the lawyers. 'Isn't any part of this thing negotiable?'

Mr Clogg looked up from the agreements and touched his necktie. Mr Masters studied the Captain.

'How did you mean, Captain Huntington?' Clogg asked.

'I mean everything we have been discussing is based on her fear of my endangering her security. Can't we agree that if I can replace or even increase the amount of the lost money within sixty days that my wife will tear up these papers. And forget divorce?'

There was an extended silence. The Captain stared at Clogg who looked across the room at Bitsy. She turned away from her watch on Farm Street and nodded almost imperceptibly to Clogg.

'All things are negotiable,' Mr Clogg told the Captain. 'Nothing is absolute.'

Edward Masters' sandy voice cut in. 'Very good of you to say that Bartholomew,' he said. 'Perhaps we can proceed as follows: Captain Huntington will sign all the transfer papers you require then we will work out an instrument now by which the Captain will be permitted to repay the money within sixty days – thus cancelling the agreements he will sign today. That is, the instrument will state that these transfer papers will not become legal documents until the passage of sixty days. Will that be acceptable?'

Mr Clogg looked to Bitsy. She nodded then turned away. Mr Clogg said those terms would be acceptable to him.

The Captain crossed to the long table and, with the help of Clogg's assistant began to sign his own name. Masters and Clogg walked to the far side of the room where they conferred in whispers. The Captain was sweating badly. His hand was trembling as it held the pen.

12

The chocolate, drop-head Rolls which the Captain thought of as his friend rather than as his car, the way a gold prospector might think of his mule, in the sense that the Rolls had extended his credit line at many a European casino, floated him out of London into Buckinghamshire.

He had had a bad morning with Juan Francohogar. They had met at the Lyons Corner House, in Piccadilly, because even if he had been seen there, talking to another man's cook, no one would have agreed that it was he, because it was hardly a place where one would expect to find a former naval person, being filled entirely, as it was, with German tourists and people who carried saxophones. Francohogar had been distraught, a most awful state for an essentially phlegmatic man.

'You see – I would honour your obligation, Captain Huntington, no matter what were to happen but – Captain Huntington – he puts something called *ketchup* on everything. It is a raw tomato sauce which combines with – '

'I think I know what it is. I think I have heard of it.' His eye fell on a bottle with red contents on the table. 'Something like this,' he said, extending it to Francohogar.

The great cook refused to touch the bottle. He nodded with horror. His voice broke. 'He wants canned pineapple. He wants fish fingers. I mean he wants me – *me* – to buy him frozen fish fingers. You cannot even comprehend these. They are batter which is stuffed with hot moist paper then he covers them with ketchup. I made him a terrine of larks and rabbit and he looked at me with loathing and told me that he did not eat cold meat loaf.'

'Why this is outrageous! The man poses out in the world as a gourmand!'

'Gourmand? Gourmand? Do you know what he drinks with my food? Portuguese red wine and sweet, unknown, execrable German white wine – and ho, ho, ho – when he wishes to have a bit of rosé – he mixes the Portuguese red wine with the rotten German white wine!'

'You cannot mean that! Surely *surely*, Juan, you are joking with me.'

Francohogar's face turned to green marble. 'I do not joke about the food and the wine, sir,' he said, biting off each word. 'He – puts – salt – on – everything.'

'Then – for any one of the things you have said here today – he has broken the contract. You may never come back to cook for me, of course, that would be incorrect, but you can return to France and open a restaurant in Paris.'

'I cannot stand Paris. There is not room for one more person in Paris and all the people are eating steak and frites anyway.'

'Then you can return to your own restaurant, the Ammej. You will make it the most famous restaurant in a region where there are no restaurants and yet there deserve to be. The Guide Michelin will send inspecteurs now.'

'I cannot dishonour you, sir. If I leave Monsieur the Ketchup Gargler, it would dishonour you.'

'I got you into this, Juan. This is my obligation, not yours. If you will permit me to call on Mr Bryson and explain why you cannot continue and if you will give him sufficient notice, you must return to the Pyrenees.'

'I am so conflicted! I love London. I have found a girl named Maudie Gonkums and I could not bear to leave her.'

'Take her with you.'

'She does not even speak English much less French.'

'Maudie Gonkums? I would have said that was an English name. What does she speak?'

'Who knows what she speaks? She says it is English. She was born in London and she has never left London but she speaks – oh, my God, how she speaks!'

But as he rode through Buckinghamshire the Captain was determined not to allow his problems to ride in the car with him. It was a very pleasant sort of day, meteorologically. And because he felt a deep love for his car he sang to it as it bore him along, swiftly and soundlessly.

> Bore four one inches,
> Stroke three point nine,
> Tappets wot pinches,
> Molybdenum wots fine,
> Austenic steel valve seats,
> Oh, let us rejoice
> For the mare who does care,
> Yes!
> Her name is Rolls Royce.

He knew where the dear thing was taking him, in a general sense, although he had never been there. He enjoyed the scenery he was occasionally permitted to see through minute breaks in the high, green hedges along the road. He greatly appreciated Gash having established the Cambridge Corporation on a tertiary road which did not tempt wide lorries. He drove slowly, savouring the absence of traffic, thinking of the luck of Hugh Villiers who had begun as a humble baron, like Lord Glandore, in 1616, to become Duke of Buckingham in seven short years, then to have a shire, a palace, and even a Seine-side gate of the palace of the Louvre named after him. He thought, in quick transition, of Baron Glandore, Duke of Glandore, Glandoreshire in western Ireland, County Cork was too big anyway, Glandore Palace and a gate, too, Seine-side or otherwise, a strait-gate or perhaps a needle's eye? – and felt contentment for about nine long, delicious seconds when he saw the neon sign which he always carried in his head: DUKE OF GLANDORE BOWLING & BILLIARDS WEINER CURB SERVICE.

His friend, the prospector's burro, wearing the stainless steel tassel called the Spirit of Ecstasy, came to a large sign fixed in concrete behind a fence made of continuous open rolls of barbed wire, an oddity on such a green and pleasant estate. The sign said: THE CAMBRIDGE CORPORATION and that line was surrounded by the fright-words RESTRICTED AREA and PROCEED NO FURTHER.

He turned his friend into the stately avenue leading to the main house which was not in sight and moved through, witnessed by a double file of ancient stag-headed oaks. All at once he realized that these were the grounds of and this was the avenue to the great Axelrod House where the minter and engraver of money for Elizabeth I had worked and lived four centuries before. Instantly he knew Gash Schute had bought Axelrod House because of his hero-worship for a mortal who could make money directly with his own hands and craft, without the costs and discounts of middlemen.

As the avenue curved a uniformed Royal Marine carrying a rifle marched smartly from a sentry box to the centre of the road to block the car's path. He stopped the car opposite a checkpoint hut from which a sergeant major of Royal Marines emerged wearing a side arm. He marched directly to the car and came to smart attention. 'Suh!' he bellowed.

'Good morning, sergeant,' the Captain said amiably. 'Commander Schute is expecting me. I am Captain Huntington.'

The sergeant stiffened. 'Suh! I had two years of sea duty aboard the *Henty*, suh.'

'I thought I'd seen you before.'

'Your identification, suh,' the sergeant said impassively. The

Captain pulled a case out of his pocket and handed it over. The sergeant took it into the checkpoint hut. A third marine appeared with a Polaroid camera. 'Your permission, suh,' he said. The Captain stared into the camera as the flash went off. The sergeant reappeared from the hut and returned the card case.

'Straight ahead to checkpoint Two, suh.'

'Two? How many are there?'

'Four visible, suh. Radar, hover balls, sonar and tower observation as well, suh.'

'Thank you, sergeant.'

'Captain Huntington! *Suh!*' Saluting, the sergeant snapped to rigid attention. The Rolls moved serenely and silently along the lovely avenue toward a sky by God and Joseph Mallord William Turner. Pheasants pheazzed, snipes sniped, and disgruntled birds groused all around him amid forty shades of lush green. How he hated the country! It was filled with snakes and holes and tiresome stone walls; nothing like the sea where there was never any clutter.

At the second checkpoint another sergeant major of Royal Marines noted the licence number of the car, then went to telephone in the hut. He pressed a red button on a wall machine then he telephoned in a normal way to check the licence number back to checkpoint one. A large, rectangular celluloid button bearing the Captain's photograph, name, and car licence number tumbled into the slot of the wall machine. The sergeant took the button to the Rolls and gravely pinned it to the Captain's lapel. 'Two sergeants major of the Royal Marines is a lot of rank for a two-hundred-yard course.'

'Mostly field rank ahead of you, Captain Huntington,' the sergeant said. Then he saluted so smartly and tensely that his arm quivered at a precise right angle to his eyebrow as he bellowed, '*Suh!*'

Axelrod House was among the stateliest of stately homes, a

palace of the Elizabethan renaissance which had been called 'the last masterpiece of the Perpendicular', that native British ecclesiastical idiom. At no time, except at Axelrod House, had the perpendicular been achieved with the same towering effect and easy assurance. Robert Smythson was (perhaps) the architect. Across the forecourt as the chocolate Rolls Royce swanned in, the house rose, tier on tier, its great, flat, long glass windows glittering like a dowager's eyes.

Oddly, there was a porch attached to all this perfection which plausibly had been ascribed to Holbein. It was worn by the great house as a false moustache might have been attached to an elegant face, rented to play a character in some historical film. Excepting for the porch – or perhaps with the porch itself viewed separately if that could be possible – everything about the Axelrod exterior was in solid, tested, unassailable English taste, unprovoked by tides of fashion.

A colonel of Royal Marines waited for the Captain in the main doorway. He wore full dress white helmet which symbolized that he had seen overseas service, a shelf of decorations, and a blood-red sash around his waist which was somewhat obscured by a gun belt. As the Captain slid out of the car, a Marine slid in behind the wheel and moved the car away.

The Captain gazed fondly upon the model Colonel. 'Clive! How bloody marvellous!' he said happily. 'I haven't seen you for seven years.' This man had shattered more clay pigeons at sea and more hearts ashore than any other member of the squadron. They had all been Asiatic ladies, as well. And he was a superb beer drinker who never lost his figure.

The Colonel was pleased. 'Rather like being back aboard the *Henty*, sir.' They shook hands warmly and slammed each other on the back. They went into the house and the Great Hall which was perhaps the first in England to be treated simply as an entrance if one could feel that stepping from the street into the Kaaba at Mecca was a simply treated entrance hall. Its axis ran counter to medieval precedent, transversely from the front of the house to the back so that, as the legend went, Lady Joan could 'preserve the economy of bidding both hello and Godspeed to her guests at the same time.' Over the fireplace in the Great Hall was the enormous heraldic cartouche with elaborate strapwork by the English plasterer, Abraham Smith, which projected the Axelrod coat of arms: ten gold coins, a ram, and a jug of mead with a quill pen rampant.

The Colonel led Captain Huntington to a wall grille surrounded by switches. 'Routine in your case, sir, but I must take your voice print.'

'Really?'

'Say the vowels into this, sir, if you will.'

'May I sing something?'

'Best to speak, sir.'

'Gilbert and Sullivan would have been proud of this security system,' the Captain said into the grille.

Imperturbably, the Colonel led the way along the transversing Great Hall to the extensive informal gardens at the rear of the house. His old comrade was so silent during the long march that the Captain was moved to say impulsively, 'Everything is quite extraordinarily formal, isn't it, Clive?'

'Commander Schute runs a tight ship, sir, where all is tickerty-boo. This is the fleetship, sir.'

They approached a trap shooting range where Commander Schute was shattering clay pigeons. As they came up, the Captain could see that he had worked out some sort of sling by which the gun was attached to his only full arm.

'Go!' the Commander cried and a clay pigeon was sent flying across the sky. His one arm swept the point of his gun along with it and fired, scoring precisely. Then the Captain realized that he was not firing a shotgun but an automatic rifle. 'Ho!' the Commander shouted and destroyed another clay pigeon.

'I say, Gash,' the Captain said with admiration, 'are you shooting with a .22 rifle?'

The Commander turned to greet his friend with enormous pleasure. 'Colin!' he cried, 'How supah!' He gave the Captain the stump of his left elbow to shake, saying, 'I mean, you can't very well shake hands with a warm rifle, can you?'

'It is a rifle, then?'

'Anyone can hit with a shotgun, can't they? I mean I've gotten so I prefer to use a pistol on the little things, but for heaven's sake don't actually *tell* anyone that.'

The Marine Colonel had disappeared. They were alone and the U-sounds of their speech, only just slightly spurious, made it as if they had been marooned within an ever-thickening thicket of croquet hoops.

The Commander was wearing dazzling tweeds with super-bags by Welchman (when Welchman had been in Sackville Street), as would befit a gentleman in the country according to strict rules by TAILOR & CUTTER. But tweeds were far from being a naval uniform which he had been raised within. They were too new. And they seemed to contain some synthetic which made them incapable of rumpling, thus negating the purpose of tweeds. Commander Schute was smaller than the Captain, endormorphic to the curve of being sigmoid. He wore a magnificent blond moustache, having shed his Royal Navy 'full set' when he shed the Royal Navy, and had formidable blond eyebrows which were like gold helmet visors. His cheeks glowed with pink health. His large blue eyes glittered, were cold rather than cool and made one vaguely think they were counting something. He had a long torso and a short pair of legs which bounced like springs when he moved. The Captain sensed that Gash had somehow become a physical culture nut.

'How is Bitsy? *Go!*' He tracked and fired, hitting nicely.

'Quite fit, thank you.'

'Marvellous gel. *Ho!*' He fired again and hit again.

'You couldn't be further away from the navy than here, could you? It is the most splendid house I have ever seen.'

A shadow of bitterness crossed the Commander's face. 'I own the house, yes, and I lease it back to them through a Canadian-Nigerian trust. But I am only a Director here, you see. I do all the heavy planning and all the hard-core abstract thinking. I bring in all the money but they get most of it.'

'Taxes?'

'Damned partners.'

'But surely, Gash – based on your character from boyhood, that is – surely, you are getting the lion's share of it?'

'Perhaps. But I deserve more. I should have more.' The Commander's face had gone heavy.

'Of course you should have more,' the Captain laughed. 'You have always thought you should have more and more.'

'*Go!*' Schute yelled and the pigeon flew out and up to be demolished. '*Ho!*' he shouted again and shot well again.

'We all have our little quirks,' the Commander said. 'I feel about money to the precise degree that you feel about gambling.'

The Captain went grave. 'I am sorry, Gash. I didn't know it was that bad.'

'What brings you here, dear fellow?'

'I need help.'

'What sort?'

'I will explain fully. First, I must make you understand that I need help desperately. I face losing everything – my wife, my life, my business, my houses,' the Captain shrugged, 'my freedom.'

'Gambling?'

'Yes.'

'I am sorry, Colin. How awful for you.'

'It all sounds hideously dull, I know. But I've thought of nothing else. That is to say I have thought about all of it –

every step of it – with all the useless anguish which always comes too late. I can allow my imagination to soar because I have nothing left to lose. And, considering everything, you are the only one who can help me.'

The Commander's eyes flickered evasively. 'Of course. That is, I mean, to be sure. I am greatly indebted to you, Colin. But – how?'

'I need your incredible mind, possibly your fantastic machines. I need the whole way you have trained yourself and your staff and your machines to approach and solve any new problem. The fact is – I might be sent to prison.'

'*Ho!*' the Commander shouted and shot. '*Go!*' he yelled and shot again.

'Colin – you see, well, I am only the Director here. To obtain abstruse counsel from The Cambridge Corporation would cost a sinful amount of money. The reason we deal with governments as clients is that only governments can afford our fees. If it were only my decision, why then of course you could have all the help from every resource we have. But –'

'Perfectly fair, Gash. Perfectly logical and perfectly fair. I would cringe to hear the charges. Further I am sure that there are nations waiting in line, hats in hand, with far more important problems than mine.'

'How very kind of you to see that, Colin.'

'I do have one other avenue of approach, Gash.'

'*Ho!*' Schute fired. '*Go!*' he hit again. 'What avenue of approach is that, Colin?'

'You have often said how much you want to own a million pounds.'

The Commander shrugged, but it was a very serious, committed shrug.

'When you hear me out, you may have a change of mind and decide to join me as a totally invisible partner.'

'Why should I decide to do that?'

'Because I have stumbled on a way to make one million pounds in one month's time.'

They sat facing each other in front of a fireplace which was high enough and wide enough to have held a roasting bullock, in Commander Schute's office which was thirty feet by forty feet, having a sixteen-foot-high ceiling. They sat on matching French baroque armchairs certain Louis XIV; heavy red velvet upon a bright gold frame, intricately worked gold brocade with two-inch-long gold fringes around the seats. The chairs were so heavy with gold decoration that the Captain glanced at the other furniture in the room. All of it was adorned with gold; encrusted or painted with gold.

'If you say we can possibly earn a gross income of one million pounds in one month's time, then I am greatly moved,' the Commander said. 'And I say this flatly – there is no one else alive from whom I would accept such a statement.' He crushed at his magnificent gold moustache with the backs of his hands in excitement. 'But how can that be? What must we do to get it?'

'You think. I execute,' the Captain answered blandly. 'There is to be absolutely no risk to you. You need never leave Axelrod House to win your share. Needless to say, there would be no financial risk to you because that would be unspeakable.'

The Commander nodded vigorously, in utter agreement.

Captain Huntington radiated confidence. Every tone of his voice was assured and reassuring. Really, he had no idea whatever of what he was talking, beyond the sum: one million pounds, magic bait for his brainy fish. His one month's time was an imaginary, pitiably arbitrary period. Beyond that myth all he had to offer, as a leper might offer his sock to a prince, was the thin straw of an idea which Yvonne had blurted out as a figure of speech to make a point – having no idea of its desperate meaning to him.

'I see,' Schute said, eager to cooperate, 'But what is it I will be required to think about?'

'About how I can steal two million pounds' worth of fine wines from the cellars of Cruse et Fils, Frères, in Bordeaux. I know every inch of those cellars. I know where every bottle of the great wines is stored and Cruse is the greatest wine warehouse in all France.'

'How extraordinary!'

'Yes.'

'I mean, really. That is to say in an abstract sense that sort of thing has been a hobby of mine for years.'

'Wine?'

'No. Gigantic robbery. I have designed, with my computers, four fool-proof stupendous robberies but of course I've never done anything about them because I've been too busy – and because they do require a certain amount of professional criminal assistance which I've no idea how I could obtain.'

The Captain smiled indulgently. 'You must leave those plans to me in your will.'

'Will do!' The Commander made a small note in a small book. 'Have you – uh – obtained the necessary professional criminal assistance for your – uh – caper?'

'I – not yet, actually.'

'Have you any idea how to go about obtaining such assistance?'

'Oh, yes. But –'

'One doesn't know what will be needed yet. We might need a safe cracker. We might need three gunmen. It is entirely up to you, all that, you see.'

'Quite so.'

'Well, just so you know how to obtain them. I decided some time ago that if one really felt one absolutely had to have a prodigious sum of money relatively quickly, one simply had to be prepared to steal it. However, in my own case, the risk

7

of exposure is too great. That is to say, I would be killing the goose, as it were, because Cambridge is a huge earner. However, as you have repeatedly said, you have nothing to lose and if you will take all the risks and be the buffer – and God knows you are the only living person I trust – then I'm all for this idea of yours. You know wine. It makes no difference to me that the bulk of two million pounds' worth of wine in its sheer size is, or seems to be, immeasurable. But that's my job. I very much adore challenges like that. Then, of course, and I think it only fair to point this out to you because you did save my life, you are my friend, then I would have this hold over you and, if necessary I could press you to execute those other four master robberies for us. I mean, we could win eight or ten million pounds and not pay one cent in taxes. You do understand what I am driving at, Colin?'

'Indeed, yes. We do these robberies and, if caught, I go to jail. Simple enough.'

At forty-seven years of age the Captain was made suddenly aware that he had left his boyhood behind. War had been a game. Automobile racing was for boys clamouring to be told they were men. Gambling was a disease but it was always a game. A few moments ago it had been right to continue to see everything that way because, in his especially limited view, all that had gotten chipped had been the hard, protective, porcelain covering which was his own life. Until he had heard Schute say from behind those hard blue eyes that he had often entertained the idea of stealing other people's money and – the Captain now admitted, though Schute had not used the words, not having had to – possibly maiming and killing in the process, he had been able to think of crime as one more romantic game.

But that had been from the outside looking in. He was inside now. Perhaps he had been well into crime from the moment he had contrived to lose to those two Chinese to have himself forced out of the navy. As though the lights had gone on at a surprise party and a few dozen of his enemies had been assembled, surrounding him with clubs and screaming 'Surprise!' he suddenly got a flash glimpse of the pain he had caused, and of the pointlessness of selfishness, but the power of the lights did not extend far enough, he could not see his way back, he did not know how he could save himself from what he had done to himself unless he did worse to himself by going forward into this crime.

War was crime with tolerant definitions. He understood war. He must bring himself to the totally impersonal, even industrial state of war so that he would be able to get through this crime, get out to the other side, then he might have time to wonder what he could do about returning to assuage the pain he had caused.

They were both committed to hard-sell, selling each other and selling themselves, and the Captain began his salesmanship at once.

'It would be like one of your scenarios. Such as the one which got the American official in and out of Peking by pretending to be a Romanian when he arranged what's-his-name's, you know, the President's visit in China in time for the election year. I'm sure you have it clearly already – one of those intricate studies which would call upon social sciences and police methods and the electronics of industrial security.'

'I quite agree. Unquestionably.'

'You may be sure, once you've developed the plan, that I can dispose of the wine to a secure buyer and we will be paid one half its value. After all, I grew up knowing the wine trade.'

'But these things – and I am speaking now of the operation itself – can be beastly costly.'

'Only relatively costly. I will provide the operating funds. That is, I will advance the funds and they will be returned to me out of the gross earnings. That is part of my job – to provide the cash.'

'Cash is one thing. And a major item. But perhaps even more important would be the availability of a professional criminal team, so to speak. I mean, you cannot be expected to know how to assemble a group of highly specialized men such as that.'

'If I didn't know how I was going to do that, I shouldn't have come to you. I will deliver those specialists to your plan. Further, all of it will be done without risk to you. I cannot repeat that too often. No one will ever know that you have created this opportunity. From your view all this will be only one more abstruse exercise.'

The glitter from Commander Schute's large blue eyes was dazzling. He rubbed his hands together so hard they seemed to glow. 'Um – well!' he said. He had difficulty beginning his acceptance speech because he did not wish to appear instantly greedy, as though he were some easily-used man. 'When you – um – pay all expenses and the specialists take their share – um – how much will be left for us?'

'My drumhead estimate would be six hundred thousand pounds,' the Captain said. 'But, of course that will need to depend on your plan and will need to be checked out by your computers. But I would say about three hundred thousand pounds for each of us.'

'Colin – let me ask you something.'

'Indeed, yes.'

'Considering the importance of my contribution to the operation – that is, nothing could possibly proceed without it – would you consider increasing my share by fifty thousand pounds?'

The Captain blinked.

Schute continued at once. 'That is three hundred and fifty thousand to me and two hundred and fifty to you?' He watched closely.

'That would be acceptable,' the Captain said.

'It is gratifying to hear you say that, Colin, because it is, after all, a symbol of your regard and confidence.'

'I have stupendous amounts of both of those for you, Gash. Always have had.'

'Would you consider increasing my share of the net to a ceiling of four hundred thousand pounds?'

'Two thirds to you, one third to me?'

'Yes.'

'I will agree to that, Gash, if it is understood that at no time is my share to be less than two hundred thousand pounds. The fact is, I must obtain two hundred thousand pounds within sixty days. That is actually the entire vital thing.'

'I will accept that. Two thirds to me. A flat two hundred thousand to you. Should the net be higher you will hold with two hundred thousand and I will get the overage. Splendid. I am very, very happy.' He extended his hand. 'It will be a privilege to serve under you again, sir.'

The release he felt was so great the Captain could feel his legs turn to water but he made himself project the very essence of relaxed joviality as he lowered himself into a chair to keep from collapsing and pulled an alligator cigar case out of his pocket.

'We'll give them a damned good show, Gash,' he said, grinning, afraid his chin would begin to wobble in a tic if he did not grasp it and forcing himself to think of the mounted brass bands playing in the Horse Guards Parade on the Queen's birthday so that he would not weep out of the sense of terrible relief.

He was saved.

Bitsy would not leave him.

He could buy his cook back – and his buildings and wine business, of course, as well.

If he ever gambled again, which was quite likely, he would gamble only with the money he would be able to earn from the wine business and he would be grateful for the chance to trade in wine because wine would have saved him and wine would have kept Bitsy with him.

He would not lose Yvonne. He would not have to send her away because he would be unable to keep up the Charles Street house. He would not lose Yvonne. He would not lose Yvonne. He would not lose Yvonne. The nightmare was over.

He snipped off the end of a cigar and lighted it. 'How shall we proceed, Gash?'

'Whenever I have a new client,' the Commander said in a new, rounder, more pear-shaped tone, 'I generally suggest that we both sleep on it, as it were, to gain a refreshed point-of-view on the problem at hand. Then – I generally ask if the client can meet with me for an intense information session on the morning of the next day. How would that suit you?'

'Very well indeed. I say, we've just gotten in some of that Pommery Fifty-Three you used to enjoy so much. You must let me send a case of it out to you.'

'Fifty-Three? My word, pure gold. Liquid gold, that's Pommery Fifty-Three.'

'You shall have it,' the Captain said, rising to leave.

13

Basil Schute seemed to have sprung full-blown from the mind of Zeus. He had been a highly regarded Intelligence officer in the Royal Navy, but no one in that service had realized what they had lost until he had gone and, almost instantaneously been recognized on several continents as a master thinker for democracy, for neo-fascism, or monarchy, the new – ugh – Left, or for any other out-dated concept with the strength to totter to him and the wealth to pay his fees for an evolving series of temporary panaceas which were fashionably called 'scenarios'.

Schute had been a child prodigy and an adolescent prodigy. He had been formally educated beyond the point most of the world ever reach by the time he was fourteen years old. He sustained his education outside England by scholarships, accumulating degrees in other countries, and made welcome in all halls of learning as already being beyond promise, already delivering results. As soon as he was able he made his way into the Royal Navy, shouldering tens of dozens of others aside to be commissioned immediately, because he wanted a life wherein he would have maximum free time to pursue his independent studies. He was able to accomplish all Intelligence chores for the *Henty* and the squadron in a total of forty-five minutes a day. In that he did not bother to sleep more than four hours a night it allowed him to devote considerable time to scholarship.

He invented, patented, and sold a speed-reading course which earned him royalties of six thousand pounds a year. He developed a short-cut system for learning all Romance languages simultaneously, all Slavic languages at the same time, and all Scandinavian at once, to the point where a really serious language student, or Common Market salesman of tractors or frozen chickens could acquire twelve languages in two years, six months. By franchising the method he earned twelve thousand pounds a year more. He developed a computer pattern for writing sex novels by computer in twelve languages, utilizing twelve basic plot situations and, because they were unnecessary to the form, no characters. He licensed one leading publisher in each country represented by each language, and the cross-pollination of having the same plots translated into each of eleven other languages delivered permutations which were incredible in terms of sales and his royalties from the software brought him forty-one thousand pounds a year on average. Then he turned his attentions to a basic investment system which, working with company shares and arbitrage and requiring no ownership of companies (which would have required the attention of his management) he used the fifty-nine thousand pounds a year as a continual investment until he had amassed a required capital of two million three hundred thousand pounds with which he had ultimately formed The Cambridge Corporation, a Guianean-Nigerian corporation, paid for with his untaxed funds from Swiss banks. All in all, financially at least, in a relatively short time he had done well for a British naval commander.

Regardless of what he told Captain Huntington, and anyone else, Schute had never had any partners in The Cambridge Corporation. There was no 'they'. He broadcast the false impression that he was only the Director and that 'they' were getting most of the money but it simply wasn't so. 'They' were merely eleven foreign bank accounts in as many countries through which the money was moved so fast that never more than two per cent in taxes was ever paid to any nation.

He made his place in the world of abstract thought and game plans by gratuitously solving problems for the Hudson Institute and the Rand Corporation by mail, in the same way William Shakespeare might have submitted his plays directly to a West End producer. The American think tanks both were grateful, even astonished. Both paid him well and, in the course of time, he exacted from them the most fulsome letters of praise a man in the Think Tank profession could ever hope to receive. The Commander took these letters to the very officers at the Admiralty who had pleaded with him to stay in the Royal Navy, in London, and they were forthcoming when he suggested that he be given a chance to solve some of their problems. The Admiralty checked him out with Washington who checked him out with Rand and the Hudson Institute. The reports were whole-heartedly admiring of Schute's ability so he began to do 'simple scenarios' for Her Majesty's Navy. The navy in turn was so smug about its find that the Prime Minister's office had to learn about Schute, then the P.M. had become so smug about *his* find that he was unable to contain the news from the French and Germans, so that CIA found out about him and passed the word back to Washington and Tel Aviv and, within a very short three years, Gash Schute was earning money at a prodigious rate.

He had based his entire technique upon the terrifying lack of interest by politicians in even the most elemental sort of reality-testing. He lunged with total thrust at the concept that there was a permanent crisis of leadership in the West. It took no genius to understand that there was not only not enough wisdom to go around but that politics was a full-time job which left no room for thinking. So few were trained to think, that what lawyers did actually passed for thinking until lawyers, together with such pondering giants as chartered accountants, had inherited the earth by preempting the leadership of the passing civilization. These gallant leaders were marching safely behind the populations whose fashionable credo, pinned on them by the renegade churches, was the infinite good intentions of man, a theory which was refuted by all man's unfashionable history because none of it, as far as Commander Schute could see, testified that man was capable of sustaining good intentions, if any.

Their leaders (!) told the savage, simple-minded people comforting stories while they arranged for their destruction. Schute, the living Think Tank, wove these stories for the savage, simple-minded leaders: twenty-minute solutions for eternal problems; make-shift, temporary escape routes; two-dimensional expedients for multi-dimensional cost. Only gold was forever, Schute knew.

Gash was a naval nickname which was conferred on any officer or rating whose name was Schute. If there were seventy-two Schutes with the fleet there would, automatically, be seventy-two Gash Schutes. In the Royal Navy any waste matter for which there is no use, which needs to be tidied out of the way, is called 'gash'. Gash is disposed of, over the side, on a gash chute. An ordinary seaman named Barry Gashe refused to reenlist (although he loved the service) because his shipmates called him Shoot Gashe and this came more and more (when he was two over the eleven ashore) to sound like an imperative sentence.

Commander Gash Schute had one ideal: gold. He had one hero: his father who had been a dealer in gold bullion. As a small boy, little Basil had thought of his father as being covered from head to foot in gold dust all through the day at his place of business and requiring, at about five minutes to five o'clock, to have himself very carefully brushed off by two trusted workmen using two large (special) vacuum cleaners which transferred the gold dust to a locked box from which it could be recaptured. As Basil grew older he would ask his father, a pious Church of England man, if the family had any Aztec blood.

'Aztec blood on what, Basil?' the father had asked, lowering the *Financial Times*. 'If we've got Aztec blood on anything, inform your mother, or Mrs Ryan. They'll take lemon juice to it, or something like that.' So Gash had never really learned what the answer was. Still, he knew they must be Aztec. Everything about the family was golden. His mother had been a shiny, blond woman who had cooked a great deal with attar of saffron. His father had rose-gold hair and great mustard coloured eyes like a carousel horse. Young Basil deplored his own dark-brown hair. As soon as he was away from home he had taken to dyeing the mousy stuff then to growing a flowing moustache and dyeing it then to dyeing the hairs on the backs of his hands; then the hair of his arms, legs, axilli and chest. At last he dyed his pubic hair because he had fallen in love. All the hairs of his body were a beautiful, light-golden colour, the very colour of the gold dust poured like salt every working day; a prince's ransom; a talking tower of gold.

The beauty, power, and allure of gold obsessed Basil by the time he was fourteen years old. At eight, he had begun to hone himself as a scholar so that through industrial chemical engineering, magic, linguistic incantations and high thermal stresses he might, with modern technology, achieve alchemy on an assembly line basis. It might be said that his pull toward gold had formed his life as a vaudeville intellectual. His parents were impressed that the boy had taught himself to speak Quechua, the language of the Incans by age nine. His father was naturally embarrassed that his boy was entering the university before the sons of his friends had finished elementary school, but proud nonetheless, remembering that his own grandfather had been able to name the jockey who had been up on every Derby winner, in or out of sequence.

By the time Basil reached Cambridge, at twelve, he no longer

107

believed alchemy concepts to be feasible but he had a grasp on the illusion that knowledge could be harnessed to earn great sums of money and that money could buy gold, no matter if illegal. The gold people of the world had the banks of Switzerland for that.

Gold became his only zest. He admired women, but only blond women with the exception of native Indian women of Bombay who converted all assets into gold jewelry. In time he came to pursue only blond, rich women, then only rich women then he put them aside altogether because they took time away from earning and cost altogether too much money.

Gash knew, because his god-like father had told him during the hour each evening he spent with his son, that gold was the only substance which had remained constant in all its values over six thousand years of endless change.

Gash had no hobbies, no family, and few interests beyond gold. He could not become a mining engineer because he was claustrophobic but also because his father had not found it necessary to labour in muck and darkness to get gold and to be able to touch masses of it daily. If he had heroes beyond his father, these were metallic such as Ballarat's 'Welcome Stranger' nugget which had been found in 1869 weighing nearly one hundred and sixty pounds, and the peacock nugget from South Africa which weighed over twelve pounds or the thirty pound nugget from the Lena River goldfields in Russia.

He would lie in darkness and measure, in golden terms, that all the gold taken from the earth in the past five hundred years could be contained in a cube which measured fifteen yards in each direction. Sometimes his heart almost burst with admiration for the Rand mines which loved gold as he loved it, although in the opposite transit that they wished to turn their gold into money and were willing to raise and mill over 60,000,000 tons of ore in order to extract four hundred tons of gold. For the Rand companies to gain a cube of gold of about nine feet meant a gigantic capital outlay on engineers, machinery, labour force and power. Fifteen million pounds needed to be spent on a mine's development before any gold could be recovered at all.

Only gold was constant against all change. There were a hundred and fifty different substances which, at different times and places, had been invested with some range of value – animal, mineral, and vegetable. But gold was more beautiful than silver as silver is more valuable than tin.

Schute cross-pollinated historical and new information about gold into his banks of computers and had been able to determine within 2 percent the amount of gold which had been taken from the earth over all time and how much was probably remaining. He had been extraordinarily cordial to his clients in the American government so that he could be sure to get a supply of moon minerals, trembling to know whether the moon contained gold.

He was certain that the Americans had sent men to the moon to assay because America had a grave gold problem. He had written a scenario, which had been taken very seriously at the top of the American government, concerning how gold could, theoretically, be removed from the moon one ton at a time but the payload of only one million one hundred and fifty-two thousand dollars could not justify the cost. He had a unit at work on the problem now. How to lift and deliver one hundred tons at a time. He knew it could be done and, as he looked into the sky at night, he saw the moon growing smaller and smaller.

But Gash Schute was not money mad, as he seemed to most people who knew him. Money meant nothing to him. Money was only something one had to earn to buy gold. Money was frivolous and meaningless to Gash Schute except as a mining force. Money got gold.

He abhorred paper money. Each minute all the paper currencies of the world lost value as the populations multiplied and thinned out the values put in by printing presses. Each moment, all the gold he traded in London, Swiss, French and Lebanese gold markets became more valuable with the real, singly-lasting value of sixty centuries. He owned and stored gold in dust, coins, bars and antique ornaments. He owned gold certificates and gold futures, gold options and shares in gold-mining companies. He had executed re-strike coups in gold coins. He and his computers had invented new leverages and escalations for moving gold prices upward in the markets of the world. As a Think Tank, he had advised and re-advised many governments into re-valuations and devaluations of currencies to drive gold prices always in the only direction they must inevitably go, upward – unless there was an international agreement to establish an international common currency, which no one who owned gold, and that designation included most of the rich of the world who controlled the governments, would possibly permit.

He stored his gold in six cantons of Switzerland, in Mexico and on the Norman coast of France because there was no inheritance tax for non-residents. There was one anomaly. He had no heirs. He had no relatives, nor any wife, nor any friend beyond Captain Colin Huntington. Because he admired Captain Huntington, because he was grateful to his bones for Huntington taking such a risk to save his life, he had drawn a will in Huntington's favour but he was unable to bring himself to sign it because even from the grave he could not bear to give up his grip on fifty-two million Swiss francs worth of gold. He did not want it to be lost in a bank vault then ultimately absorbed by the banks, but he could not allow anyone to own his gold because he knew they would immediately transform it into passing values such as the ownership of buildings, or citrus farms or Caribbean islands or motor cars or – too, too sadly this, in Colin's case just gamble it away.

Gold was forever. Gold was immutable. Its proper disposal was the only intellectual problem which The Cambridge Corporation had been unable to solve.

14

The Captain rolled off Yvonne very, very slowly in the enormous bed. Yvonne was glorious and correctly naked. The Captain wore hideously striped pajamas.

'Oh, my darling,' Yvonne gasped.

The Captain was breathing altogether shallowly. Much too shallowly in fact to be able to answer at all.

'I don't mind, you must understand that,' Yvonne said weakly, 'but why do you wear pajamas?'

'Some inate shyness, I suppose,' he answered at last, his stomach rising and falling like an exhausted pugilist's.

'Modesty do you mean?'

'Yes, I think so.'

'Pfui. You are worried about your pot belly.'

'My – pot – belly! You are joking. I am as flat as a board! I only wore these damned pajamas because I thought it might pleasure you more.'

'Why should it pleasure me more?'

'Bitsy always enjoys it best when I have all my clothes on.'

'Bitsy is an American! They are used to doing it in the backs of airplanes and in telephone booths. I am a Frenchwoman. I do it on a bed!'

'Oh, well.'

'Besides, the colours of your pajamas always clash with the colours of the sheets.'

'Everything clashes, darling. Everything is in conflict. And a good thing too according to Toynbee.'

'I will wait for you.'

'When?'

'When she puts you in prison, your wonderful wife who does it with the clothes on, I will wait for you and you will see who loves you and who you love.'

He regarded her blandly. 'There is no possibility of prison,' he drawled. 'Everything is arranged. I am going to pay both of them back.'

'Oh?'

'Everything will be as perfect as before.'

'How?'

'I have a plan.'

'I see.'

'It is a flawless, fool-proof plan.'

'There is no such thing. There are too many fools.'

'Furthermore, you are perhaps the entire key to the plan.'

'How can that be?'

'I need you to succeed with it.'

'From me you can have anything. You know that.'

'I want you to arrange a meeting with your father.'

Yvonne gasped so deeply and suddenly that she began to cough. 'What do you know about my fazzair?' she was at last able to say, thinking all at once of France and almost in French.

'Under less urgent circumstances,' the Captain said primly, 'I should never have permitted the matter to come up. But, one night about a year ago, on my way back from Bordeaux, I had to stop over in Paris to get an opinion on some champagne from Henri Emmet at the bank. I had left my car at the Paris airport. I flew from Bordeaux to Paris intending to drive into town to see the Emmets for dinner. I went to find my car in the parking lot – and I found your father.'

*

The Captain spotted the chocolate-coloured Rolls in the airport parking lot. He made his way to it through aisles of cars and got in. He started the engine and began to move out of the space. The way was blocked by a long, black Mercedes 600SEL limousine which glided to a stop in front of him. He reversed the Rolls back out of the space but another long, black Mercedes 600SEL blocked that exit.

The Captain's position behind the right-side steering wheel of the Rolls was immediately adjacent to the man who sat behind the left-side steering of a Mercedes 600SEL. It seemed longer, sleeker, and blacker than the others. It was parked directly beside him.

The driver was burly with a shock of white hair, a high-pink complexion, a stolidly-sensual, expressionless face and enormous shoulders which were covered by exquisite tailoring of the sort which no Englishman would think of wearing.

'Good evening, Captain Huntington,' he said. He spoke it in English but with markedly French diction. He had the weary, inexorable voice of a movie gangster. He seemed utterly disinterested in anything he might, himself, say. 'I see you are imbedded in the traffic.'

The Captain was nettled that the man presumed to know his name, in fact that anyone vulgar enough to drive such an enormous German limousine himself would have the cheek to speak to him in such a casually familiar way. He looked at the lumpy faces of the men in the car with the burly man and said, with some asperity, 'What sort of traffic do you people handle? Whores or narcotics?'

'Watch it, Captain.'

'Watch what, sir?'

'You know what I mean. Watch it with my daughter.'

'This is all a mistake, sir. I don't know anyone who might be even remotely related to you.'

'I am Charles Bonnette. My daughter is Yvonne Bonnette.'

8   113

The captain was aghast that this thick-necked hoodlum should present himself as the father of a girl of Yvonne's quality and sweetness. This was either some wretched practical joke or something far more serious was involved. They were hoodlums. They must have been attracted to the Rolls and were after his money. They had entirely too much information about him. They must have planned this for some time, excepting the whole thing was very peculiar.

'I find that impossible to believe. It would be best if you showed me formal identification.'

'Why?' Bonnette asked.

'This looks like a stick-up to me.'

'A stick-up?'

'A robbery. Stick-up is an American criminal designation.'

'I know what a stick-up is,' Bonnette answered indignantly. 'What kind of identification?'

'Oh – your Diners' Club card. Anything like that.'

Bonnette fumbled in his clothing jammed behind the steering wheel. With some difficulty he extracted a card case. He found the card he wanted and extended it to the Captain.

The Captain read the card. 'Ah – you are a member of the Cercle de la Chance.'

'I own it.'

'Odious food but first class croupiers.' He returned the card. 'Well, good to meet you, Monsieur Bonnette.' He re-started his car engine.

'Well, watch it with my daughter, you understand?'

The Captain provided a withering look. 'Nothing would make me take less than hallowing care of Yvonne.'

'Just watch it, that's all.'

'Signal your man to clear the way, please.'

Bonnette made an exasperated gesture at the driver of the car in front of the Rolls. It moved out of sight.

'Good night, Bonnette,' the Captain said. 'And watch it with that awful food at your club.' He drove away with all the ensuing silence that only a Rolls advertisement could command, leaving the clamour of the car's ticking clock behind him.

Bonnette turned to the hoodlums in his car. 'Pretty classy guy, eh? You know who he has for his personal cook, right in his own house? Francohogar that is who is his cook. And this guy happens to be a very good friend of my daughter, Yvonne.'

The Captain was tying his shoelaces. Yvonne said, 'Papa just happened to do it that way to show you how many Mercedes he has.' She giggled wildly. 'He was only trying to make a nice impression for me.'

'I had the distinct impression they were rented cars.'

'How terrible he would feel if he knew you thought that!' She rolled over in bed with glee, squalling with laughter.

'I certainly will never mention it.'

'No, no! Never!'

'I also got the indelible impression that he was a big-business criminal.'

Yvonne became sober at once. 'Yes. He is a big-business criminal. He makes his fortune from the misery of other people. He sells them dope. He gives them chances to gamble. He steals whatever he can from them. He corrupts police and judges. He demands perjury. He extorts money from the weak then he lends it back to them at ten percent a week.'

'But he does all these things successfully?'

'Oh, yes. He has a genuinely talented criminal mind which is organized because he is a genuine, organized criminal.'

'I had hoped he was. That is so very important to me.'

She stared at him with hard eyes. She was beginning to be frightened. Having a weakness like Colin's was one thing. Vices and kinks were nothing to the British. They felt no guilt. It was their own lives and no other British really judged them because the vices made them all the more human. The British hadn't been Catholics for such a long time that guilt was not *à la mode* anymore with them. But – a big difference – if they weren't trained into guilt they were trained not to break the law. If he ever had anything to do with her father it could have terrible consequences for him.

'What are you saying?' she asked harshly. A rage was gathering behind her lovely young face. 'No matter what else may happen to us in this life, I would pray that you would never get mixed up with him.'

'I am only asking you to introduce him to me – less formally.'

'Why?'

The Captain shrugged.

'I ask you – why?'

'I think it is best that you never know why.'

'Do you know what you are doing? Do you know what kind of people these people are? I know. He has murdered men and he has had them murdered. He has had people tortured. Are you listening to me? He was in opium growing to make heroin to sell to children. Then he came to France and he, himself, was their big executive in charge of manufacturing the heroin to take the future away from people and cities and to make crimes and more crimes so they could squeeze enough money out to pay my father for the heroin. Is that what you want? Do you want to study how to die? Do you have any feeling left? Because if you have any feeling, if you have one scrap of feeling then you cannot have anything to do with my father who does not believe in hope or love or people. Only in money. Only in power. Mostly in money. Go to him and you will be dead.'

The Captain exhaled slowly. He had been holding his breath to hear her answer. 'If you refuse me in this,' he said with a still voice, 'if I do not meet your father, my wife or Bryson will send me to prison and when I come out our hearts will long have been empty of each other. I will be an old man and you will be on the other side of the world.'

She was out of bed, her naked body flashing across the space between them. She pulled him into her arms. 'I love you so. I can't help it. I can do nothing about it. I love you so.'

The Captain's hand moved downward along her naked back. It patted her pink bottom soothingly and gently. His face was framed over her shoulder. His eyes stared out into the far distance into a memory of long years before, into a Valentine of sentimentality which he always took out and gazed upon when he wanted to sharpen the teeth of his misery.

There was a long, wide lawn at the front of Rossenarra which he had brought to a beautiful shade with one part sulphate of ammonia to one gallon of water for each square yard and by covering it with the finest manure at the end of October on each even-numbered year. He had produced that lawn from sacks of fescue seed the way the weaver in the *Arabian Nights* had produced the magic carpet. The lawn was greener than Ireland, softer than baby food. Beyond the lawn the high box of Georgian house, as lightly-whitely pink as a child's ear, stood behind its massive limestone porch with many tall windows, sixty-seven of them, all of them needing to be washed on the first day of spring. The Georgian box had long arms ending in a garage on one side, stables at the other. A many-layered waltz was playing inside the house: layers of violins and horns, layers of percussion and woodwinds then the forest of sounds would part and the soprano saxophone would break free to run like a young girl across the open field of the 'Valse Vanité'.

The massive front door opened. The Captain, wearing a tropical, white uniform of the Royal Navy with a captain's stripes, was dancing with Bitsy in the main hall. She wore pale green chiffon with only the outlines of deeply purple flowers printed upon it. Her luminous black hair and her large, green eyes were the focal point of the room. Her face was a great bowl of happiness as it stared upward at his — as a child has watched the evening star.

They whirled through a door to the billiard room then through it and beyond, into the large salon where her portrait by James Richard Blake hung bewitchingly above the fireplace. They waltzed gaily through the furniture which had been her dowry, past a photograph, in a silver frame, of King Edward VII speaking conspiratorially to Lord Glandore, then through the doorway and on into the main hall.

He could hear the music. He could remember it note for note forever. They danced into the dining room. He whispered something and she laughed deliciously. He let her sink slowly into a chair. They clinked glasses, sipped, adored each other.

15

The chocolate-coloured, drophead Rolls Royce with the Hong Kong licence plates made its continually arrested approach through the security maze which surrounded Axelrod House. The Colonel of Royal Marines stood to greet him as before at the massive porch. He was taken to the voice print grille where switches were thrown.

Unaccountably to himself but, he thought afterward in the measure of recognizing that he was leaving his innocence behind him, the Captain recited the passage of Matthew Arnold's 'Dover Beach' which began:

> Ah, love, let us be true
> To one another for the world which seems
> To lie before us like a land of dreams
> So various, so beautiful, so new,
> Hath really neither joy, nor love, nor light
> Nor certitude, nor peace, nor help for pain
> And we are here as on a darkening plain
> Swept with confused alarms of struggle and flight
> Where ignorant armies clash by night.

The light flashed green.

'I had forgotten those lovely words,' the Colonel said.

'I wonder what they mean,' said Captain Huntington.

The Colonel led the way to the memorable staircase down which Lord Axelrod had tumbled servants for allowing his posset to grow cold. They passed two marquetry doors; each quarter ton leaf was carried smoothly on only two brass hinges.

There was no record remaining of the man who had created the splendid amalgam of frail marquetry and delicate ironwork which was the broad staircase. The treads and risers were of mahogany inlaid with satinwood, teak, ivory and ebony; the soffits were elegantly panelled and inlaid. As they climbed they could hear the rustling of the iron ears of corn against the wreathes and rosettes of the balustrade.

At the top of the stairs, the Colonel moved them in stately procession through the Long Gallery, a peculiarly English architectural development, whose walls were covered with seventeen Brussels tapestries depicting the story of King Midas. The Gallery was also banked with IBM magnetic tape typewriters, about two dozen of them, all typing on steadily with nothing living in sight. The armed Colonel said, 'I am told these typewriters can memorize the contents of every book in the British Museum and type out each word of them without flaw twenty years later.'

He opened the door at the far end of the Long Gallery and passed the Captain into it. The Colonel did not enter. He shut the door and switched on the light of the panel which said: COMMANDER SCHUTE IS CONFERRING.

The Captain was euphoric. The recovery of the two hundred thousand pounds was now so virtually certain that he had been moved to take the bull by the horns and had visited Bitsy at Farm Street the night before. He had rung the bell twice in their special coded way then he had let himself in with the scrollwork key.

Bitsy was in the bedroom watching the fourth re-run of the *Forsyte Saga* and sorting out purchase orders for woollen socks from Special Service in the Pentagon which admired the sort of socks her plant in Northern New Jersey could turn out for ski borne and Arctic troops, thanks to Cousin Harry's generous endorsement of them. As the Captain came into the room she grabbed her throat and cried out his name, looking helpless and ravishingly beautiful, as though she had not heard the doorbell and had been greatly surprised.

'Have I startled you?'

'Oh. No. It's all right.'

'I rang. The special way.'

'You did? I didn't hear it.' She was treading water frantically to decide which position she should take. What should her policy be? Why did men always think in terms of surprises? But he was walking steadily toward her as she sat up in the bed. He hadn't hesitated in the doorway which might have helped her arrive at some positive position.

'What are you *doing* here?' she tried on for size.

'Doing? Nothing – yet.'

'What do you want?'

'Want? I am your husband.'

'Oh, no, Colin. Not that. Not that.' But the truth was it had been such a long time and Soames being so miserable on that TV screen had made her think how miserable Colin must be and since she knew how miserable *she* felt the whole thing made her sort of ropey.

He had seen that light glaze from over those eyes before, making them look like the glass eyes in Cuban religious statues. He understood all her languages. He knew she felt it was merely etiquette to tell him that love making was out-of-the-question because that was a reflex of her generation, in her country, the generation before they spread their legs to do it for an apple. She had to declare that there was no possibility of their ever, ever copulating again – in tones which said such action had been outlawed by the Attorney-General on the grounds that the Director of the Federal Bureau of Investigation was too old to cut the mustard. He sat down beside her on the bed and she began to move her hands all over him while she protested, as though they were not her hands, but all at once they became her hands as he guided one of them and she

121

moaned 'With all your clothes on, darling. This time with all your clothes on.'

She asked him to leave at once when it was over – it had taken a joyfully long time to be over – because she was expecting a conference call from Daddy and Uncle Jim and simply had to be able to concentrate.

He had floated along Chesterfield Hill to Charles Street feeling so free of pain and tension that even though he thought of gambling, he had no interest in it.

Yvonne was waiting for him naked under the blue sheets. He thought that it was as though these two women had antennae which could pick up the signal from him from rather far-off Buckinghamshire, that their world was saved, that everything was going to be wonderful forevermore.

He had slept as he had not slept for many years that night. He had never been more sure of himself and the future, nor more happy.

As the Captain crossed the enormous room to Schute's desk the Commander, being now the two-thirds owner, did not spring to his feet in welcome but pulled himself slowly up, shook hands, then pushed a large coffin filled with overlong cigars at his guest.

'Ah, thank you, Gash. I didn't know you smoked.'

'Don't actually. But your fantastic Pommery arrived this morning and I felt encouraged to do something hospitable.'

'How very kind.' The Captain snipped an end off and lighted up. 'But, speaking of hospitality, must I have the same struggle with your security arrangements each time I visit Axelrod House? After two such processings surely I may be considered safe?'

'I am *so* sorry, Colin. But, no. You must go through the agonies every time.'

'How awful.'

'We have a desperately pukka security committee – the CIA people, the Foreign Office, the navy chaps, the West German Federal Police, Japan's Kampei Tai people, the French SDECE and Israel's Sherutei Betahan fellas and they set the rules, not I. Further, I too must suffer through it each time I leave and each time I return, hence I refuse to budge.' That was all a lot of bumf, of course. The Commander had designed the procedures to merchandise his business.

'Well, thank heaven for all that expertise, then,' the Captain said. 'This room must be entirely safe.'

'My dear fella. Every room in the world is bugged. Nothing we can do about it really. I mean, every little schoolhouse, every church is bugged. But we'll only be chatting about a robbery in France. My clients couldn't care less.'

The Captain went giddy thinking of Daddy, Uncle Jim, Uncle Pete and Harry and Larry listening attentively to a tape machine while his voice discussed stealing two million pounds' worth of wine. 'Then we must continue our meetings in a moving car,' he said earnestly. He was so stern that Gash laughed aloud at his discomfort.

'I was joking actually. No one can bug this room. This is a transparent glass room which floats within another room whose very power source is a battery pack. This room cost the CIA forty-two thousand pounds, for heaven's sake. Do you know anyone in the CIA?'

'I am not permitted to say.'

'They are most thorough. You may speak right out. What are your orders, sir?'

'This is your cruise for the moment, Gash. When you develop the way to take the wine, then I will take over.'

Gash's manner changed as it had the evening before. He became portentously professional, plucking at his sober aplomb as though it were a harp. His voice dropped into a middle-belly tone of mysterious self-importance and his eyes rather gave away that his ears were listening intently to the sounds he would make.

'It can be done, you know, Colin. The theft most definitely can be done. I allotted forty minutes of intense concentration to the problem last night – to sort out our approaches, as it were, and I decided, after due sifting, that the time is certainly here for Big Business crime to borrow from the expertise of the social scientists, the psychologists, the engineers, the electronicists, and the police themselves for the solutions to the myriad problems which beset the crime industry. My own analytical behaviorists, I am sure, working with advanced statistics and sampling techniques together with all the software I happen to have designed and filed concerning criminal methodologies can – for the purposes of this project – turn my fleet of sturdy IBM computers into temporary master criminals, as it were. I really think we can, Colin. I mean I have slept on that statement, as it were.'

'I slept on what I slept on as well, Gash, and I can tell you that I am utterly gung-ho about the entire thing.'

'In my view,' Gash said, not having listened to the Captain for a second, 'our human criminals have been too deeply immersed in intuitive analyses, however cogent. But the prisons are full up, aren't they? Further, it seems perfectly clear that there can be no doubt that really great criminal action – war and nominating conventions being pertinent examples – must have more scientific means to test its theories. We, here at Axelrod House, we of the Cambridge Corporation, are prepared to provide that.'

'Fascinating,' the Captain said.

'I mean we really can.'

'How?'

'What do you know about computers?' Gash asked.

'Nothing at all. Oh, I used them on the *Henty* but I merely told someone what I wanted and the technicians did the rest.'

'I would like to re-arrange the computer in your perspective. It is not a magical thing, you see. It must have specific reporting of real information and the machines can then co-relate that. I mean to say, to oversimplify, we tell it how many bottles there are to steal, what each bottle weighs, what a case weighs and measures, the various approaches to and from the repository of the wine, the security techniques used to guard it, the temperatures it must rest at, the relative market values of different vintages et cetera, et cetera – then we can begin to ask it basic questions. Such as: how do we lift the most efficient number of cases within the optimum period of desirable time lapse? And so on and on. You will relate, I will co-relate. I will tell you what information we must have. You will provide that. Each day as the ratios of information increase we will be able to ask more precise questions about the plan we will require. I'll have it set up check lists so that we can know we have overlooked nothing. I'll have it inter-relate various time and motion studies. I'll have it give the specifications for the sort of criminal specialists we must have and what the minimum number of these will be. We will be able to ask it for the correct way to share out the gross with these specialists – although I have definite ideas on that myself. It will give us a breakdown on all projected costs down to the last farthing. It will advise us on the yield of the unit value per case, per vintage, for the disposal of the wine. It is a gradual process, you see. The computers and I must think together and I must guide their thinking. I have already undertaken the feasibility studies. I know it can be done.' He stood up. He balanced himself delicately upon the tips of the fingers of his only hand, pressed into the tabletop. 'Come with me and meet the computers,' he said, 'which will tell you how to steal two million pounds' worth of wine.'

*

They went into the Great Chamber of Axelrod House which, in Alexander Somerset's opinion was 'the most beautiful room, not in England alone, but in the whole of Europe'. With its Elizabethan plasterwork and tapestries it should have been one of the most homogeneous and untouched in its culture were it not for the furnishings which Commander Schute had added. However, the room had lost that sense of contact with the past which other sections of the house repeatedly conveyed. The marble fireplace was of splendid restraint (and comparable in this respect with the great fireplaces at Bramshill in Hampshire). Authenticity, then, was indeed the note before the Cambridge Corporation – before the room had been populated by bank and bank of computers, contrasting painfully with the 'other' Elizabethan effect. Two queens; one name; two confabulating styles of decoration.

As they walked along the files and between the rows of the machines Commander Schute said, 'These computers can speak to each other. They exchange information at almost incalculable speeds. They can absorb two hundred and fifty billion bites of information per second. Everything they have stored in their memory cores is instantly retrievable. We no longer need human storage clerks shifting reels from place to place. The machines do it all: to themselves, by themselves, for themselves and their masters. Any one of these beautiful, almost divine machines, can dispense medical diagnoses to forty-one thousand hospitals classifying eight hundred odd different diseases and malfunctions simultaneously. They can translate all the technical journals of all the industry and the military of Russia, Japan, the United States, China and Germany, also simultaneously, while conducting a constant inventory of two million businesses and all the military services of the world, sort their payrolls, build their cost predictions, design their complexes of factory and production, regulate road traffic, aim extraordinary weapons, and send out one billion, twelve hundred million monthly statements of account all at one and the same time.'

'My God,' the Captain said.

'Precisely, dear Colin. We have here either a deity or the ultimate weapon for fascism.'

'If the former,' the Captain said, 'let us hope He has certain criminal tendencies.'

As the days and nights went on they worked facing each other on either side of the programming table, the Commander operating the in-put communicator. They sat in shirtsleeves, damp and rumpled.

'Total storage area,' the Captain droned, 'two million seven hundred thousand square feet. All regional varieties of wines are stored, all grades and all classes.' As Gash fed in the information, the Captain puffed on a long, black cigar and refilled his glass from a bottle of Pommery floating about in an ice bucket. 'Total capacity about three million bottles and perhaps twenty thousand hogsheads. Altogether about fourteen million five hundred and seventy-five gallons which the Cruse firm sells regularly to one hundred and one countries.'

He took two sheafs of documents out of an attaché case and pushed them toward his partner. 'Files thirty-one and thirty-two. They list the bin numbers of the most valuable wines by name and by wholesale market prices. Having been given the dimensions of a single case of twelve bottles, as well as weight, and taking into account the varying sizes of bottles and cases among the Bordeaux, Burgundy and Champagne classifications, will you ask the computer how many cases we will be able to move out of the Cruse warehouse effectively with the minimum staff it has assigned us for maximum efficiency in forty-seven minutes?'

Schute grunted and typed the input. It seemed to the Captain that the print-out began to emerge almost before Schute had finished asking the questions. Schute read from the print-out.

127

'Two hundred and twenty-three thousand four hundred bottles – which is eighteen thousand six hundred and sixteen and two-thirds cases.'

'Splendid,' the Captain said. 'We can easily average fifty-five pounds a case.'

'Net? Net to us?'

'Yes.'

'My word, that is one million seventy-eight thousand eight hundred and eighty pounds.' He began to re-programme rapidly.

'Now what?'

Typing furiously, the Commander said, 'We must find out how this money should be shared. We must know what that filthy pack of crooks is going to cost us.'

The print-out emerged, Schute read from it aloud: 'Outstanding formula for sharing out by unskilled and skilled criminal labour and executive criminal management other than proprietors should be based on equity formulae used for sharing proceeds from robbery of German national gold reserves in Bavaria by U.S. military personnel and native civilians in June 1945. This is entirely workable and universally applicable because it is based upon international marine salvage agreements for sharing by officers and crew in cargoes of distressed ships rescued at sea.'

'What a sensible approach,' the Captain said.

'Let us wait to judge that until we get some numbers,' Gash said.

'Read on, please.'

'Um – recommended sharing out,' Schute read. 'For unskilled labour: drivers, mechanics, forklift operators, et cetera, a flat payment of five thousand pounds apiece.' Schute looked up and stared at the Captain. 'By God, that's awfully high for forty-seven odd minutes of work.'

'In a way.'

'Um – eighteen unskilled labour required at cost of ninety

thousand pounds. One semi-skilled arsonist needed. Fee lower than going rate because of pleasure principle implied. Arsonist: seven thousand five hundred pounds. Alarms expert: ten thousand pounds. Essential to recruit two experienced executive criminals. Payment to executive criminals: one-third of total.'

Schute was outraged. 'I think this is utterly disgusting,' he said. 'We do all the work and two thugs and their helpers walk off with the lion's share. Paying those two men one-third is simply out of the question. Then, on top of all that, whoever buys the wine from us – the fence I think it is called – makes a one hundred percent profit. It simply is not fair.'

'Wine is alive. Wine has a face and a personality which are as clear as any finger prints. It can be recognized anywhere. Whoever buys it will be taking a big risk after investing the substantial sum of one million pounds.'

'And we are supposed to rejoice over his leavings.'

'Dammit, Gash. We are hardly on our way yet you insist on staging a classic falling out of the thieves.'

'I have the right to protest, you know,' Schute bridled.

'We don't have the buyer for the wine we have not yet stolen. Nor do we have our splendid criminal organization. I must add, in passing, that I don't yet have the capital to swing any of this. Now, if you will consent, please ask our friends, the machines, how much money all this is going to require.'

'Very well,' Schute said sullenly. He banged the inquiry into the computer, his lower lip protruding like a Ubangi plate. Soon the print-out began. Schute scooped it up and began to read from it: 'Maximum capital requirement: forty-one thousand eight hundred pounds.'

'My *God*!' the Captain cried.

'Minimum capital requirement: eighteen thousand pounds, ninety-three new pence including previous estimate of four thousand two hundred pounds of costs for transportation,

9

meals, tips and laundry.' He looked up in a rage. 'Why does the blasted thing always insist on including laundry? If laundry, why doesn't he charge us for their blasted haircuts?'

'How did it arrive at minimum costs?' the Captain asked.

Schute read on. 'Difference between maximum and minimum dependent on: One: whether criminal staff can steal such heavy equipment as lorries, heavy duty Mercedes tow trucks, forklift trucks, endless belt equipment and weapons. Two: whether bribery will be necessary. To average out the maximum and minimum capital requirements: twenty-nine thousand five hundred and nine pounds and fifty-two new pence.'

The Captain had turned ashen.

'Can you raise that sort of money?' Schute asked.

'Have to, old man.'

'Well – '

'I don't suppose you could – '

'Awfully sorry, Colin.'

'No. Of course you couldn't.'

'You did guarantee no risk, Colin.'

'I apologize for asking. And you are quite right, too. No matter.' He stood up and put on his jacket. 'I am certain I know who the fence, as you call it, will be. I think I know how to handle establishing our professional criminal organization. Therefore, all I need is about thirty thousand pounds. Very well. Good night, Gash.'

The Captain finished his glass of wine, put on his bowler, took up his case and left.

He came out of Axelrod House into a wet night. The Colonel was on the porch to see him off. The chocolate-coloured Rolls was driven up. He nodded good night with a considerable amount of distraction, and moved the car out of the courtyard.

The green velvet grass among the old trees of the great park had sunk into a sea of blackness beyond the two-hundred-yard ring of high-poled lights which surrounded Axelrod House from a distance of eighty yards. Anyone unauthorized who stepped into that circle of light would be shot down by tower snipers and his corpse questioned closely afterwards. The Captain turned his fourteen thousand pound burro off the mile-long avenue after he had satisfied the checkpoints with identification and had turned in his celluloid button, then into the tertiary road to London.

Like the edges of smoke insisting itself under a closed door he could feel the stirrings of gambling lust scratch its talons upon the inside wall of his stomach. Yvonne insisted that lust was too profound a word for it. She said it was a substitute for masturbation.

Then he realized that he could not gamble because he had nothing to gamble with: no cash, no credit, no possessions portable enough for a gambling house manager. In fact, he had nothing but his luck. Captain Huntington was a mature man in one sense. He was never fooled by the surface worthlessness of his luck. He knew and cherished that he had been born with a healthy mind and body, that by missing the peerage by the mere accident of having an older brother he had gained the incentive which had put him through the navy as a substitute meritocracy through which he had found Bitsy. He had had the great luck to leap from strength to strength for, because of Daddy, that living part of Bitsy, he had gone into the wine trade and he had found Yvonne. All of it had been a chain of luck so golden as to, at last, be the cause of his salvation from the minor negative forces of his life. He had lost money, yes. If one could lose money, one could win it back. His true luck had been being born as he had been born. God's finger had reached down and had touched him and had chosen him to win out of hundreds of millions of faceless others who were sacrificing their pasts by cursing their luck.

He needed only thirty thousand pounds. Repeat: only thirty thousand pounds. Because of his incredibly good luck that

131

was a sum of money which would be ineffably easy to find. It was true he would have to make certain compromises, however temporary, with things such as honour and dignity to drill himself into the understanding that, in losing the wine company to John Bryson, in signing over the same wine company – the identical wine company – to Bitsy, he had merely lost/signed over the company itself: i.e. its goodwill and its long list of active customers, not the wine stocks which it owned. The wine stocks were clearly his to sell if he chose to sell them. He would have to make himself understand that. Being his and only his he would therefore sell them off at auction – careful not to touch any of Daddy's wine stocks of Chateau Ambreaux – to get the money to finance the theft of eighteen thousand cases of wine so that he could buy back from John Bryson what Bryson might consider Bryson already owned, in order to give to Bitsy what he had already disposed of, so that he could repay Bitsy about two hundred thousand pounds to add to her thirty-odd million dollars (always growing).

Charles Bonnette had been born in Sicily as Carlo Bonnetti. He had run errands carrying blackmail notes at five to begin to learn his trade and had slouched in the dust and baking sun of the country villages in the west when he had grown taller, as a symbol of intimidation. He had made his bones when he had been fourteen. He was admitted at twenty to the Fratellanza he would serve for the rest of his life. He was a clever boy and very charming; tall and strong and very convincing. He was not afraid of anything except his leaders, which was only traditional. He studied the art of demanding respect, of projecting the touchy need for great respect the way other boys might study surgery or the law. At twenty-two he had been moved by the Brotherhood out of Palermo to Turkey, a rare honour because it was an expression of high confidence which had passed over many older men who had sought the post. He had learned French in Turkey, taught by a series of beautiful ladies with pliable Parisian accents. No matter how many stern announcements might be made by the Attorney-General of the United States, Carlo Bonnetti knew there was a Mafia.

In Turkey, he began as an enforcer for the manager of the agricultural side of the little brothers' opium interests and, while murdering when necessary or maiming when that would do, he had learned how the world's most fantastic cash crop was grown. Then, because he spoke French, he was appointed Agricultural Manager for Indo-China, where he learned supple

English on the pillows of colonial ladies. Almost at the moment when he could have gone on to real riches as the boss opium farmer in a country which understood the crop, he saw the very fields themselves wrested from his hands by the new Vietnamese government after France had been forced out and Foster Dulles had come skittering in to save the little enclave of nations (which the Brotherhood could have turned into one productive opium field) from itself.

Instead of moving him to Laos or Thailand or even allowing him to open up Indonesia with modern farming efficiency, he had been moved closer to the great money mine, into the responsible work as production manager for the heroin factories of southern France, with eleven depots in the Marseilles area and a production quota which called for an 11·78 percent increase per year per plant which he was able to exceed by 2·34 percent on plant average.

Wealth brought him enormous aplomb. He became the quintessential man of respect. He killed with aplomb and he maimed with aplomb. He moved across any scene like a king stag in a painting but he had a dangerous weakness for an organizational, big business criminal who needed only to listen for what the public wanted, then to supply it to bring in riches and power. Bonnette had a need to be engaged in risky, intricately-timed armed robbery, to be accepted by the recognized aristocrats of crime not as a hustler, pander, and extortionist who lived somewhere way down on the totem pole, but as a man cunning enough and brave enough to survive and win big numbers with a gun in his hand, defying society on a braver scale than any of the safe, fat-cat mafiosi.

Because he was from the south, Bonnette posed as a parfumeur on the fringes of French flash society, where he was sought after as an elegant man of affairs welcome (almost) anywhere, the friend of titled film stars and other famous people with much more clout. He was not unknown to politicians. He was admired by The Friends in North America among the biggest of the best. He was respected and listened to with all attention in Sicily. He was Charles Bonnette, parfumeur, with the large private airplane and the dangerous gambling club; celebrated fin bec and friend of great wine for although he used women like a trencherman, he sipped at the vintages with delicate sensibilities and, like most Frenchmen, could fake his way through the wines of a six course dinner with the best of them. Most of all, Charles Bonnette, whether as a murderer, a social lion, or a businessman, was eager to please himself, eager to provoke himself into newer and more tantalizing feats of living. It had doubled his bulk in twenty years. His was the quintessential appetite which had killed all the great bull fighters and racing car drivers – all men whose mirrors had convinced them that they could do no wrong.

The maitre d'hotel bowed low as he came out of the lift on the restaurant floor of the Tour D'Argent in Paris. It was not Charles Bonnette, mafioso, who was welcomed. That was merely a rumour and perhaps, they thought, a myth. If the Mafia did not exist in a barbaric country such as the United States, on the authority of its prime legal officer, they reasoned, then why should it exist in such a civilized country as France?

Bonnette was ushered across the beautiful room, nodding blandly, smiling occasionally, as he moved to the table where Captain Huntington was waiting for him. The men shook hands and seated themselves.

'So – we meet again,' Bonnette said.

'Sorry about not keeping in touch,' the Captain said. 'I say – I hope you don't mind. I ordered this lunch from London before I left this morning.'

'Food cannot be harmed even if it is ordered in London, if it is cooked in Paris, Captain Huntington.'

The first course was hot venison paté with fresh foie gras. The venison was out-of-season and had had to be flown in from arctic Sweden. The two men ate in hoarding nibbles, as cautiously as ladies in a tea shoppe, as if there might be ground glass within. With it they sipped exquisite Meusault, a Blagny of '61, big and ambitious; a wine of murmured luxury. When that food had disappeared Bonnette said, 'I was surprised when my daughter telephoned me then I was surprised again when she said she wanted me to see you. And I have not been surprised for twenty-five years.'

'Very interesting.'

'Is she well? Yvonne?'

'In the pink, I would say.'

'I am glad. You must give her my best. Also please tell her that her sister sends her best.'

'Ah – a sister?'

'A twin sister – eh? They are very different in every other way except they look alike. Claire is in Australia now. How did it happen that you wished to have this meeting, Captain?'

'A *twin*. Think of that. Well!' He wrenched himself away from the wonderment of having two of Yvonne. 'How to explain? You see, Monsieur Bonnette, the first time you and I met I gained what could be called an intuitive grasp of your position and influence. I have need of that now.'

Chewing daintily, Bonnette raised his eyebrows. 'You wish to buy perfume?'

'Ah, you have perfume, too, do you?'

'Perfume is where I made my name and such fortune as I may possess.'

'I put it this way, Monsieur Bonnette. I have need of a number of experienced men in your field to share approximately ten million francs with me.'

'A good day's pay.'

'For most of us.'

'What kind of work? It must be very dangerous work to offer so much.'

'I like to think that most of the danger has been foreseen and will have been removed.'

'You make it sound as if you are asking me to help you to rob a bank,' Bonnette said blandly. 'What else could yield ten million francs?'

'Wine.'

'The wine is here, Captain Huntington,' the sommelier said, pouring into an empty glass beside the canary Blagny. The Captain regarded the wine, inhaled it, then sipped it. 'It is not only noble, it is royal,' he said to the wine waiter. 'As you commanded, Captain.' He poured the red wine into the glasses of both men as the *commis* cleared away the Barquette of Mussels. As Bonnette sipped the Clos du Vougeot '34 he rolled his eyes like an apprentice minstrel man to indicate that he wanted to praise the wine, but first to business.

'What kind of work if not a bank?' he asked.

'Eighteen thousand cases of the finest wine in France. Ten million francs worth of wine – our share.'

Bonnette worked away at the saddle of lamb as he answered. 'You will need an army of men just to lift it.'

'I will need eighteen unskilled labourers, two skilled technicians, two executives, two trucks, eighteen forklift trucks, three long moving belt mechanisms, four walkie-talkie units, twenty-seven feet of nylon line, two three-inch rolls of adhesive tape, nine telephone numbers, one hypodermic needle, two heavy duty Mercedes tow trucks, four car mechanics, and certain other things I will provide myself.'

'You don't sound like you need help to me,' Bonnette said.

'I need people, reliable, experienced people.'

'What kind of technicians?'

'An arsonist and an alarms man. The alarms man has to have daring and physical strength.'

137

'All alarms men have to have daring, my friend. They go in first and feed on their own nerves. The job depends on them.'

'Indeed.'

'What do you pay this daring alarms man out of the ten million francs?'

'Fifty thousand francs.'

'Never.'

'I won't be making the arrangement with him, you will.'

From across the room, they were two businessmen beating the stockholders out of an expensive lunch. Bonnette sipped his wine and rolled his eyes again like a burnt cork darky. 'If your job turns up more wine like that, my friend, I'll take a case.' He burped discreetly into a napkin. 'Is that all you want me to do? Make your deals?'

'Much more. You would be in charge of the entire operation directly under me. You would procure the men and materials. You would be in charge of security.'

'For how much of the ten million?'

'One-third to you, including your assistant. You pay him whatever you work out with him.'

'What does my assistant do?'

'He should steal all necessary transport and equipment for one thing. He should be in charge of loading, we think.'

'Who is we?'

'I have a friend who is an I B M computer.'

'Why should you get two-thirds?'

'I don't actually. I get one third for originating the idea and running the operation, for financing it as well, of course. Only I am qualified to run this operation as it is organized. The other third goes for the manner in which it has been organized – for the fool-proof, super-detailed, incredibly complex plan.'

'When do I see the plan?'

'Probably never. But if we should decide to reveal it that would happen on the morning of the day we leave.'

'How do you dispose of eighteen thousand cases of wine?'

'Well – that would be part of the plan, wouldn't it?'

'I am very sorry. That is something I have to know.'

'You will know that part. I did not say you would never know. I will tell you one hour before we make the transfer. Which will be eleven hours after we have the wine.'

'Hot wine.'

'What?'

'The whole country will be looking for us. It would be like stealing the secret formula for Coca Cola in the United States. Eleven hours with eighteen thousand cases of classic French wine will be like a lifetime.'

'Not really. That is, you won't feel that way when the time comes, I assure you. They will be looking for us on the other side of France.'

'You don't give me anything. How can I judge if it is good for me?'

'Monsieur Bonnette, I will tell you everything, except the buyer and the disposal of the wine, on the morning of the day we leave. You must have guidelines, no doubt. But, as you can well appreciate, if you knew what I know you wouldn't very much need me, would you?' The Captain shrugged. 'I will take a chance with you. If you don't like the plan on the morning of the day we leave and you go home, you'll be leaving me high and dry. I have no place else to go with it.'

'I don't know. I don't like blind operations. I am no kid looking for a thrill. I am a businessman at these things.'

'It must be as it was at D-day, Monsieur Bonnette. Higher executives than you or I had to work entirely in the dark until the party started.'

'It is not like hiring a cook, hiring an arsonist.'

'It can't be very much different. My wife engaged a cook when we were first married who burned almost everything.'

'If these people go along it will be only my say so. The egg will be on my face.'

'Not to worry.'

'When does this crazy job begin? What famous morning is it that we are supposed to leave?'

'Ideally, two weeks from Friday.'

'You know, you have a lot of nerve stiffing me like this. If it wasn't for Yvonne asking for a favour –'

'No favours,' the Captain said curtly. 'Your end will be close to three million francs, one side or the other. Furthermore, Yvonne says you have never done a favour for anyone in your life.'

'She said that to you?'

'Are you in or out?'

'All right. I'm in as far as the meeting on that famous morning – eh? Come to my club three days from now at eleven forty-five in the morning and I will have the three technicians waiting for you.'

'Excellent.'

'And I suggest you bring some earnest money with you.'

Neither man had looked up to see the breath-taking view of the cathedral, the Seine, and Paris which spread out under the restaurant. They had seen all that before. And only talking about ten million francs was a beautiful thing in itself.

17

Juan Francohogar was waiting at one of the tables set out on the pavement in the Shepherds' Market when Captain Huntington came hurrying along. 'Sorry. Dreadful mess, parking. Why do I do it? It isn't as though a car needs exercise. Are you all right? You look so pale and seem so still.'

'We leave in one hour.'

'Who?'

'With Mr Bryson in his private jet.'

'Where?'

'To Spain for the bulls, to Italy for the sculpture, to Geneva to dine with a man who draws something called "Dennis the Menace" which has Mr Bryson greatly excited – we will also buy watches in Geneva – then to Vienna for the operetta, not the opera, which shows unexpected good taste in my employer, then to Copenhagen for three days of unrelenting pornography and for this he has organized expert guides. We are to sleep and eat in Hilton Hotels throughout the voyage, I understand, for this is to be a holiday for me as well, you see. I am not to cook at all, only to eat that Hilton Hotel food, except on the plane, *en route*, when he will permit me to make him the snacks. What is a snacks?'

'How do you spell it?'

Francohogar shrugged, 'S-n-a-x.'

'It must be some Pittsburgh dish. Get him to block it out for you then fake it.'

'I am desolated.'

'Juan, I got you into this and it is my responsibility to get you out.'

Francohogar covered his face with his hands and leaned forward on the small table.

'As soon as you return I will call on Mr Bryson to tell him in no uncertain terms that he has violated spirit and letter of the agreement,' the Captain said. 'I shall tell him you wish to return to your own restaurant, will suggest that he invest fifty or seventy thousand francs for repairs and repainting and that in return you will cook him one splendid dinner for himself and his friends each summer, naming the main dish after him with printed menus which he may send on to the American banking trade papers.'

'Thank you. You have been so kind. Always such good advice.'

'I thank you. And I will tell you something else, Juan. You are doing me a decided favour to keep Mr Bryson out of England for the next week or so and I will ask you to be sure that he does not read the newspapers during the little holiday because what I am about to do, what I must do, may make him very cross.'

'Not one newspaper, sir. You may depend.'

'I have to sell the wine stocks of my wine company which I lost to Mr Bryson and it is possible that he would take exception to that, believing, as is possible, that he also won the wine stocks when he won the wine company.'

'Preposterous. Every day he does something more preposterous.'

'If the meals get too bad for you I think it would be perfectly all right to put a sedative or two in his snax.'

'Then he would sleep through dinner?'

'It would be worthwhile doing in Rome and Vienna, perhaps. You would enjoy the *Rigatoni con la Pagliata* at Checchino across from the slaughterhouse in Rome. And, of course, Sellahettin's in Vienna.'

'What is it – *con la pagliata?*'

'It is part of the tubular intestine of beef that contains juices of indescribable flavour.'

'Which sedative?'

'I feel sure a man of his age must travel with a pharmacy of sleeping pills. And vitamin pills. What you must do at once, Juan, is to put the sleeping pills in the vitamin bottle and the vitamins in the sleeping pill bottle.'

'I will never, ever be able to thank you for all you've done for me, Captain Huntington.'

'I must go now, Juan.' The Captain arose, patted Franco-hogar warmly on the shoulder and strode off in the general direction of Bond Street.

The Captain put ten new pence into the tray of an orchestra of elderly street musicians who owned most of the real estate on the block and entered the building. The world-famous auction rooms were crowded because what was about to be held was a 'first' auction. The Captain Colin Huntington Collection of French wines was to be auctioned simultaneously in New York, San Francisco, Tokyo, Geneva and London by Telstar satellite.

Telstar had been Gash Schute's idea. He had produced costs, availabilities, and methods for the Captain to pass along insistently to the auctioneers who had protested that there would not be enough time to mount it properly, but Gash had anticipated that. The Captain explained to the auctioneers that the fact was there would not be enough time to mount an ordinary auction in terms of his willingness to sell his wine but, because of the historic nature of the planet's first spontaneous, round-the-world wine auction by satellite, all news of it must be held back until the day of the auction itself, privileged customers notified by telephone the day before, and the press invited to attend that morning, as a true 'news' event. With some uncertainty which grew into much bold confidence after

143

the telephone invitations had been extended, the auctioneers had agreed.

As he knew it must, the Captain's great, good luck held. Bitsy was called away to Mexico City to investigate an invention for making linen out of the skins of bananas which as she said excitedly, if it worked would mean that she could sell the canned bananas to the armed forces in Viet Nam and might even be able to negotiate, through Uncle Pete, Uncle Jim and Harry a possible test order of ten or twenty thousand uniforms made out of the banana fabric. So she would not be in London where, if by any accident of Job's comforter telephoning to bring news of the proposed sale of wine stocks, she might have sought an injunction to stop the auction.

The crowd was poring over the catalogues and bottles on display. It was very thick. The Captain felt it looked like a winning day. He sought out the chief auctioneer to modify his reserve prices upward. The auctioneer protested but the Captain was firm. 'This is a thirsty crowd,' he said. 'I can feel it.' They haggled like Arabs over the figure the Captain insisted was his bottom price or no sale for the Gaffelière-Naudes and an intensely whispered bitter wrangle developed over what he considered must be the absolute floor for the Beausèjour-Duffau-Lagarrosse '45. They were interrupted when the press decided who the Captain must be. They took pictures of him and the auctioneer with still and television cameras. The next day in *The Times*, and other newspapers of the world not excluding *Novedades* in Mexico City, Captain Huntington appeared as a very model of an aristocratic (retired) British naval officer with bowler hat, medium-weight, eight year old worsted suit which fitted him as the ocean fits the shoreline. In the photograph he appeared to be lightly amused, eyes crinkling mildly, lips together and smiling (no vulgar display of teeth) as though he were selling his wine stocks simply because the Telstar notion had been something no really forward-looking wine merchant should allow himself to ignore – progressive, interesting, possibly profitable, in all an idea worth exploring.

The photograph was so impressive that his brother, Lord Glandore, put it up with Scotch tape in the front window of his bowling alley building in Boise and had written with *Bon Ami* on the glass: LORD GLANDORE'S BROTHER and had done forty-two dollars and ninety-five cents more billing for that weekend. It was a blessing that the Captain would never see or know of it.

The auctioneer was banging his gavel on the platform which was flanked on either side by two five feet square television screens marked, from left to right, San Francisco, Tokyo, then on the other side, Geneva and New York. 'In fifteen seconds,' the auctioneer said, 'these auction galleries will make history by conducting the first planetary auction of fine wines ever held. As Telstar satellite, JEK, circles the earth three hundred and eight miles above us, the system of which it is a part will televise bids for the lots to be offered from the Captain Huntington Collection of fine wines. These bids will be recorded on the telly screens on either side of me but all lots will be knocked down in London, by me, with this action being transmitted to the screens in San Francisco, Tokyo, Geneva, and New York.'

A loud buzzer was sounded. The auctioneer managed to look sufficiently portentous. 'The auction is now open for bidding on Lot 36 shown in the programmes as ten cases of Bonnes Mares, a Burgundy red wine of the district, Côte de Nuits, France. The official classification of this wine is Grand Cru or Great Growth. For some reason this very great wine is not known abroad. It is the peer of most red wines of the Côtes de Nuit. This is a soft wine with much of the elegance and delicacy of Musigny. It is richer in tannins than most Burgundies giving it the strength to age and round out beautifully. What am I offered for ten cases of Bonnes Mares nineteen hundred and sixty-one?'

Tokyo bid first, followed almost instantly by a large African lady in the skins and silks of a princess, in Geneva, and a highly excited German bidding from the auction rooms in New York. The Japanese bid in yen, the princess in Swiss francs, and the German in dollars which was something everyone at hand seemed to have overlooked and men had to be rushed to offices for charts which would instantly translate these various currencies into pounds sterling and the auctioneer made perfectly wretched jokes and comments and the Captain steadfastly made a note in his small book that he was not going to pay for this hiatus as his share of the Telstar rental. He timed it carefully; three minutes, thirty-eight seconds were lost.

Unflappable, the auctioneer knocked down the wine to the German in New York, sold forty cases of superb Ducru-Beaucaillou '55 to the Japanese, who seemed to be bidding from the most desperately crowded, yet the largest of all the television rooms shown on the four screens, and Japan won the bidding on lots two through nine in succession. As the lots were sold, the Captain made price notes serenely in his small black book as though he was bored. Occasionally the auctioneer would look at him for instructions on violating reserve prices but each time the Captain would shake his head and force the bidding higher.

He had an enthralling sense of winning, of being chosen above all other men to win. As always, it transcended any other emotion he had ever felt. He knew at these moments that gambling was his reason for being. He felt majestic. He was the man they all kept turning their eyes to see: the incomparable gambler poised at the very centre of the planet, his amiable pleasure made possible by his incredible luck, his endless run of luck which broke roulette banks and stood down craven millionaires at chemmy. He was the hope of every chancer who had ever ruined himself and who would ruin himself again, the hope of that unattainable category to all but himself: the gambler who had everything.

When it was over strangers poured over him from everywhere to shake his hand, to touch him as they would an amulet. He suffered it. When the room had cleared he and the auctioneer had a row over the gaffe about the currency bidding procedures but at last they agreed to split the cost of the lost time. The auctioneer said he would have the Captain's cheque ready in two days' time. 'It would be just right, I think, if you could come by at just before seven – if you are sure you don't want us to bring the cheque to you.'

'Thank you,' the Captain said, 'but I shall be in France most of the day. Seven will be fine, thank you.'

18

Elevating himself in stately measure at six o'clock on the afternoon of the following day, the Captain ascended the stairwell leading to the large sitting room in the Farm Street Building, rising as Neptune might have come out of the sea for a Fishmongers Convention which is to say with considerable dignity. Not until he reached the top did he turn his head and body toward the possible occupants of the room, having put the bad moment off as long as possible.

Bitsy was seated on the sofa beside Mr Clogg. Her face was contorted with barely controlled fury. She may have either intended or hoped to keep close control over the rage she felt but the sight of the enormous bouquet of flowers he was carrying caused her to break. Her voice was far too loud and it trembled badly.

'What are those ridiculous flowers? I suppose I have paid for those, too. Have you lost your mind? Give them to me!' She got up and wrenched the flowers out of his hands, rushed with them to the window, flung it open and threw them violently out into the street.

'You should have looked at the card first, Bitsy,' the Captain said only slightly reprovingly. 'I didn't bring the flowers. They were propped up against the front door.'

'You are lying!'

'It was easily ten pounds worth of flowers so I should imagine – '

'Spare me what you imagine! All right, *Captain* Huntington, we have definite proof that you have sold off the entire wine stock of Huntington Fine Wines and we are going to impound payment from the auction people tomorrow morning.'

'Well! I am glad we talked it over. Had you done so I should have had to file a countersuit against you and that would be messy.'

'A countersuit. Ha. Ha. Ha,' she laughed mirthlessly. She turned to her solicitor and said elaborately, 'He would have had to file a countersuit. What else is new, *Captain* Huntington.'

'You are being a bit hysterical, Bitsy. Because you read about the first wine auction by satellite on some front page in Mexico City or Washington you have leaped at an entirely faulty conclusion.'

'It was on every front page,' Bitsy sobbed. 'With that smarmy picture of you. I've been on a conference call with Daddy and Uncle Jim and Uncle Pete for twenty minutes this afternoon. I'm a goddam wreck. And Uncle Pete was all the way out in Seattle.'

The Captain sat down calmly and spoke sensibly. 'What did you tell them?' he asked pleasantly.

'What could I tell them?'

'I have no idea. What did you tell them?'

'I told them you were exploring a new, world-wide method of merchandising fine wine.'

'What did they say?'

'What could they say?'

'They must have said something. I have never seen you this upset.'

She began to weep. 'They said it was the smartest thing they'd heard all week,' she wailed. 'Uncle Pete wonders if we could auction off war material by Telstar?'

'Then why are you so upset? If they are all pleased you should be pleased.'

'Because I know it's a lie. You aren't exploring new methods. You stole that wine to get money to gamble.'

'That is not true, Bitsy,' he said with patience. 'And I did not steal the wine. I sold the wine, yes – to create capital I must have to make everything right between us.'

She shook her finger at him violently. 'You stole my property and sold it. You will go to prison for that.'

'Not true. I don't ask for your apologies but that is not true.'

'It doesn't matter,' she said wildly. 'I don't care what you say. I don't care what you do anymore because you are not going to have any scope in which to do it. I am going to impound that auction money and I am going to get a warrant for your arrest. You are going to prison.'

'On what grounds?' the Captain asked mildly, so sure of himself, so self-righteous that Bitsy became hesitant.

'Now just a darned minute here, Colin. Are you telling me you have forgotten the papers you signed here just ten days ago which made me sole owner of those wine stocks?'

The Captain crossed his long legs deliberately. He took a long, black cigar from the alligator case and clipped the end off it. He lighted the cigar, blew smoke at Bitsy and Mr Clogg, then addressed himself to Bitsy. 'Let us review. Firstly, those transfer papers do not become effective for sixty days from the day of signing, as you well know. Secondly, those papers made no mention of turning over wine stocks as a part of that business. You have only to read the agreements. What you are acquiring – if you do – is Huntington Fine Wines, its place of business and premises above, and its goodwill.'

Bitsy looked in panic at Mr Clogg who cleared his throat. 'Whereas one might say that what Captain Huntington has stated is true insofar as the letter of the agreement, we must also give our opinion that he overlooks the spirit of that agreement and in my opinion – '

'Do you mean you goofed?' Bitsy demanded. 'Are you telling me that you don't know how to draw up a simple agreement and that his twit of a lawyer outsmarted you?'

150

'Now, now. Now, now, Mrs Huntington.'

'Thirdly,' the Captain said with sudden bite, 'I ask you to please work hard to get this through your beautiful head, Bitsy. I must have capital if I am ever to be able to return to you all the money I lost for you and which you seem to want more than anything else.'

'That isn't fair, Colin! I will not be made into the monster of this marriage. I have pride. I have myself to face. And Daddy –'

'And Uncle Jim and Uncle Pete and Harry and Larry. I respect that. It gives me all the more reason why I must have capital.'

'So you can squander it at the Denbigh Club?' She had worked herself into a distraught state. 'Have you gambled away Rossenarra?' she asked hysterically. 'If you have, Colin, I swear to you I will spend everything I have to put you in prison. I want the deed to Rossenarra now – in my hand, now, tonight – to prove you haven't gambled it away.'

'That is not the spirit of our agreement,' the Captain said loftily. 'If I must do that I need not do it for some eighty days.'

Bitsy turned on Mr Clogg. 'What kind of a lawyer are you? They have bilked you. He has the best of us.' She picked up a book and threw it violently into the fireplace. She wheeled on the Captain.

'I want the deed to Rossenarra now!'

'I must insist on the period of grace,' he said gently.

'Now! I want it now!'

'Surely, Bitsy, you know I could do nothing to harm either you or Rossenarra.'

She wept with frustration. 'You could and you have,' she sobbed. 'You don't love either of us. You never could have. Perhaps you loved me once but you are in love with some memory of me, not with me.'

19

At five minutes to seven the following evening, Captain Huntington stopped off at the auction rooms to receive the cheque for the sale of the wine. The cheque was thirty-one hundred pounds short of thirty thousand which the computer had decided would be best to put aside for expenses. Even though he had been assured that most of the equipment required could be stolen, he worried about the difference in cash as if it were a real deficiency. Providing the money was his responsibility and, being an aberrant responsibility, he took it most seriously. To fail was glorious, of course, that was the entire essence of gambling, but to fail for the reason of not meeting one's responsibilities was not sporting at all.

He was driving slowly and even aimlessly through Mayfair when the solution, the clear vision of what he had to do, came to him. He had been on his way to Yvonne's house but instead he stopped at the first telephone box and called her.

'Where are you?' she asked anxiously, nude beneath the ice-blue sheets. 'I worry about you all the time since you met my father.'

'I've been picking up the auction proceeds cheque.'

'That's nice. It is legitimate so it is nice.'

'I have one more little errand to run. It won't take an hour. I'll just get it done then pop round to you.'

'Where are you going?'

'I'll tell you all about it later.' He hung up.

Yvonne rattled the receiver and yelled into the phone. 'Colin! Colin, you can't! No! You can't, you can't!'

The doorman at the Denbigh Palace Club took the Rolls for parking. The Captain went into the club, to the back of the building, to knock on a door marked MANAGER. A weary-looking man in dinner clothes was seated behind a desk piled with slips of paper. He was chewing on a cigar. He did not remove the cigar. He shook hands with the Captain while sitting which was very annoying.

'Good evening, Captain Huntington,' he said with contorted speech which he had either learned from a phonograph record or from gargling metal asterisks. 'It is always good to see you.'

'I should think so.'

The Captain took the large auction cheque from his pocket and dropped it on the desk. (Shaking hands while seated, indeed!) The manager gaped at the numbers on the cheque then looked up at the Captain for an explanation, as though he were not the manager of a gambling house.

'It is too late to have this cashed anywhere else,' the Captain said. 'I would like a gambling credit against it, please.'

'Certainly, Captain Huntington. How deep?'

The Captain shrugged. He could not resist showing off in circumstances such as these. 'All the way, if necessary,' he drawled. He decided he really did detest these fellows and their abominable manner learned from some book. His distaste showed and the manager became solicitous all at once.

'Very good, sir. Count on me to call ahead, sir.' He was on his feet. 'What would your pleasure be tonight, Captain Huntington?'

No matter what spurious patina had been guaranteed by the upper-class-speech phonograph records this man had studied, the Captain knew, there was simply no way to hide that he had come from somewhere north of the Liffey in Dublin and there-fore felt much better about having had his hand shaken from a sitting position.

'Roulette, I think,' he said and left the office.

*

153

He sat down at the roulette table, the only player at such an early hour of the evening. He greeted the staff by name and was greeted over-cordially in return. 'A thousand to start, please, Bocca,' he said. The croupier's stick pushed the fifty pound plaques to him. The Captain was composed, even serene, except that when he tried to lift a plaque to place his first bet his hand trembled so violently that he had to withdraw it to his lap. He turned in his chair with a most natural movement and called for a waiter. He ordered a half-bottle of Pommery '53. He felt nauseous and dizzy but when he turned back to the table he began his play with a steady hand.

Naked, Yvonne ran to a clothes closet and ripped a dress off a hanger. She threw it over her arm and raced to a bureau drawer to snatch out a silk scarf and a pair of silk panties. She pulled the panties on with frantic speed, her face taut with tension. She pulled the dress on over her head, not bothering with a brassiere. She took up a brush, gave her hair a few strokes then ran out of the room, tying the scarf around her head.

In Charles Street she tried to flag an empty cab but two went by before an empty one turned out of Queen Street. She spoke abruptly to the driver as he lowered the front window. 'The Denbigh Palace Club, please. In Debo Terrace. As quickly as you can.' She leaped into the cab and slammed the door. The cab took off.

Before the cab had come to a full stop in front of the Denbigh Club she had paid the driver and had the cab door open. She raced up the steps of the building. When she was almost at the top, the front door opened and the Captain came out.

'I knew it!' she cried with a triumphant sort of bitterness. 'I knew you would come here. Did you lose everything?'

He looked at her with something like pity. 'Lose? Because I

have lost now and again, surely you don't think I always lose?' His mood was Jovian.

'You mean you still have all that money?'

'Indeed, yes. And six thousand pounds more. We have more than enough, more than we may have needed now.'

She stared at him with furious contempt. 'You know what you are, Colin? You are one of those men who must bring pain and ruin to everyone else but they never seem to get touched themselves.'

'I might say I wish that were true.'

'You were meant to destroy. You belong in command of a fighting ship.'

'Yes, quite true. I did belong there. But now we must go off to an elegant dinner at The Club in the Halkin Arcade because Bitsy never seems to go anywhere but Annabelle's. How pretty your dress is.' He kissed her lightly on the forehead. She took his arm. They went down the steps and up the street together.

20

John Bryson telephoned him the next morning to ask if the Captain could join him for dinner. He didn't sound a bit troublesome so probably he hadn't seen a paper or his attention span was worse than usual.

'I'd be delighted to dine with you, John, but it must be a very early evening. I'm off to Paris by the earliest plane in the morning.'

'Oh, indeed an early evening.'

They decided on the Caprice because the walls and the service had a cheerful effect on Bryson. When they were seated in the restaurant, without any preliminaries, Bryson said he needed some substantial advice.

'It is about your cook,' he said.

'Francohogar?'

'Yes. You see – I don't quite know how to say this without appearing aged – but the fact is that, whereas he is undoubtedly a fine cook because everyone who knows about those things says he is, what he cooks is altogether too rich for me.'

The waiter came. Bryson ordered a soft boiled egg and some toast. The Captain ordered some terrine then aiguillettes of beef in a sauce which he asked to be made with a good Chambertin and a purée of string beans with an *epigramme* of mashed potatoes and celeriac. The waiter departed.

'Did you know that I passed out – I mean I just went out cold – in Rome and in Vienna on this trip we were just on?'

'No! How perfectly awful. Have you seen a doctor?'

'Yes. But not about that. On the flight from London to Madrid I asked him to make me some snacks. He asked me what sort of snacks I had in mind. I said – well, you know, like hors d'oeuvres except preferably in the form of a burger. Well, you wouldn't believe it but he hadn't packed any burgers or any franks and he turned out a platter of *French* hors d'oeuvres which were so rich that they made me sick. Then on the flight to Rome he did it again and I just plain passed out that night. I leaned over to tie my shoelaces and just kept going. I mean, I didn't come to until the next morning. Then it happened again in Vienna.'

'How frightful, John!'

'The point is, I've had to do something I'm afraid you won't like very much, Captain. I discharged Francohogar.'

'No!'

'Yes. I respected that he had a long contract but I was so woozy most of the time from his damned food that I had to take the bull by the horns. We negotiated an annulment of the contract for a payment of fifty thousand francs – not much, I agree – which he will use to refurbish a restaurant he has his eye on in France although I had to agree to allow him to cook me one superb meal a year there, free of charge. Superb to someone, no doubt.'

'I must say I think you handled that beautifully, John.'

'You aren't angry, then?'

'Angry?'

'I don't happen to like that kind of cooking and you do. I didn't want him but you made a great thing about him being your cook and perhaps I should have insisted that he return to you.'

'What is done, is done.' The Captain shrugged. He reached out reflexively to catch Bryson who had almost slumped into his egg cup. 'It's that damned rich food,' Bryson said yawning cavernously. 'I can hardly remember to take my vitamin tablets.'

157

He scooped a vial out of his pocket, opened it and slid a pill out upon his hand, popped it into his mouth and washed it down with ice water. The Captain made it a point to look the other way. No harm done, he felt and there definitely seemed to be not more than three sleeping pills left in the vitamin bottle.

He landed at Orly, for Paris, at ten fifteen. At ten forty-five he was ringing the doorbell at Charles Bonnette's Club de la Chance, which was known as a 'dining club' which was very daring, considering the food. The established reason why the food was so bad was that the croupiers had to take turns as cook every night. Everything came out of cans and not the sort of cans which could be bought at Fauchon, rather cans which had been run up by a failing dog food company because, although its charter said it was a dining club, Charles Bonnette did not want his members and their guests sitting around chewing on things ecstatically when they could be gambling.

The club was in the best part of the 16th arrondissement and if not the very best (because Bonnette ran a six storey *maison à rendezvous* across the street) it was surely in the most convenient section, in the rue Paul Valéry.

The Captain rang the bell firmly. An unpleasant-looking man, too pale by far, opened the door and since he did not ask the Captain who he was and what he wanted the Captain walked into the building and kept walking until he came to the dining room where Bonnette and a black man were waiting for him.

He and Bonnette shook hands. He was introduced to the black man who said his name was Ford McHenry. He was an American. The Captain had a certain amount of feeling for West Indians who, after all could play cricket, but he did not at all like the idea of going into business with an American Negro who had shown more and more that they did not know their place and who were known drug addicts. Instead of shaking hands he put his hat and his case on a nearby chair.

He was not pleased. Among other things McHenry was no jock-strap, Greek God, Olympic team, black man such as one sees in films. He was a pip-squeak, pumpkin-faced, bulgy-eyed runt of about five feet six inches tall with a face like a basketful of warts.

They spoke in French because Bonnette had introduced them in French. McHenry spoke French with a variety hall, New York accent and it determined that his home speech had never paid much attention to Whitey's rules of grammar. The Captain thought it extremely odd that, out of an undeniably wide choice of cunning, native born criminals, Bonnette had chosen this man.

'It may strike you as odd,' the Captain said to McHenry, 'but I had definitely thought Monsieur Bonnette would have produced a Frenchman as his assistant.'

'The fact is, baby,' McHenry said, 'I am a lot more versatile than the cats here. I mean like I can handle any kind of work. Heavy or mental – you know? I mean lemme run a fleet of big trucks or guys you gotta have to do rough stuff an' you got yourseff a master sergeant what runs with the ball – dig? Or gimme demolitions. I done four years with demolitions out in Nam. I blew up maybe eighty Cong hooches. Under orders, a-course.' He grinned broadly and to the Captain's surprise, in that the only Negroes he had ever seen close up had been in photographs, McHenry had very poor teeth. They were like so much roquefort cheese. The Captain felt let down.

'Cap'n, baby,' McHenry was saying, 'my country taught me how to blow up anything, wreck everything, ruin anything.'

A repellant thought entered the Captain's mind. 'Are you a deserter?' he asked with maximum disapproval.

'I ain't only a deserter like, but I am what you would call a war criminal. I am what they tagged Calley but they ain't taggin' Ford McHenry – you know what I mean?'

The Captain was appalled. He did not approve of McHenry's colour. He felt little confidence in the way the man sounded.

But the thought that the man was a deserter from his country's armed forces and that he bragged about being one of their ratty little war criminals as well was simply too difficult to be accepted.

'I take it you are a deserter as a by-product of being a war criminal?'

'What else?'

'Why are you a war criminal?'

'Just you guess at it and leave it lay there.'

'How do you get by with it?'

The Captain was making a comparison and learning something about himself. He had felt no rejection of the criminal classes whatever, when he had met Charles Bonnette. That had been surprising, really. Bonnette stood for implacable anti-authority and if there was one thing the Captain truly believed in, institutionally speaking, it was a devout view of authority; such as the Royal Navy or any other militant protector of class. But Bonnette had excellent speech. He dressed moderately well and knew food and wines. He was a man of poise and charm. McHenry was something else. In a way, he made clear to the Captain why more people of aristocratic background had not turned to crime in any of the many moments of their desperation. Flatly, the reason was that they simply would not have cared to have associated with men of McHenry's ilk. He detested the word ilk, but ilk was the only word. It was a Scottish word and he did not approve of the Scots either. Colour, he supposed, had something to do with it as though McHenry, knowing he simply didn't have a prayer of being accepted by the right people (probably because of colour) just hadn't made the effort Bonnette had made – not that he accepted Bonnette in that sense by any means. But courtesy forced him to listen to what McHenry was saying about being a deserter.

'I bought me a clean set of papers and got myself a stable of eight broads out workin' for me and they showed me how to speak le Fransch as she is spoke.'

Great *God*, the Captain thought, I am now on the verge of having a pimp as a business partner. 'Managing eight women must be dangerous work,' he murmured. Did the whores of all the world work for men like this: scum with respect for nothing or anyone? Eight women paying homage and fear to this miserable runt was an incomprehensible thing to the Captain. He wondered if he had ever known women who were capable of renouncing pride and self-respect, to give up everything under the pretence of need to allow themselves to be used by a man? He thought not. He most definitely thought not. A woman who could throw herself away on a parasite like this was merely proving that it was a good thing that all classes and worlds were separate. Captain Huntington did not include his women or himself in that broad indictment of manners because he had never looked at it in just that way where his own sector was concerned.

'What else do you do?'

'What I got like very big, baby, is like a lot of enthusiasm for makin' a hunnert thousand dollars.'

'You have many of the qualifications we need,' the Captain said, rising. Again he did not offer to shake hands. 'Let me talk it over with Monsieur Bonnette and we'll get back to you.'

As soon as McHenry left the Captain asked Bonnette with some irritation, where he had possibly found such a man and how he could possibly have chosen him. 'There was no reason to produce absolute dregs,' he said. 'I cannot help but feel that you are trying to make some sort of comment, offering me a man like that, to be your executive officer.'

'What do you know about it, Captain? This is a different world. We are not looking for someone who dresses well or speaks nicely. We want someone who will kill without hesi-

11

tation, someone who can handle men. McHenry is very much of the milieu. He is the man, right now, whom the rough element is most afraid of. He is afraid of nothing. He is very intelligent, as well. He is also a killer.'

'You are right, of course. And a very pleasant chap for a killer. But then, so was an old Admiral of mine. I'll take him on your recommendation. Who is next?'

'The arsonist. Hector Schraum. Arson is not a usual speciality for a professional.' Bonnette showed the sort of distaste a Muslim would show to a pork chop.

Captain Huntington expected to meet someone far more unacceptable than McHenry because of Bonnette's ill expression, but the Captain liked Hector Schraum instantly.

The man spoke perfect French although he was German and he offered to speak English if the Captain chose. He was an extremely well-kept fellow; small but with good carriage, impeccable manners, grave dignity. He was attentive, courteous and no braggart. The Captain felt he must be one of those unfortunates with whom the prisons must be filled, someone whose back had been pushed to the wall and who had had to defy society to survive.

'How long have you been in your work?' the Captain asked briskly. Bonnette had settled down with a copy of *Paris Match* and seemed to be ignoring them.

'I cannot say, really, sir,' Schraum replied. 'That is, I kept no records. But I know my work. I prefer the jellied alcohol bases because of their endurance and I admire napalm. It is so difficult to extinguish and can do extensive damage.'

'I see,' the Captain said judiciously. 'The fact is, we will require three fires in three large public buildings.'

Bonnette put *Match* down.

'They will need to go into flame within seven minutes of each other.'

'I can do that, of course,' Schraum said confidently. 'I will

162

organize everything precisely. I can set the fires roaring by remote timer. Naturally, I would prefer to fire them myself, by hand, but it can work either way without flaw.'

'Good chap.'

'You said public buildings. Could that include a hospital or a hotel perhaps?'

Bonnette looked across at them quickly, staring at Schraum with hard eyes as though only heroin should be permitted to kill strangers. The Captain spoke reflexively and with quickened emphasis (in that he felt the best way for the strangers was by bomb from a plane which had roared off the deck of a carrier) 'Good God, no!'

'As you wish, of course,' Schraum said. Then Bonnette took over to say that he would talk to Schraum about terms that night and that he wanted Schraum to come back at eleven. After Schraum left he said, with disgust. 'It would make no difference who the man was. Arsonists are all alike. They are monsters.'

'There is one thing I would like you to pass along, please.'

'Certainly.'

'Please tell Mr McHenry that he is not to call me baby.'

'I will try.'

'Were you able to locate an alarms man?'

'He is waiting.' He pushed a button on his telephone.

A tall, powerful man who wore a polo neck shirt and a blue blazer came in. He looked like a tennis racquet salesman. His eyes announced that he would not volunteer anything but if they phrased the questions correctly he might answer. He had a hard, nervous face which did not twitch perceptibly but which seemed to be moving as if there were torrents of water under the skin. Bonnette was very easy and jovial with him.

'Henri! How does it go?' The men shook hands and Bonnette clapped him across the shoulders. 'Here is the best man I have ever worked with,' he said to the Captain. 'He is the one you are glad to have with you when it gets hard around the edges. Henri Fouchet. Henri, this is the Captain.'

Fouchet nodded in a remote way, sat down and crossed his legs. He lighted a cigarette which had a gold tip.

The Captain sat facing him in a straight-backed chair. Bonnette propped himself against the wall with his arms folded.

'I have the blueprints of the alarms system you will have to solve,' the Captain said. 'It is not a very modern system, not a very sophisticated one because wine is hard to steal in any interesting quantities.'

'Wine?' Fouchet asked Bonnette the question.

'He wants to take the caves of Cruse et Fils, Frère in Bordeaux,' Bonnette said drily.

'How did you know that?' the Captain asked Bonnette. He was startled.

'Easy, my friend. No other warehouse in France could spare that much great wine. It makes no difference. Don't get into an uproar. Henri would have found out in a few days where these alarm blueprints had been installed.'

The Captain shrugged. 'It is just another warehouse. There are four watchmen. We will want you to take out the watchmen after you have deranged the alarm connections to the police, then on a precise time table we will want you to open the warehouse doors on the quaiside.'

Fouchet nodded.

Bonnette said, 'Henri has the easiest job but that is only because he, himself, is doing it.'

Fouchet smiled suddenly and brilliantly at the compliment. 'What does it pay?' he asked casually.

'Seventy-five thousand francs,' Bonnette said. The Captain looked at Bonnette sharply. 'That is Henri's price.' Bonnette said to the Captain. 'Do you have the blueprints with you?'

The Captain nodded. He reached for his case, opened it, and

took out a large manila envelope. He tossed it to Fouchet who did not trouble to open it.

Once again the Captain and Bonnette were alone in the large dining room with all the bare wooden tables and the cheap looking gilt chairs which had not been designed for daylight.

'Thank you,' the Captain said. 'They are three satisfactory men. The alarms man was the most impressive, surely the most professional. Am I right?'

'How could you tell that?' Bonnette said in mock amazement. 'All he said was one word "Wine" until he asked how much.'

'After years of a service command one becomes a pretty good judge of men.'

'Henri is better educated than the others. After all a muscle-worker or a pyromaniac doesn't have to go to a trades school. But Fouchet is a cocaine addict and he has to screw himself into some pretty bad tensions when he works. Sometimes he kills when it isn't necessary, he gets so tense.'

'You are pulling my leg,' the Captain said, smiling.

'No, no. He kills mostly when one is not ready to have him kill.'

'Then we must make sure that he is not armed,' the Captain said. 'Further some incentive plan could be applied. If he kills then we fine him – he is paid less. I most certainly do not anticipate – nor would I sanction – even what you call "necessary" killing.'

'Yes. I will tell him.' He inhaled deeply and exhaled slowly. 'He has never been arrested. He is clean. Nobody knows his face. I personally know of four big jobs he has done. All that counts for something.'

'No murders, please.'

'Don't think about it. We are all alike in this business. Everyone of us has some hang-up. You are in the business now, Captain. What is your hang-up?'

The Captain smiled with genuine amusement at the man's effrontery. 'I am a professional naval officer and a wine merchant, Monsieur Bonnette,' he said. 'I don't believe in hang-ups. This operation is just another shore raid to me. Nothing more.'

'Then we are going in from the sea?'

The Captain turned away abruptly to his attaché case. He opened it with an irritated snap and removed a large manila envelope which he handed to Bonnette.

'These are the trucks and equipment we will want Mr McHenry to get for us as well as where they are to be delivered. Do you think he could find eighteen forklift trucks?'

Bonnette shrugged, 'Of course.'

'Please note that the tow trucks must be the especially powerful and reliable Mercedes trucks and you will find expense money in there for false plates, advances, laundry, lunches and tips.'

'Laundry?'

The Captain waved the question aside with an irritated gesture which told his own bafflement. 'In any event, please study it carefully. It will tell you where we will meet again.'

Bonnette opened the envelope and scanned the top sheet.

'This looks as if it were typed by computer.'

'It does, doesn't it? Good day, Monsieur Bonnette. Keep well.' The Captain put on his bowler hat, took up his case and left. Bonnette sat down at a table near the window. He put on silver-rimmed eyeglasses which were a jarring note and began to study the bulky instructions. There was a knock at the door.

'Entrez,' Bonnette said.

McHenry came in.

'Did you listen?' Bonnette asked.

'Yeah.'

'What do you think?'

'Jesus, he's kinda fogged in, ain't he?'

'He's in the wrong business if that's what you mean.'

'Still, he's mighty cool. Like cold all the way in. Make me shiver.'

'Why?'

'It's like a man who ain't got nothin' left to lose.'

Bonnette held up the sheaf of papers which the Captain had left with him. 'He has plenty to lose and we are going to win it.'

'Hey, I'm kinda gladda hear you say that.' McHenry grinned horribly, his spotty teeth breaking out into the open like un- disciplined cavalry.

'I now believe him that this job can make ten million francs.'

'Wow.'

'He's figured this job with computers. I thought this was like some game they packaged for kids but then I read this stuff and it adds up better than I ever worked before. I think he can knock over Cruse. I think he can win the ten million.'

'Pleasure me more.'

'I'll do that. When he tells me how he is going to fence the eighteen thousand cases of wine, we will take the ten million francs away from him.'

The Captain walked to the garage under the Avenue Georges V, admiring the way butchers arranged their meat in a manner which made one know they were proud of it but which no other butchers, outside France, bother to do. He admired the way the fruit and vegetables were displayed as though each had a separate reputation to be kept spotless, shining and interesting in designs of fruit, lettuce, nuts, beets and endive, as though the vendor cared deeply that one wanted to eat well, as much as he hated to part with such food.

He drove the Rolls out along the Autoroute West toward Cherbourg. He had an appointment at Le Britannique, a café on the quai Caligny with a Captain Pappadakis and a Chief

Engineer Kullers whom the computers had pulled out of the joint security file as being outstanding (and available) men for sea-borne operations.

The road was good. The weather was fine. The Captain thought it through and approved of Francohogar going soon to reopen his Restaurant Ammej because he would have it entirely in shape by September and he, himself, would not require Francohogar back in London until mid-October, at which time some nephew could be brought in to run the place and Juan could go back once a month to be sure everything was running well.

He was slightly depressed about the outlook on the robbery which was to say that with so much expertise assembled much of the gamble was being taken out of it. He had needed Gash Schute because he didn't have that sort of mind himself and they had needed Gash's little machines and his abstract research staff. But because of statisticians, professors, samplers and thinkers the risk had been reduced heavily. Charles Bonnette was far too professional. The technicians he had found had been too slick and sure and even the damned wine auction had gone too well for that matter. Everything was just jelling too quickly.

He knew he could not have reasoned this way with anyone else but himself, not even Yvonne. He was a desperate man who had to have two hundred thousand pounds within seventy-eight days or he would lose his wife, his cook, his real property and when either Bitsy or Bryson sent him to jail, Yvonne. Therefore it was vital that everything which should shape up be allowed to develop to optimum strength, reducing risks, because there were always invisible factors lurking at the edges of every bet which made winning impossible.

Then he knew why he had been drawn to Hector Schraum. The arsonist was hopelessness and defeat. Schraum did not admit any odds whatever in favour of himself or mankind, not

168

odds of one hundred to one against man's chances for serenity and, if Schraum could get control, he would increase those odds to a thousand to one. People like that made the gamble more attractive because when in spite of the intentions of Schraum and reflexive killers such as Fouchet, one had achieved something of value, one had been chosen out of the millions to win and to survive. All in all he was satisfied that the odds against succeeding with the robbery were over thirty to one. That would be a bet worth winning. Less than the odds at roulette but still a bet worth winning.

Captain Pappadakis was a stocky man with a George V beard and very clear eyes. Chief Engineer Kullers was a red-haired man with a seamed face and horn-rimmed glasses. Both were dressed in watchcaps and peajackets. They declined dinner but preferred to sit on the café terrace outside. Captain Pappadakis agreed to accept a half bottle of Vichy. The Chief had a bottle of beer and a marc.

Captain Huntington presented the credentials which Gash had prepared. Being credentials prepared by a government espionage group they were not in straightforward form, such as a letter or a business card, but were a gypsy playing card on which had been cemented a Spanish duro. Captain Pappadakis put the thing in his side pocket without glancing at it. He had been briefed with a description of the Captain by telephone.

'I need a two decker freighter,' Captain Huntington said.

Pappadakis nodded.

'I'll want the holds cleared out and fitted with temporary bunks for nine hundred and forty-two people.'

Pappadakis nodded.

'This envelope contains five thousand Australian dollars, as you requested, although we had the devil's own time rounding them up.' He passed the envelope to Pappadakis who dropped it in his side pocket. 'The envelope also contains the latitude and longitude for our rendezvous at sea one week from Friday, on July 16th. When we rendezvous I will off-load passengers. When they have been secured aboard your ship you will head due west, out to sea, following the course set down in that envelope, then, on the morning of the third day, you will put the passengers ashore at the North African port named. Our agent will be waiting there for you with the remaining forty-five thousand dollars. But why Australian dollars?'

'I buy Australian wine and ship it to Copenhagen. The performers in the pornographic shows tell the press that Australian wine is what keeps them going and the Swedes soon hear about it so there is a big market for Australian wine in Sweden. There is one more thing, not about wine. No paying me by your agent in North Africa. By passenger in the first lifeboat.'

Captain Huntington felt the jolt of exhilaration. Here was a marvellous example of what could go wrong. A distraught passenger would be handed forty-five thousand Australian dollars wrapped in oilskins and told to deliver it to the captain of the rescuing ship. The passenger, in the continuing panic, would naturally drop it over the side of the lifeboat and Pappadakis would refuse to take anyone aboard and sail off.

'Not possible, I'm afraid,' he told Pappadakis. 'Much too much risk.'

'Then no dice.'

'My dear Pappadakis. Surely you talked to Gash Schute about me. He and I are old colleagues. I am no land-locked thug. I am Captain Colin Huntington, retired commander of her Majesty's aircraft carrier, *Henty*.'

Pappadakis brightened. Chief Kullers slurped his beer, then burped like Krakatoa. 'Well!' Pappadakis said. 'That is a different story. I thought you were just another espionage fink.'

'No, no,' Captain Huntington said. 'Nothing like that at all. This will be an armed robbery.'

Kullers' eyebrows went up. 'At sea?'

'Of course not at sea. I wanted to make the point that this is not more dreary spy stuff.'

'I was Royal Navy myself, for a while. Torpedo boats,' Pappadakis said.

'Perfectly awful duty.' The Captain addressed Chief Kullers. 'Do you know car ferries of the Bergquist class below decks, Chief?'

'Sure. One Chief, three engineers, one electrician, one repair man and four motormen.' Kullers had an old-fashioned New York accent. The words seemed to drop out of an oblong slot at the side of his mouth. 'They got De Laval fuel pumps, English Hindmarch M W D reduction gear and Asea generators. Lovely stuff. Engines run off at about fifteen hundred litres an hour driving Lindholmen boilers.'

'Good. Please join my unit at the Hotel Canute on the Canute quay in Southampton at ten ayem on July 15th. The drill is set down in this envelope together with one thousand American dollars as earnest money. Full instructions at the Canute.'

'How much does it pay all in? I got a helluva dentist bill.'

'Fifteen thousand dollars.'

'Could I get it in Belgian money?'

'Why?'

'My dentist is in Antwerp.'

'You must be having quite a bit of work done.'

'Listen – please! It hurts just to talk about it.' He let his attention veer away because a girl in a sheer dress was standing between him and the sun.

Captain Huntington drove aboard the night ferry from Cherbourg to Southampton where they docked at seven o'clock the following morning. He made a sauntering tour of the waterfront then found a cab and drove to the hotel which the computer had selected where he made the arrangements for his group who would be checking in a week from Thursday night.

21

It was late at night when the Captain entered the Great Hall at Axelrod House. Schute was in his shirt sleeves, sweating profusely at the computer-programming table.

'Evening, Gash. Awfully warm in here.'

'Do you have any idea what it would cost to air-condition a place like this?'

'Still, heat like this can't be awfully good for the computers.'

'That's what the bloody committee says but they don't offer funds to cool it down, do they? Seven bloody government agencies but not one puts his hand in his pocket, does he?'

The Captain hated to work in shirtsleeves. He was certain that, day after day in Boise, Idaho, Lord Glandore never put a jacket on. 'Making progress?' he asked. He willed himself to remain cool and comfortable.

Schute smiled thinly and nodded. 'The machines have developed keenly criminal minds.'

'How very kinky.'

'We've just finished a study of the shoals along the Gironde river. It isn't navigable without a pilot.'

'I've been swotting up on that myself. I'll qualify as pilot.'

'Not a chance. You'll have to take the pilot aboard. The whole coast would be up in arms if a ship of that size started up the estuary without all the business of contacting and taking aboard a pilot.'

'What a surprised fellow he is going to be.'

'The computers are worried about the cars as well. They say

once the ignitions have been locked and the brakes set on two hundred and sixty cars it could be very difficult to move them and take entirely too much time.'

'What do they suggest?'

'You have engaged – or someone has engaged – four car mechanics. They must be told to bring with them sets of master ignition keys which can start any kind of car. It's the only way they can move that many cars in the time they will have.'

'Will do.'

'We've finished the elapsed time studies and the computers want the warehouse alarm systems – which your man will have dismantled – to go off after you have made it away and out to sea. That means he will have to re-cycle the alarms rather than merely knocking them out. We're working on an exact time right now.'

'I will handle that.' The Captain made notes in his book.

'There is only the one police patrol in the warehouse area. It cruises past at irregular intervals. I'm afraid the diversions on the other side of the river aren't going to discourage these chaps from sticking their noses in. The computers have decided they must be taken. If they give you the routes the patrol car generally follows can someone handle that?'

'Indubitably. I would say let us have them come right out on the quai demanding to know what the hell is going on. Then we'll take them and stow them aboard.'

'No rough stuff.'

'No rough stuff is the watchword.'

'We'll give you the precise solution of morphine to keep the watchmen asleep until the police come. Very efficient of you to get their exact body weights.'

'Thank you.'

'The loading time schedule has come through on a print-out in four sections – for the roules and the endless-belt machines

174

then the forklift trucks and the heavy lorries and the computers have coordinated that with the human time and motion rates. We'll need far fewer forklifts because the warehouse is crawling with them which means we can cut the overland down to one large truck.'

'And one less driver.'

'Quite so. Now – for your good friend the easy-going wine buyer –'

'Might as well call him the Fence. Never have that chance again.'

'Quite so. The coordinates for the rendezvous with the Fence will need to be passed along for his navigator.'

'That's for me. I'll do it by cable in the morning.'

'The computers have asked you to hold out three passenger cars – preferably a minibus or some estate wagons to move the labourers out to the terminals when the job is over.'

'Will do.' The Captain made a note.

'How did the meetings go?'

'Very well altogether. Bonnette's people were perfectly terrible but quite professional. Big surprise was that Captain Pappadakis had been Royal Navy.'

'Oh, yes. I should have told you. He was torpedo boats.'

'So he said. But it makes me wonder. Is there an honest man left with the fleet?'

'My dear Colin!'

'At any rate, during the Bonnette meetings, I did get the distinct impression that professional criminals may think differently than we do.'

'How do you mean?' Gash put the question with considerable interest because he had future plans for these professional criminals.

'Have the computers issued warnings of any sort?'

'Yes. They did. As a matter of fact.'

'About people?'

'Not about specific people, of course. About professional criminal psychology in general.'

'What is recommended?'

'I'll read you some of the print-out.' He rummaged in a large box.

'Key reference supported by all other cross-reference authority,' he read aloud. 'Key reference title: Professional Criminal Reflexes by Richard Gallagher, professor of criminological studies, New York University. Cross-refer, same author, Specialized Criminal Reactive Associations. Relevant extract colon Quotation: The advanced professional criminal whose work is of a pervasive industrial nature, i.e. crime established as a regularly remunerative business employing seven or more persons for normal procedures, regard non-professional criminals as being vulnerable and non-essential after the fact of the crime has exhausted their utility.'

'What does that mean, Gash?'

Schute put the print-out back into the large box. 'It means that when you disclose how you will be able to dispose of all that wine or the moment you are paid for the wine, your executive criminal echelon will, most likely, have worked out a plan to take it away from you.'

'I had thought of that. Does the computer say how we prevent that?'

'Oh, yes.'

'How?'

'It recommends an invisible sort of bodyguard for you, actually.'

'Who?'

'Someone utterly unknown to the executive criminals.'

'How do I do that? I mean, one more criminal with a gun will just be one more criminal who will want to take the million pounds away from me.'

'Precisely true, but it can be done.'

176

'How?'

'I shall be your invisible bodyguard.'

The Captain stared at him while he registered the new concept. 'That is impossible,' he said flatly. 'From the very first I guaranteed that you would have no risk in this. We agreed that you would not have to risk as much as leaving this building.'

Gash smiled his benevolent appreciation. 'You will recall, dear boy, that I am not entirely a thinker-researcher. You may recall I was the best marksman in the squadron. That is to say, I do have a certain flair for action.'

'I most certainly do not deny that. But this new plan violates our agreement. There must be some other way for me to defend myself.'

Gash shook his head sadly. Clearly he had given the matter a good deal of attention. 'Unfortunately, there is not, dear boy. Only I can bring the protection unnoticed. Only I can conceal myself among the other passengers until the time comes for the transfer of the wine. Only I can shoot them down to protect you – if necessary.'

'Shoot them down?' It wasn't entirely that the Captain rejected the idea of shooting people down because that had been his training but, on the other hand, Charles Bonnette *was* Yvonne's father and shooting him seemed somehow insensitive to her. Further, Bonnette and McHenry were his business partners. Among British businessmen, at least he felt he had reason to believe, shooting down would be out of the question.

'Circumstances alter cases, Colin. It may become highly necessary.'

'But it gives me the odd feeling that if we rationalize killing them to defend ourselves, thus eliminating the need to share out the profits from the crime, we will have banded together against them in the same sort of criminal plotting described in that book the computer quoted. Each side, you see, will have

12

become self-righteously convinced of the need to murder.'

'Nonsense. Besides, the occasion for such violence may never come up. They may be the exceptions, and entirely satisfied with the amount of their share. It is a fortune, after all.'

'Yes.'

'But – and we must have a clear, mutual understanding on this – if they would kill you to steal the money, I would shoot them down to protect your life. That, my dear Colin, is the morality of it.'

'You are right.' Captain Huntington extended his hand. 'Thank you, old friend, for volunteering to take such a risk.'

22

Yvonne sat bolt upright against the backboard of the large bed, mostly under the blue sheets, her lovely bosoms staring implacably at the Captain. He was dressed for travel, packing a case. He removed a Navy issue automatic pistol from a drawer. He inserted a clip of bullets.

'Do you have to load it now?' Yvonne asked.

'Pistols are like cameras. There are shots one hates to miss.'

'Have you ever killed anyone?'

'In war, yes.'

'From a ship at sea to the land – with big shells?'

'I was with the carriers.'

'Did you ever kill someone up close? With a gun in your hand?'

'In the Korean police action, I think they called it. I was with the U.N. force.'

'Who did you kill?'

'I killed five Chinese fellows and I got a medal for it because they were taking an American general somewhere. About an inch or so across, a small ribbon and a little pin as a memorial for five dead Chinese fellows.'

'How did it feel?'

'When it happens?'

'Yes.'

'One feels surprisingly relieved that one is alive and they are dead.' He engaged the safety on the pistol and wrapped it in a silk handkerchief which he stuffed into the side pocket of a blue, cashmere topcoat which had been lying across the bottom of the bed.

Yvonne watched him, memorizing everything about him – how his wrists turned, how his hairs lay, how his torso moved. Her face was sad.

'I have this bad feeling that we will never see each other again.'

'You mustn't.'

'But I do.'

He stared at her tenderly, remembering walking beside her in Green Park that first day and he could feel her strong fingers eagerly interlaced with his hand. Everything was green except her scarlet dress and her large brown eyes which had such power when she looked up at him, a long, slow sideways look of rapt attention that he had to tense himself, even in memory, not to lay her down upon the grass among the other lunchtime lovers. He remembered the lunch they had not eaten and the wine they had drunk as though it were being served before him now. He heard her odd voice singing at the Ritz piano. She made him exultant in everything she did.

'Yvonne, do sing that song – "*L'important c'est la rose*".'

Her face became sadder. 'That means you feel you will never see me again,' she said.

'I don't feel that way at all. I swear to you, I don't. But – just the same – isn't that how life should be lived? By expecting to die? Nothing blithe about it, I'll admit, but it does add enormously to what one should be doing at any given moment, which is living. Isn't that true?'

'Yes.'

'Then sing. Expand the moment. That is what songs are for and why the slightest of them is more important than the greatest painting.'

She leaned back, all at once content, on the pillows of her

bed, her sweet bosoms expressive and sang the song while he sat beside her.

'That was very good,' he said. 'If possible, I would say it was even better than the first time.'

'When will you come back to me?'

'I shall be walking through that doorway at fourteen fifty o'clock on Monday afternoon next. Only six days.'

'Will you be unharmed?'

'In body, yes.'

'What do you mean?'

'I suspect my soul will have been damaged somewhat. From associating with evil companions. That always stains, you know.' He smiled at her.

'Kiss me, Colin.'

He grinned. 'With all these bulky clothes on? Won't it make you feel like Bitsy?'

'No matter how we did it, I couldn't feel like Bitsy because I love you.'

He kissed her. They clung to each other. Then Yvonne's mouth was at the Captain's ear. She spoke softly. 'No matter what else you will do, look out for my father. Be careful, my love. Don't trust my father.'

23

Captain Huntington went into the conference room at the Hotel Canute well over an hour before the others arrived. The room was on the top floor of the building and, staring out the window, he could see the enormous car ferry at its pier, taking on ship's stores for the evening departure. There would be over a thousand people aboard the ferry, counting the crew, and something between a hundred and fifty and two hundred cars. Once he boarded that ship and the operation got underway aboard her, which was essential to his being able to take the wine, there would be no turning back. It was the only climax of his life which he had recognized before it had happened.

If he turned away now and went back to London and collected Yvonne and emigrated to Australia or enlisted in the army or took any one of the hundreds of alternatives which existed he could move toward a different climax. He did not want to be a White Rabbit hurrying mindlessly to his own destruction. If he stayed here for one more hour he would be conducting a briefing session for four professional criminals who could be just a shade greedier than he was. Once that meeting started it would be too late to work out alternatives such as working as a pin boy for Lord Glandore in Idaho or going back to Keamore to sing chanties to Texans in the Kerry taverns.

But it seemed more likely that there were no alternatives; that they were illusions. He owed two hundred thousand pounds; no illusion. The true climax had happened far back there, when he hadn't known it was happening, when he had been gambling away the buildings and his business and his cook. It was too late to boggle on about alternatives. He had always believed that there was free will. It was the only ethic taught in western society on which Mammon and the priests could agree. Surely at one point in his life he must have made at least one choice of free will which had freed consequences which made all that followed inexorably foretold?

He had entered the Royal Navy as an act of free will. From that act he had met Bitsy and he had, but unconsciously, not by free will, tried to cut Bitsy's gigantic fortune down to size by gambling for greater amounts than he had even seen before which had led to irremediable conditions and to consequences which had dragged him like a handcuffed man tied to a running stallion to this room overlooking the Southampton harbour; overlooking violences and darknesses which he could not foretell but which would lessen him. But had entering the Royal Navy been an act of free will? Or had he merely been fleeing the heavy hand of Aunt Evans's husband's sister's husband, the Bordeaux wine merchant and had known no other escape route? Had he ever taken a step which was an originating point? Yes! Yvonne. No. There had been no other choice but Yvonne. There had been nothing else his senses would let him do. When he had met her he was in the wine trade as a consequence of having failed as a naval officer which had been the result of fleeing Bordeaux to which he was now about to return. A full circle. Had he ever undertaken an act of free will? Did free will exist or was it merely another politician's jest by which man tried to separate himself from the other animals?

They sat facing him in an attentive arc as though they were billiard-ball salesmen attending an area sales convention:

Charles Bonnette, prominent narcotics manufacturer, pander and murderer, internationally fashionable in an electric blue suit. Beside him Ford McHenry: deserter, boasted war criminal, pimp and thief who had been so highly commended because he would kill without hesitation. According to the computers, both these men had evolved their little plot to murder him and take everything.

Next to McHenry, meek and mild, sat the timid grey-white little man called Hector Schraum who believed devoutly in murder by fire, probably for sexual reasons. Beside him, tall, straight, silent and resolute: Henri Fouchet, an electronics wizard who murdered only when he got a little irritable or overtense for which conditions he took a patent medicine called cocaine to gain instant relief the quick, new, easy way. These were his partners. Chief Kullers at the far end of the arc was such a square he simply wasn't in it. He did not know and cared less what the next two days would evolve because he would be where he had chosen to be long years before: down in the bowels of a ship, keeping an engine running, separated by noise from life and uncaring unless someone tried to over-involve him. He, Captain Colin Huntington, R.N. (ret.) was Chairman of the Board. Who was Lord Glandore now? Who had respected that family title more now? Who was the peer of whom? He wondered mildly if he were even the peer of these four men gathered before him.

Why was he always seeking, the Captain wondered, differences of fixed station on shelves, each of which needed to be slightly higher than the last, with himself, in all his purity, at the top, above all shelves, for reasons of proof of moral and material merit? After all, he had done a bit of murdering himself in Her Majesty's Service. Murder was a natural turn of the species, legally and otherwise. Bryson and Bitsy could prove he had stolen as much or more than any of these men. Why must he insist there was such a difference between them and

184

himself? He made an effort of free will. First he admitted that his brother Lord Glandore was to be preferred between the two of them. Second because it had become vitally important for survival he admitted that he was one of this band of sick ruffians, *pares cum paribus*, so that he could strike harder, survive longer and get out of all of it with Bitsy's and Bryson's money.

He held a pointer as he stood before a large easel, a projection screen and a rear screen slide projector. He began to speak in the manner of a college lecturer.

'Chief Engineer Kullers will handle the engine room crews below decks. The engine room crews will be the only people other than ourselves to remain aboard after the operation gets underway. That includes cooks and galley crews, all seamen, all stewards and stewardesses, all officers. The first assignment of Mr McHenry when the capture of the ship gets underway and while we will be off-loading the passengers will be to have the galley prepare and refrigerate ninety-six sandwiches, a sufficient quantity of salad, a large pot of stock, and one dozen cold cooked chickens before they are off-loaded.

'Mr Bonnette and I will take the bridge where Mr McHenry will join us as soon as the work of the food has been completed. The radio room is directly off the bridge and we will silence that when we take the bridge. No radio report is to be made to base. However, if messages for the ship or its passengers are sent from the base this signal must be answered or an alarm will be spread to search for the ship. Therefore I shall spend all my time on the bridge as navigator, radio man and Captain from the time we strike until we complete the raid on the Cruse cellars and put to sea again.'

He propped up a large map on a stiff board upon the easel. It was a clear black and white map of the Bay of Biscay which the Spanish call the Cantabrian Sea. The map showed the south of England, western France, and northern Spain. Using his pointer, the Captain said, 'This is the Bay of Biscay, the second roughest body of water in the world, may you never find yourselves sailing upon the first. Here,' the pointer tapped, 'is the mouth of the Gironde river which connects the city of Bordeaux with the sea, a distance of about forty land miles.'

He flicked on the rear screen projector. The audience blinked as an aerial photograph of the city of Bordeaux appeared on the screen. 'This is Bordeaux,' the Captain said. 'The area within this white circle is the warehouse of Cruse et Fils, Frères, the enormous and vastly prestigious house of wine growers, shippers, and brokers. This warehouse extends for seven city blocks under the river and the Quai des Chartrons. The warehouse and cellars are our strike area.

'Mr Schraum,' the Captain nodded amiably at Schraum who moved forward eagerly to the edge of his chair, 'will set three major fires inside three public buildings which will, of course, have been deserted for the night, which are situated at acceptable spacings on the far perimeter of the city and well across the city from the Cruse cellars. These fires will serve to divert police activity and attention because Mr Schraum and Mr Fouchet will call all principal police posts to generate police attention.'

Schraum's eyes glittered. His mouth twitched unpleasantly. He seemed to be experiencing some unspeakable ecstasy and the Captain hastily looked away from him.

'We will need to deal with one police patrol car in the course of its normal rounds, as it checks on external warehouse security. This patrol car should show itself on the quai between the warehouse and the ship at approximately twenty-two minutes after we have docked and the loading has started. Mr Bonnette, coming from the ship, and Mr McHenry, coming out from the warehouse will secure these police and drive the car aboard the ferry where they will be stowed on the car deck and released to roam the ship before we go ashore into Portugal. There is to be no violence. Is that clear?'

Bonnette and McHenry nodded solemnly.

'Mr Schraum and Mr Fouchet will fly ahead of us to Bordeaux. Mr Fouchet will disable the alarms system at Cruse which is connected directly to the headquarters post of the Prefecture of Police and will re-set it to go off at eleven twenty-five the following morning. As well he will tie up the four watchmen inside the warehouse whose patrol routes have been marked. With your permission, we will now proceed with the check list. Mr Schraum and Mr Fouchet may be excused to get off to catch their planes.' The two men left without a gesture or without acknowledging that they knew the other was leaving.

'Mr McHenry, is the lorry now on its way to Bordeaux from Paris with the labourers and the equipment?'

'Yes, sir.'

'Where are the two Mercedes tow trucks?'

'Right down the street, Cap'n. We board with them at three o'clock. We got us two trucks, four mechanics, four sets of master ignition keys.'

'Thank you.' The Captain flicked the rear screen projector. The picture changed to show a ten-thousand-ton ferry at its pier in Southampton. The prow of the car ferry yawned like a dragon's mouth, as though it was feeding on the minnow-sized automobiles which were driving into it.

'You are looking at the one reason which allows us to be here now, planning everything we plan. It is the ten-thousand-ton car ferry, *Bergquist Laura*, which runs between Southampton and Bilbao. Only this car ferry, or perhaps a less available aircraft carrier, has the immediate accessible loading space – on its car deck – for eighteen-thousand-odd cases of wine. We must take this car ferry in order to take the wine.'

He turned again to the large map of the Bay of Biscay and

187

circled Southampton on it with a red paint pencil. 'We are here,' he said. 'The wine is here.' He circled Bordeaux then he drew an arrowed red line across the Bay of Biscay to Bilbao. 'This is the normal route of the car ferry.' He drew a circle on the ferry's route-line at a point just below the Cotentin peninsula. 'Here is where we will capture the car ferry and off-load the passengers, crew, and cars into the sea.'

'Into the sea?' Bonnette spoke the shocked astonishment of the men in the room as though mass murder were the only homicidal sin, as though it were natural and correct for people to engage from time to time in small murders but that this sort of heinous, mass, wet murder simply was not done.

'You are gonna throw a couple of hundred cars into the ocean?' McHenry asked with awe.

The Captain was not amused. 'Your concern over the fate of life and property is touching. I hasten to explain that all passengers will be off-loaded into the ship's life-boats, by the trained ship's crews. They will be rowed approximately two hundred yards to the double-decker freighter, *Benito Juarez*, which having rendezvoused with us at this point on my orders will appear to be coming to the rescue in answer to an SOS.'

'The freighter is ours?' Bonnette asked.

'It is a rented Drive-Ur-Self freighter under our control,' the Captain said. 'Two days after we have disposed of the wine, the passengers will be landed on a beach in North Africa near a Club Méditerranée, our captain claiming delay due to a broken rudder which would have to be re-rigged. He should receive a decoration from the Swedish government for his part in the rescue, the *Bergquist Laura* being a Swedish ship.'

'But like what about all them cars?' McHenry pleaded.

'Mr McHenry – if we do not dump the one hundred and ten or one hundred and fifty automobiles there will be no vast, immediately accessible storage area in which to stow the wine. Therefore, the first job of this – uh – hijacking will be putting

188

the cooks to work and the last job will be dumping the cars into the sea.'

He drew a green-arrowed line with a paint pencil across the Bay of Biscay from the capture point to the Gironde estuary. 'We will sail up the Gironde at twenty-three hundred hours tomorrow night. We will moor at the Cruse warehouse on the Quai des Chartrons at fourteen minutes after two o'clock on Sunday morning. We will load in forty-seven minutes and go down the river and out to sea again. That is all there is to it.'

'How do we dispose of the wine?' Bonnette asked stolidly.

'As I said, I will tell you that one hour before it happens. Your turn to speak has come. Are you in or are you out?'

'We are in,' Bonnette said.

The Captain stepped down from the platform and walked to the window, thinking that Bonnette had a much better-formed sense of free will than he did. He had proposed but Bonnette had disposed for all of them. They were all committed now.

'Please pick up the envelopes with your names on them on the table by the door,' he said without turning, staring at the enormous car ferry. 'Study them carefully. We leave in four hours. Good day, gentlemen.'

He listened to them leave. He had been the son of the intimate friend of a King of England. He had been a captain of one of Her Majesty's carriers but he had failed so he had become a wine merchant but he had failed so he had become a criminal. The margin for failure in this new work would be slender. He would be dead or he would be in prison for the rest of his life if he failed at this career. He felt a hardness settle within him, throughout himself. He was finished with failure.

Gash Schutc carefully secured the bottoms of his tweed bags then buttoned his tweed waistcoat carefully. He stood before the full-length mirror at Axelrod House and slipped into his tweed jacket. He placed his matching tweed fedora on his head so its brim lined up parallel with the line of his shoulders.

He gave each side of his golden moustache twenty-five brisk strokes with a military brush then he took a key from his pocket and unlocked a steel filing cabinet, took out a heavy steel box, unlocked that, and removed a large, brown, manila envelope which contained the four major fool-proof crimes which he and the computers had developed so painstakingly. He took the envelope to the modern, L-shaped desk in the large bedroom and dropped four blobs of blue sealing wax upon the flap at the back of the envelope and sealed each of these with his heavy ring. He turned the package face up and, writing in a rapidly moving italic hand in red ink marked: 'In the event of my death, the contents of this envelope will become the property of my friend, Captain Colin Huntington, R.N. (ret.),' then signed his name and the date under that.

He had no premonition of his own death, what he had just done was merely one of the tidy things he did. He took his unsigned will out of the desk file and stared at it for some time. It had been written by an attorney. It was all quite properly worded, he felt sure. It was brief, running to one and one third pages, and stated that he thereby left all his worldly goods to his friend and saviour, Captain Colin Huntington, R.N. (ret.) who was resident at Farm Street, W.1, London. The will was unsigned. Commander Schute's relentless tidiness caused him to take his pen in hand again and to lower it over the line which blankly awaited his signature. But Captain Huntington had never expressed any interest in gold. Captain Huntington, for all his good and sturdy qualities, was a frivolous fellow with thoughts of women, French cooking, fine wines and the peerage. Captain Huntington was, further, an unlucky gambler.

He could not make his hand sign his name so he compromised. He initialled the will and dated the initials, then addressed an envelope to his attorney in London, sealed the will within it, then stamped it properly and dropped it in the

OUT basket on his desk. It was only semi-tidy, he mourned and disapproved, but it was the best he could do.

He packed a black satchel with two 9mm Luger pistols which could deliver such tremendous impact when they hit, a pair of pajamas, two shirts, a change of underclothing and a copy of Wynne-Edwards's 'Animal Dispersion in Relation to Social Behavior'. He left the room through the tall French windows and sauntered out across the broad lawn to the Cambridge Corporation helicopter which flew him to Southampton.

It was a hot, brilliantly sunny July day and there was no breeze from the sea so near at hand. The Captain regarded the long lines of cars waiting to board the car ferry in lines which were seven abreast and his rough count estimated that there were about one hundred and twenty cars and about eleven heavy trucks. He could see Ford McHenry seated in the cab of a heavy Mercedes tow truck in the fourth position of the number three line, wearing a white jumper. The second Mercedes tow truck waited just behind him. The long lines seemed to be packed with every variety of holiday paraphernalia, the Captain thought. He remembered a Frenchman who had refused to learn English because of the word 'paraphernalia'. The man had asked him what the word meant in English and he had said, 'Oh, I suppose it means semi-useless baggage.' The man had crowed. 'That is what you say! That is why English will never approach French in precision. Here is the dictionary definition of the word paraphernalia: The property which, at common law, remained, more or less, under the control of a married woman and which did not pass into the administration of her husband's estate upon his decease before her.' If French were a precise language, the Captain thought, we might as well all give up trying to communicate altogether.

He felt the heat. The hundred odd cars seemed to be painted on a mirage. He stared out at the hundreds of water skis, beach blankets, butane stoves, tents, mattresses, and playpens which were lashed to car roofs and fenders. He had begun to worry about where Gash Schute could be. He had looked at his watch twice before he realized that somewhere in the vicinity Bonnette was undoubtedly watching him so he stopped looking out over the crowd and at his watch and strolled along the pavement to the foot passengers' waiting room where he could buy a few paperback novels as his own contribution to paraphernalia.

The foot passenger terminal was new and cool with a high arched ceiling, a café-bar and two news stands. As soon as he entered he spotted Charles Bonnette and Chief Kullers in different parts of the large room ignoring each other and him, among the herding of sixty or seventy passengers who would sail to Bilbao without cars: campers with enormous haversacks which had knapsacks on top of them, wearing enormous shoes below matchstick thick legs. He could see dozens and dozens of cameras. He turned his back to the crowd after he had bought two paperbacks to be able to stare out at the avenue along which a taxi should soon be bringing Gash Schute and from which he could watch the lines of cars.

The eighth car in the line contained a shiningly handsome young couple who were exquisitely placed in a long, macaw-red Jaguar with its top down. The shining girl with every hair in place and no baggage showing anywhere said to the beautiful young man beside her, 'It's not only just as though we were going to romantic, bloody-marvellous Spain on our honeymoon, but we are going to bloody-marvellous, romantic Spain in the most fantastic car any girl's Daddy ever gave her for a wedding present.'

'Gave us,' the young man said. 'Us. He gave the car to us.'

Car nineteen in line six contained a pinkly endomorphic driver in his undershirt, his wife, Brenda, whose hair was in sky-blue rollers, who held twin babies in her lap and had actually found places on the floor of the car for her two feet, among the bottles of milk and Ribena and quires of packaged nappies. On the back seat of the car there were three suitcases and a small, tow-headed boy holding a toy tractor, a toy fire engine, and a Koala bear doll on his lap.

'I cannot believe we are having a holiday, Gareth,' the sweet-faced woman said for the ninth time that day. 'First we saved to get married, then we saved for the kids, then we saved for the car and now we are off on a glorious holiday with a bank loan.'

'That's as it should be, Bren,' her husband said, 'so that when we get back we'll be strong enough to save to pay back the bank loan.'

Car forty-seven was a Kelly-green Mustang with Illinois plates. There was a man and a woman in it, but only incidentally. Mainly the car seemed to be in use to transport scuba diving equipment for one, one set of gold-plated golf clubs, one tennis racket, one large pair of riding boots, one cased shotgun, one pair of water skis and pieces of matched Vuitton luggage. The man was a snarler because he was a tax lawyer specializing in Guiana corporations which transferred to Ontario trusts which off-funnelled into Luxembourg companies which controlled Nigerian storage battery factories and he spent his life, even when he was sleeping, in a deep sweat that the IRS was going to catch up with every one of his clients, because of his fantasies, and his entire world would come tumbling down. This pressure had had a terrible effect on his disposition.

'What the hell do I have you for?' he snarled at his wife. 'When are you going to learn to pack a car? How could you possibly lose my handball glove? You hang on that goddam telephone talking to your goddam mother all day like she was around the corner instead of in Oak Park. Am I right or am I right?' His wife bit her lip, held back from unpacking the shot gun and firing it at him, and looked out the window.

Car thirty-one, line three, was a Triumph two-seater holding one woman of about thirty-five. She was pretty and she had a giddy look. Her husband had given her a Diner's Club Card, a Barclaycard and an American Express card and she spent as much time as she could at sea because she loved the feeling of being cut off from the world with new people who had never heard her limited supply of patter and adorable tricks. Also, the sea did something to peoples' inhibitions. They would board at three and she would unpack then stretch out to read 'The Great Resorts' to focus her conversation. At six she would dress and walk around, making new friends. Then at about ten o'clock she would return to her cabin, spread out flat on her back and more or less stay that way for the rest of the voyage, entertaining the new friends she had made. Then she would take in the bulls at Bilbao, get limbered up again, and drive back on the next car ferry to make more new friends.

First in line on the sequestered heavy vehicle side was a large tourist bus which carried sixty-four passengers including Miss Erle Mae Gammidge who weighed three hundred and eighty-one pounds and who occupied two bus seats when an arm rest had been removed.

The boarding whistle sounded. Gates were opened. The foot passengers shuffled past the ticket window to board the ferry and Captain Huntington, in order not to alarm Charles Bonnette into thinking that he was waiting for someone to arrive who was not supposed to be there, made his way to the head of the line where he was able to help an elderly woman who was trying to support her husband while coping with a valise. She was most grateful. 'He has a bad heart,' she explained, 'and this heat makes him feel very weak.'

'It will be much cooler when the ship gets moving,' the Captain said.

The old man said, 'My heart is all right. It's just the heat. I thank you for helping my wife.' Captain Huntington stood on the far side of the man, helping to support him and carrying their case.

'You are very, very kind,' the old woman said. Their speech was strongly Spanish.

The Captains, Charles Bonnette and Chief Kullers were well aboard when Commander Schute's taxi let him off in front of the passenger building.

'Looks like a crowded crossing,' he said to the Purser at the embarkation gate.

'We are full up, sir. Absolutely full up.'

Schute boarded and found his way toward his cabin. The corridors were well lighted and well marked with arrows and cabin numbers. On the way he passed the ship's nursery where eighteen or twenty little tootlers were playing at the top of their lungs. He glared at them and kept moving. He moved approximately two and a half feet when he found himself at his stateroom. He stared and listened again to the shaking, terrifying noises which came shrilly and unceasingly out of the playroom then he went into his cabin, closed the door and sat down to rest. The noise seemed louder and shriller with the door closed. He rang the bell for a steward, leaning on it viciously. He sat down directly facing the closed door until she arrived.

'Sir?' she said, putting her head in. 'Can't help you now. Too rushed until we sail, sir.'

'You will help me now,' the Commander said. He got to his feet and extended a five-pound note. 'Get me out of here,' he said.

She stared at the money. 'I don't understand, sir.'

'Can't you hear those little bastards? Get me out. Put me as far away from that screeching as the ship's plan will allow.' He jammed the money into her hand. She fled.

In ten minutes, following what could have been an addition

of ten more small children to the happy horde, the Purser arrived at the Schute cabin. He was cold and stiff. 'The stewardess has told me your problem, sir,' he said, jamming the five-pound note back into the Commander's hand. 'There is no possibility of transfer, sir, unless you wish to share a cabin with three rock musicians. We are full up, sir.'

'Full up? What about that dreadful racket?'

'The children are generally in their beds by seven, sir.'

'Seven? For heaven's sake, man, it isn't yet four o'clock. What time does the infernal place open in the morning?'

'Not until seven sir. You may rest assured of that.' The Purser smiled cruelly. When he left, the Commander removed a 9mm bullet from the cotton he had wrapped it in and stuffed the cotton into his ears. Then he put the bullet between his teeth and, biting down hard, sat down to read the Wynne-Edwards book, a volunteer prisoner in his cabin for the rest of the voyage.

The cars then the big trucks rumbled aboard the ship to their places on the car deck through the enormous, yawning jaw at the front of the ship. Then the high, steel upper jaw closed into full bite and was locked. The lines were cast off. The ship's whistle hooted. The ferry moved slowly out of her pier then out into the great, deep-water harbour to seek the roads which would take her round the Isle of Wight and then steadily out to sea.

The Captain played the slot machines steadily and found himself in conversation with the pretty, possibly giddy, lady who had begun on her sweep to accumulate friends. 'Wonderful day for it, isn't it?' she said.

'My word, yes,' the Captain said continuing to feed the metal bandit. 'Have you made this voyage before?' he asked.

'Oh, yes. Dozens of times.'

'How is the food?'

'Oh, I don't know really. I could say merely abominable and be kind.'

'I was afraid of that.'

'Why don't we have a pre-prandial?'

'A –'

'A drink before dinner. To get acquainted. To stave off in the bar before dinner?'

'How very kind of you.'

'It's not that.' She smiled as lewdly as she could and that was a problem for all her plans, really, because she could not smile lewdly. 'I just find that I like you very, very much. Cheer-o!'

'Cheer-o, madame,' the Captain said.

Charles Bonnette inspected the tax-free shops to see if there was anything he might want to take after the hijack. At six o'clock he went to the Purser's Desk and sent a coded radio-gram to a realty company in Palm Springs, California, which raised the price of heroin in continental United States by the equivalent of four dollars a deck which would, in its turn, raise the crime statistics in American big cities.

Ford McHenry cased the cash flow in all the bars as nine-hundred-odd people began to slake their thirsts and he became deeply interested every time a cash register opened and he could look into it. He was still wearing his white jumper suit and so were the four car mechanics. At six-thirty all five got into the line at the cafeteria, looking like a circus flying act.

'What do you chaps do?' a small boy asked McHenry.

'We racing drivers. We goin' to Spain and win everything.'

'You are?' the lad said, 'I thought you were bakers.'

Chief Kullers conducted a professional examination of the ship's lifeboats, then went below to find the engineering duty officer. It was a long climb down on hot iron ladders and across catwalks. He showed the duty officer his union ticket. 'I'm a Chief myself,' he explained, 'kinda takin' a little vacation before I pick up my ship at La Coruna. I'd sure like to see your set-up here.' The engineering officer was delighted to oblige.

Reluctantly the Captain entered the ship's dining room for the second sitting at nine o'clock, expecting the worst. He regarded, smelled, and tasted a glass of available red wine. 'This is perfectly sound Algerian wine,' he said to the wine steward. 'Why should they put this Beaujolais label on the bottle?'

'Our passengers enjoy trying to pronounce the French, sir,' the wine steward explained.

The Captain tasted the soup which the waiter had placed before him. He blinked. 'This is superb soup!' he exclaimed.

'It *is*?' the waiter said with confusion.

'The carte says tonight's soup is mulligatawny. This isn't mulligatawny.'

'It isn't?'

'Of course not. Its the best Aubergine and Crab soup I've ever tasted.'

'I – I don't know what could have happened, sir.'

The Captain tasted the fish. 'Whatever is this?' he said to the waiter.

'It's our Dover sole, sir. And very popular.'

'It is sole, yes. But it is a *mousse* of sole and it takes four hours to prepare.'

'Oh, no, sir.'

The Captain consumed two rapid forkfuls. 'It is magnificent – simply magnificent.'

When he tasted the duck ('What is that?' – 'That's our special today, sir, the duck') he had pushed himself away from the table. He started to stride out of the room, stopped and returned to the waiter. 'If anyone else should ask you what that is,' he said, 'you may say, on my authority, that it is *Le Canard à la façon du Docteur Couchoud*,' then wheeled away, crossed the room and went out through the door to the galley.

Juan Francohogar was at work in the kitchen.

'Captain Huntington!' he almost shouted with astonishment.

'I knew it,' the Captain said. 'I knew it was you. What are you doing here?'

'I am going home. This is the best way to go. I can work, so there is no cost and when we dock France is only two hours away.'

'I must talk to you,' the Captain said. 'When do you finish?'

'In one hour, sir.'

'I will come back.' The Captain left the galley. He felt cheerful. Here was a typical thing which always promised to go wrong no matter how much planning. He could not off-load Francohogar because the man would not understand why he, Captain Huntington, had not been off-loaded as well. If he kept him aboard Francohogar would be incriminated should the entire thing fail. He stood at the ship's rail and stared out into the black night. He decided that he would keep Francohogar aboard, never allowing him to leave the galley, which it would not occur to the cook to do anyway. If the whole operation failed they would be under French jurisdiction and no French policeman or officer of the court would ever believe that a cook as exalted as Francohogar would have anything to do with stealing wine so he would be safe.

Commander Schute refused to permit himself to eat, although he was prodigiously hungry, before the nursery room closed for the day and wondrous silence returned. Then he allowed the stewardess to bring him a platter of four double roast beef sandwiches and a bottle of Beaujolais. He did not renew his offer of the five pounds. In the first place he had offended himself by attempting to give away that amount of money for what amounted to the woman's duty so she would now have to be that rare pussycat who went to sea without a beautiful five-pound note. He thanked her gravely then propped his feet with the high, hiker's shoes, the long woollen socks and the tweed superbags upon the berth, gnawed at the sandwiches thriftily to make them last longer, sipped wine and read avidly of how the male fiddler crab stood outside its burrow when the tide was out, beckoning and signalling other fiddler crabs with its semaphore-like chela, pivoting to look like a fiddler playing his bow. The Commander always found relaxation in the world of fiddler crabs – or birds or whales or rabbit – anywhere gold had no meaning and did not insist upon inexorable pursuit.

The wrist alarm went off eleven hours after the car ferry had left port. Captain Huntington had been asleep in seaman's work clothes. He awoke and swung his feet over the side of the berth. He reached for the telephone and called the galley. McHenry answered and said all was secure. The Captain asked if he had made certain that Monsieur Francohogar was asleep and then locked in his cabin. Mr Francohogar was sleeping like a baby.

'He can sleep through anything,' the Captain said. 'What is the weather like?'

'Wet and rough, Cap'n.'

'Too bad.'

While the ship rolled and pitched, the Captain put on a watchcoat and a Royal Navy cap with captain's insignia. He dropped the Navy issue automatic into his side pocket and left the cabin. He felt hard and calm and sick at his stomach, just as he had felt when a naval ship prepared to move into action. He thought of the difference between thinking of nine hundred and twenty passengers on a computer print-out and seeing them all aboard this ship; he had never seen so many people swarming over such a confined space. He felt a dread of whether he could move them safely out and a greater dread of whether

Pappadakis would bring the freighter to the rendezvous point on time.

As he stepped out into the companionway, Charles Bonnette was leaving his cabin ten yards ahead. They made their way forward, single file, holding hard to the handrails because the ship was pitching so violently. When they moved out on the deck the force of the wind made it necessary for both men to use all their strength to get the outside door open and when they did the sound of the fury of the wind was a gigantic noise as it whistled in out of the totally black night. The heavy rain drove at their backs as the Captain led the way up the bridge ladder. When they made it to the top they struggled against the wind and the bucking of the ship to tie black silk kerchiefs over their faces. They entered the bridge, causing the door to bang heavily against the bulkhead, with Charles Bonnette showing a gun in his hand. The quartermaster and the duty officer stared at them blankly. No one spoke while the Captain crossed the enclosed bridge and went to the radio room which was just behind the bridge on the port side. He walked to the couch on which the radio officer was stretched out under a light blanket, took him firmly under the right armpit and pulled him up. 'Come out to the bridge with me, please,' he said. The man came out of sleep instantly and got to his feet. The Captain moved him forward and planted him beside the radar screen then said to all three men, 'I am taking this ship,' he said.

'That is piracy,' the duty officer said dully; automatically. 'We will hang you.'

The word itself jolted the Captain, not the penalty for having committed the word. The computers had used the word 'capture' again and again. McHenry had always said 'hijack'. But they were merely coy, convenience words for the most ancient baseness he had ever been taught to understand and it jolted him. He was a British naval officer who had suddenly become what he had been trained to regard as vermin; a pirate. The fall had been sudden but it had taken him downward thousands of miles into other depths. He had said to Yvonne that something was 'a new low'. It had been a dizzying pinnacle whatever it had been. Yes. Captain Colin Huntington, Royal Navy, retired, was a pirate. He heard McHenry burst into the bridge house, snarling for intimidation. He saw two of the car mechanics behind him. They were all armed.

'The officers' quarters is one deck below. Take them out through the bridge house and lock them in the cabin with the ship's captain. When the ship's deck officers leave, make sure they leave by the captain's gig, not by passenger lifeboat. If they mix with the passengers and tell them the ship is being hijacked we will only create panic. As it is now, the passengers will follow the lifeboat drill instructions and the crew will see that they are all right. Put the deck officers off last. That is the best way.'

McHenry and the two mechanics herded the three men below. The Captain checked the ship's position and the radar. He telephoned to the engine room. Chief Kullers answered.

'The bridge is secure, Chief. Are you on schedule?'

'The engine room is secure.'

'I am coming down.'

'Aye, aye, sir.'

The Captain reset the coordinates for the ship's course and switched on the automatic pilot. 'Stay here,' he said to Bonnette. 'No one must be out of hearing of the radio room. If there is any kind of sound out of it telephone me at once in the engine room.'

Bonnette grunted. 'Who steers this thing while you're gone?'

'It's on automatic pilot. Rest yourself. I'll return in ten minutes.'

He went down the bridge ladder to the officers' quarters and moved rapidly and confidently to the elevator which was waiting for him most conveniently. He punched the engine room button and dropped rapidly. When he came out, far below decks, he climbed downward on the iron ladders which were almost too hot to touch. He crossed a catwalk and entered the engine room bridge. A Swedish engineering officer and a motorman were seated on the far side. They were covered by two of the car mechanics who had guns.

'I am in command of this ship,' the Captain said. 'I control the bridge and our own crew is abovedecks enforcing our intentions. I came below to make sure that you understand what the situation is. Now hear me. This officer is an experienced licensed chief engineer who is familiar with all your equipment. Do as he orders and you'll be all right. Keep working and each man will get a thousand kroner bonus. Stop working and you will be shot. Acknowledge that you understand me.'

'We understand,' the engineering officer said. 'You have committed piracy. After piracy what is murder because they will hang you anyway. So we will do as you order us.'

To the Captain, the heat in the enclosed bridge was prodigious. What had been rain on his face was now sweat. The Chief and the engineering officer were working in shirt sleeves with gold epaulets on their shirted shoulders. 'The motorman will instruct the Chief when there is a change of watch. Twenty minutes before the change of each watch, the next watch will be brought in here at gunpoint to work and you will be taken out and locked in your quarters. In a few moments you are going to hear my voice on the public address system,' said the Captain, 'calling the passengers and the crew to abandon ship. Pay it no attention. It will be a false announcement. We will off-load all officers, crew and passengers, except yourselves, to another ship within the half hour. That is all.'

The telephone rang. The Chief picked it up. He listened

then handed the phone to the Captain. 'It's the bridge,' he said.

'Yes?' the Captain said into the phone.

'The radio room is making all kinds of noises,' Bonnette said. The Captain hung up and left the engine-room bridge, going up the hot ladder as fast as he could move with sweat-slippery hands.

Passengers were dancing in the lounge. They were the die-hards who had decided long before that it would cost them money to go to bed as most of the other passengers had. They were having a marvellous time by travel agent guarantee. Stewards were rushing drink trays large enough to require two hands so that when the ship rolled or pitched or did both, they would pause expertly to brace with their legs against the nearest firm surface. A three man combo of long-haired kids was playing guitars and drums and singing in the new grotesquely ugly way which not only requires shouting but had forced the two east London boys who did the singing to study records by Elvis and Ray Charles through a thousand playings so that they could scream out the words in the flawless accents of central Mississippi field hands.

There was still a small knot of people in the roulette room at four twenty-five that morning. Two card games were going in the lounge, one British and highly demonstrative, the other Spanish, and stolid. But it was the bar which pulled the biggest crowd. Not that any of them particularly cared about drinking but it was six whole hours later than the licensing hours at home where the pubs closed at half past ten and that was a distinction they were not prepared to miss.

Dawn was thirty-two minutes, nineteen seconds away.

The Captain sprinted the last twenty yards along the companionway in officer country then up the ladder. He dove through the doorway into the radio room and sat at the

204

equipment waiting for a break of silence. Then he began to tap rapidly on the sending key. There was an exchange.

'What is happening?' Bonnette said.

'Southampton was getting very worried because we didn't answer for twelve minutes. They were about to ask the French coast guard to make a search.'

'Jesus.'

'It's all right. I told them I had an abscessed tooth. Here comes the message which caused all the uproar.' The Captain slipped on a pair of earphones and began to write down a message. His face, which was taut, got grimmer. He signed off and removed the earphones, staring numbly up at Bonnette. The noisy room was quiet again.

'What happened? Why were they trying to get us?' Bonnette asked.

'This is a passenger ship. It was a message for a passenger.'

'What message?' Bonnette's habitual, professional cool had again taken mastery over his terror. Terror plus cool produces criminal anger. 'What does it say, this goddam message?'

'It's from Beverly Hills where it is now eight o'clock at night. It says,' the Captain read from the pad in front of him, 'Missed you on Flag Day, missed you on Mother's Day, so happy July 17th Vicky dear Signed Herm.'

He got up abruptly and strolled past Bonnette to the bridge. 'How is it the computers didn't anticipate Herm,' he asked himself and a thrilling sense of horror ran from his stomach through his arms and legs. This was what lengthened the odds. There had to be other Herms and there had to be many other Herms. He grinned with the pleasure of possible destruction.

'How come they aren't all vomiting down there,' Bonnette asked, 'with weather like this? I'd be vomiting myself if I didn't have so much on my mind.'

'They're heaving it up in the cabins,' the Captain said. He looked at his watch. 'Two minutes, five seconds to the beginnings of dawn, and then you'll have a preview, my dear Bonnette, of what Hell will be like.'

'Where the hell is McHenry?' Bonnette said. 'My feet are killing me.'

The Captain alternated his gaze between the watch and the western, not eastern, horizon. Bonnette stood behind him and stared too, not knowing why. 'Now!' the Captain said and, as if by the signal of his intense whisper, a rocket exploded high in the air over the sea somewhere out in front of them.

'Thank God,' the Captain said.

'What was that?'

'That was a very good mariner named Captain Pappadakis aboard the *Benito Juarez*. The rescue is at hand.'

He leaned with all his weight upon the alarm button. Instantly, gongs throughout the ship began to ring out the message of desperate trouble; seven short gongs, one long gong. The ship's whistle began to blow in the same cadence. The Captain gave the sounds a chance to hammer the fright in. He looked ahead. The faintest glimmer of dawn made it possible for him to make out the bow of the ship dipping into the sea as all exterior lights followed with his hand switch and the flood lights showed the running, rolling sea with eighteen to thirty foot waves all around the ship.

Below decks the crew was turning out into souwesters and oilskins. Stewards were racing from switchbox to switchbox to make the ship ablaze with light. Ship's officers on one deck below, just under the bridge, came tumbling out of their quarters strapping on side arms and racing to the lifts or rushing down companionways.

An excitable Shropshireman from Ludlow named Hunt was playing cards with four other men in the ship's lounge, holding his discard high before slamming it upon the table. His arm froze in the air as the gongs and whistles began to sound.

'What does that mean?' he asked, not moving. 'Odd time of

night for bells.' Then the Captain's voice came booming out clearly through the ninety-one loudspeakers on the ship, cutting off the gongs and hooting.

'Do you hear there?' the Captain's voice said. 'Do you hear there? Attention all ship's officers and crew. This is your captain speaking.'

On the bridge, Captain Huntington took a bos'n's pipe from his pocket and blew it into the microphone.

'This is the captain speaking,' he repeated. 'Do you hear there? All officers and crew will proceed to stations to abandon ship. Do you hear there? Prepare to abandon ship. This is your captain speaking.'

He pressed the alarms button again and the noises which were crazing, because they had been identified, shook the ship. Hunt, the frozen card player unfroze with shock, slammed the card down upon the table, and got up so frantically that he overturned his chair. He sprinted toward the deck exit, the other card players right behind him.

Passengers lay on their berths green with sea sickness, forgetting it instantly as the Captain's voice crashed into staterooms.

'Attention all passengers. Do you hear there? This is your captain ordering you to prepare to abandon ship. You will proceed to muster stations without delay. Do you hear? Do you hear there?'

The elderly Spanish man whom Captain Huntington had assisted aboard in Southampton came out of his stateroom and plucked at the sleeves of people rushing past him in the companionway.

'What it say? What it say?' he asked everyone, getting no answer until the Captain's rusty Spanish repeated the same announcement, as under international shipping requirements. '*Oyé! Oyé! Atencion por el Capitan! Oyé! Ponga cinuron salvavides. Atencion pasajeros! Atencion por el Capitan! Aprisa*

voya al estacion de asamblea. Urgente! Urgente! Abandonar
el barco!'

The elderly Spaniard was transfixed with fright. He turned
to go into his cabin to rescue his wife, his eyes rolling in his
head, then clutched at his chest and leaned against the bulkhead for relief. His wife came out of the cabin with his topcoat
and hat. She put her arm around him. They were thrown from
side to side in the narrow companionway by the bucking of the
ship on those seas.

People in every stage of dress and undress began to foam
across the salon which was heaving like a wild horse. Furniture
was slammed out of the way. Women were knocked sprawling.
On the starboard side of the lounge a most orderly group had
formed at a muster station. At the centre of the forward muster
salon the three raggle-tag, long-haired rock musicians had
assembled and had plugged in their electric guitars. They were
frightened almost rigid but they did what they decided they
had to do by playing into a microphone which fed the ship's
public address system whenever the Captain had not pre-
empted it. Over and over again they played rock arrangements
of 'Mairzy Doats' and 'The Eyes of Texas Are Upon You', the
drummer no longer as bored as he had been all night. 'For
Christ's sake, Cecil,' he yelled at the leader, 'can't you move it
into "Sweet Georgia Brown" or somefink?'

'Do you hear there? Do you hear there?' the Captain's voice
exploded everywhere. 'There is serious leakage in the forward
bulkhead which is now beyond control. This ship cannot be
saved. This ship will sink within thirty-five minutes. Go at once
to your muster stations and prepare to abandon ship. This is
your captain speaking.'

At the first announcement, four decks below, the handsome
young couple who had seemed to be a living part of the red
Jaguar sports car were honeymooning avidly on the upper bunk
when the first gongs had sounded, then the Captain's announce-

ment slammed into them. Charmian stiffened convulsively in her husband's arms as she listened.

'The car!' she screamed as soon as she understood what was happening. 'What are we going to do about the car?'

Jeremy withdrew abruptly and she gasped. He almost hurt himself badly scrambling out of bed because the lights were out and he had forgotten they were in the upper berth.

'Are you all right?' Charmian called down. 'Darling! Answer me! Are you all right?'

'Yes. Yes, I think so.'

'Then, please darling, do something about the car.'

'My God – I hope your father insured it.'

'You hope *Daddy* insured it? Jeremy, are you saying you did not insure my car?'

'Darling – it was natural to assume that if a man gives a new car on the day two people get married and are scheduled to leave for a foreign country, he would either have insured the car or have instructed the bride and groom to insure it.'

The gongs began again. Charmian had to scream to be heard over the awful racket. 'Never mind, darling. We must get dressed and get down to that car deck and save that car.'

Gladys, the pretty, somewhat giddy, woman was well under a bulky Spanish fellow who travelled in figs and dates, on the lower berth of her cabin. He was the most accomplished and enthusiastic new friend she had made on several voyages. Then the gongs went off and the captain's voice interrupted them. She tried to pay it no attention but men are like small boys, she began to think, and anything can divert their attention. Her new friend was actually trying to pull away from her but she had a firm scissors hold around his waist with her two sinewy legs and she resisted frantically. 'No, no! Not yet. Please, Estaban! Not just yet, darling. Just a few little seconds more, Estaban! *EstaBAN!*'

14

*

The ring of light had definitely lifted across the eastern horizon. The sea was becoming more and more visible and, in the distance, one could see the *Benito Juarez* begin to loom up as a vessel whose every feature would soon be distinguishable. The Captain went out on the docking bridge and operated the signal light, telling Captain Pappadakis: LOWER CLIMBING NETS AND BREAK OIL BAGS OPEN ON SURFACE WHEN WE LOWER OUR FIRST STARBOARD BOAT ACKNOWLEDGE. He waited for the freighter's blinkers to signal MESSAGE ACKNOWLEDGED.

Below decks most passengers had been mustered by the ship's officers and crews and were standing in almost orderly rows at their muster stations, dressed in lifejackets, while on the deck immediately outside, seamen removed the railings so that when the lifeboats were lowered on their davits from the boat deck above they could be entered at deck level, even if twenty-eight feet above the sea. At the after muster station on the port side a group of iron lunged singers began beautiful vocal harmony with Bertha Moore's 'A Child's Thought' which wrestled and fought the rock band's now constant 'Sweet Georgia Brown' for the minds and souls of the frightened passengers and the effect was cruel buffeting fright and horror with 'If I were God up the sky/*Sweet Georgia Brown*/I'll tell you all what I would do/I would not let the babies cry/*Sweet Georgia Brown*/Because veir toofs was coming froo.'

People were still sprinting zig-zag across the salon and back seeking members of their family or afraid to stay still in case they began to think. The elderly Spanish man clutched his chest tightly with his eyes closed in agony and fell heavily to the deck. His wife tried to pull him to his feet by his arm, screaming one piercing note. The lights began to flick on and off, on and off, to warn that the lifeboats were ready to be boarded.

Miss Erle Mae Gammidge, three hundred and eighty-one pounds, lay on her back in a lower bunk staring at the ceiling, unable to move herself out of the berth to get to her feet. The gongs, the Captain's voice, and the inane music had been hammering her fear and shaping it into wilder and wilder panic. She tried desperately to reach the wall bell but her arm was too short. Her shrill screams became weaker as she cried out for help. She strained and tried to lift herself, gasping to breathe.

The Purser and the stewardesses were coming along the hall making a systematic check of each room. Commander Schute crouched on top of a toilet seat in the public Men's Room of his deck, feet well up off the floor so that the steward's sweep of the area failed to find him.

The stewardess burst open the door of Miss Gammidge's stateroom and found her. She took one look at the size and weight of the agonized passenger and went back to the alley to call for help. Another stewardess rushed along under the pressure of the Captain's voice jabbing through the loud speakers. Together they were able to lift Miss Gammidge out of the berth, put on her slippers and somehow guide her out of the room, talking to her steadily to comfort her, as the Captain's announcement was repeated in Spanish for the third time. It was tremendously difficult, slow work to get Miss Gammidge up the bucking companionway to the boarding deck. As they pushed and pulled and moved her enormous, almost paralytically frightened bulk up the stairs they decided not to take her to a muster station but to bring her directly to a lifeboat station to put her aboard first, as the first lifeboat was lowered.

They battled the wind, the rain and the pitching ship to Station No. 7 on the starboard side. The older stewardess decided that Miss Gammidge must sit on the deck to wait because her own weight was too much for her to support in that sea. The heavy cross winds were moving the ship into a pronounced roll while it pitched. The seamen had removed the ship's railings. The stewardesses ran off to get Miss Gammidge a blanket from a stack at the nearest muster station but, when they were about twenty-eight feet away they heard her scream and turned in sudden panic. The ship had gone into a contorted roll as it came out of a deep, high pitch and Miss Gammidge, screaming, was sliding on her behind across the polished teak deck towards the open, unprotected ship's side. The stewardesses reversed and began to sprint to save her. Four feet before they could get there, Miss Gammidge slid, screaming, into the wild, engulfing sea.

The American tax lawyer from Illinois, Mustang owner and snarler, was in the loo when the gongs began to go off. As the Captain's announcement was coming through, his wife was pounding on the closed door and crying out with shrill fear. 'Harry! Harry! The ship is sinking. Harry, for God's sake! The ship is *sinking*!' As she spoke she was pulling on gloves calmly then she reached over as slowly as a sleepwalker and took a fire axe down from the wall of the cabin.

Snarling to the end, Harry stuck his head out of the small room. 'What the hell is this, Gertrude? Can't you even let me have a little peace in here?'

She whacked him across the forehead with the axe moving in fullest baseball swing and he went down like two hundred pounds of beef, his head in the head. She stared down at his torso with a small, satisfied smile, sighed contentedly, checked the wall chart for the position of her muster station and left the cabin.

Captain Pappadakis, on the bridge of the *Benito Juarez* gave the order to fire the star shell to encourage the passengers of the *Bergquist Laura* by letting them know that rescue was at hand. The first lifeboats were on the sea. The climbing nets were over the side of the freighter and the oiled waters for ninety yards around it were relatively calm. Fore and aft, flood-lights opened up, illuminating the sea all around the lifeboats showing a mere two hundred yards between the two ships.

Dawn was up full and strong. In Lifeboat No. 4, the sweet-faced young woman named Brenda was sobbing brokenly on her husband's shoulder as she held two babies with her arms. 'I've lost my little boy,' she sobbed. 'He let go of my hand and I couldn't find him in all that crowd. What am I going to do? What am I going to do?'

'They'll find him, Bren,' her husband said. 'They'll have him by now. He'll be on another boat, Bren. You'll see.'

Bonnette and McHenry were playing pinochle at the chart table on the bridge and McHenry was cheating by using a stripper deck which let him pull out aces on every cut and because he had persuaded Bonnette to agree that the first twelve cards dealt in each hand had to be dealt four at a time, every time it was Bonnette's turn to deal, McHenry gave the deck four running cuts which brought the four aces to the top of the deck. Because Bonnette was dealing the aces he thought McHenry was very, very lucky.

'Monsieur Bonnette?' the Captain said from the ship's wheel. 'Turn out the ship's captain and the three other men in his cabin and take them to the stern. Put them in the gig. They'll know how to get it over the side.'

'What about the other officers?' Bonnette asked.

'They were running to their stations when the first gong sounded. They command the lifeboats.'

Bonnette and McHenry got up. McHenry objected that if all the lifeboats were gone they'd need the gig to get ashore themselves.

'We go ashore on a rubber life raft. Get moving,' the Captain said.

Bonnette and McHenry went below to the officers' quarters.

The Captain watched passengers stream up the two ladders which Pappadakis had lowered from the deck of the *Benito Juarez* and watched the men passengers clambering up the suspended climbing nets. The wind was dying, the sea was calmer.

One of the mechanics was on guard in front of the door to the ship's captain's cabin. Bonnette rapped on the door. 'You are coming out now,' Bonnette said. 'Keep your hands high over your head. Come out one at a time.'

A loud, hard Scandinavian voice shouted, 'You yust come in and get us.' A gun was fired. Its bullet splintered the door and passed through air between Bonnette and McHenry. Bonnette flattened against the bulkhead and fired through the door. McHenry ran to the end of the corridor then, turning left, made his way out to the boat deck. It was a simple tactic which created an ambush and a crossfire at the same time. As Bonnette shot occasionally through the door to hold the officers' attention, McHenry fired directly through the glass of the porthole. As he killed the ship's captain and the first officer, turning the other two men to face him, Bonnette burst in through the door and shot the remaining two men in the back. To be sure he reloaded and delivered the standard assassin's bullet into the backs of their heads without fuss or bother. Then McHenry came around through the corridor again and they locked the four corpses in the cabin.

McHenry looked at his watch. 'Time we off-loaded them cars,' he said. 'Come on. Down to the car deck.'

Commander Schute sat with his feet up on the berth reading Wynne-Edwards. 'The requirement for social integration,' he read, 'as a prerequisite to the homeostatic control of dispersion, offers a simple explanation for the production of many sounds by animals, the purpose of which has not previously been understood, and this perhaps is nowhere more obvious than those made by animals under water.'

24

The distance between the *Bergquist Laura* and the *Benito Juarez* widened greatly as Captain Huntington began to beat inshore toward calmer seas to jettison the one hundred and ten cars and trucks into the open ocean and Captain Pappadakis headed the freighter westward. When the heavy seas stopped crashing against the car deck level, McHenry called the bridge to say they were able to begin unloading. The Captain signalled for Full Speed Astern on the engine room telegraph and when that manoeuvre had been accomplished, he pushed the button which operated the electric winches which opened the jaw of the prow of the ship. As the ship moved backward out of the weather, the ship's prow separated and the line of the car deck was fourteen feet above the open water. The mechanics worked steadily under the direction of McHenry. The front line cars had their engines started with the master ignition keys and were rolled to a marking line four feet before the rim of the deck then the driver leaped out and one of the powerful Mercedes tow trucks came up behind it and pushed it forward over the edge of the deck into the ocean where it disappeared at once. Working smoothly they were able to off-load four cars a minute, two on each side, from two triple lines which extended all the way along the length of the ship.

To the west, the hysterical exhausted passengers stood at the rail of the *Benito Juarez* staring at all of their possessions which were somewhere inside the car ferry which they kept expecting to sink before their eyes. Men and women were weeping uncontrollably, sitting or lying flat on the steel deck. Children were stony-faced with shock. Brenda kept moving dazedly among the hundreds of passengers, asking if they had seen her little boy. The handsome girl called Charmian, no longer on her way to bloody-marvellous romantic Spain, pulled at her husband's sleeve as he stood dazedly with a pair of binoculars hung around his neck, staring across the mile of ocean at the retreating car ferry. 'What are they doing? Why is its mouth open?'

'I imagine it has something to do with taking on more air,' Jeremy said, 'so that the middle of the ship can be lighter and they can keep her floating.'

'Let me look at it. With the glasses.'

He handed the glasses to her numbly. She sighted through them. She screamed. 'They are dumping the cars into the sea!'

'Not possible.'

'They are! They are!'

'They must be fighting to make the ship lighter.'

'My God! Oh, Jeremy! They are throwing away a magnificent Rolls!'

'How perfectly awful!'

'Jeremy! Jeremy, darling! My God, oh my God, they are killing our beautiful Jag. It's going! It's over the edge!' She gripped the binoculars sobbing wildly. 'It's gone, it's gone!' She crumpled to the deck. Jeremy stared at the faraway ship and pressed at his temples with both hands.

25

'We are precisely on schedule, I am happy to say,' Captain Huntington told his associate as he laid out a new chart on the table. 'Somebody said an old man died of a heart attack,' Bonnette said.

'He probably fainted. Witnesses overdramatize. I'm sure he'll be all right.'

'No doubt.'

'Did you remove the ship's captain and those other officers without a hitch?'

'We removed them.'

'It was a perfect operation,' the Captain said. 'And a very tricky one to perform at sea.'

'Nowhere else could you perform it. There was also a rumour that a small boy fell over the side trying to get into a lifeboat.'

'For heaven's sake, Bonnette! That sort of myth always occurs in panic situations. It is *non*sense. If there was a small boy, he had a mother. If he had a mother she had a firm grip on him, you may be sure.'

'I hope so. It's the little things like that which make the police nervous. And it upsets the insurance companies and they stir up the newspapers so if you're caught, you're cooked, the trial is all over before it starts.'

'How is Chief Kullers?'

'He is fine. I brought him six bottles of beer and liverwurst. His men are working like watches.'

'I say – I had completely forgotten about Francohogar.'

'Who?'

'My former cook, Francohogar, turned up as a passenger on his way back to the Pyrenees.'

'*Juan* Francohogar? Yes, I know,' Bonnette said with excitement, 'he was your personal, private cook, I remember.'

Ford McHenry entered from the docking deck grinning broadly. 'I got the Purser's safe open,' he said. 'Pretty good. About forty-three hundred pounds and there was three hundred and twelve pounds in the cash at the bars from the late business. The boys are working on the roulette cash box now but that ain't gonna be great, if you know what I mean. After I get a sangwitch I'm gonna go through all the baggage in the cabins which oughta be good for another five thousand and some stones. I mean, nine hundred passengers.'

The Captain excused himself and went down the rear stairway to the elevator in the officers' quarters as Bonnette said, 'We haven't looked into the ship's captain's safe yet. Altogether it should yield about fifty thousand pounds, if the jewelry is anything.'

The key to Francohogar's cabin was hanging in the lock. Captain Huntington turned it and opened the door. Francohogar was buttoning his white cook's tunic as the Captain came in and, not having attempted to leave, did not know he had been locked in for the night.

'Good morning, sir.'

'Good morning, Juan.'

'It seems very quiet out there this morning.'

'Yes. It is very quiet. We've had a frightful storm in the night. Almost the entire ship is in bed, dreadfully seasick.'

'The cooks? The cooks are seasick?'

'Alas, yes. No one is working actually. I came down to ask if you could make lunch and dinner for seven.'

'Only seven?'

'Yes, please. In two sittings. Just ring the bridge when you

218

are ready to have it served and someone will come down for it. That would be one sitting for three and one for four. I don't suppose there's any decent wine aboard?'

'Oh, yes sir. In the cook's locker there is always the best wine.'

'Jolly good. Now – for lunch I was thinking about the shape of something such as lamb. Could we build the meal around lamb?'

'Oh, yes sir.'

'Splendid. For dinner – '

'Would you like a roasted loin of pork with rhubarb, sir? They have the rhubarb in the freezer. We could have it with a barley casserole, perhaps, and some braised celery.'

'That would be very nice in the middle, as it were. More than anything else, however, I would like to have you start us with a spanakopita, one of your wonderful spinach pies, although I don't suppose there is any feta cheese aboard.'

'If there is no feta cheese then I will make it with something better than feta cheese. Anyway, with spanakopita, the pastry is everything.'

'And some carrots and grapes.'

'I will finish you with cantaloupe stuffed with a purée of its own pulp combined with blueberries and kirsch. It will be a lovely balance.'

'We are in your good hands then. Lunch about one all right?'

Francohogar nodded sombrely.

Two of the car mechanics brought the food to the bridge and set it upon the charts table. Bonnette and McHenry ate with dumb awe, occasionally bleating with ecstasy, while the Captain chatted on, chewing merrily away on what was, for him, a perfectly normal meal.

'I had the signal from your efficient alarms man, Fouchet, at four o'clock this afternoon while you were sleeping off your lunch. The truck is moving on time and he will begin to dismantle the alarm system just' – the Captain looked at his wrist watch – 'in just seven hours' time, as soon as the day crews are gone and the night watchmen begin their patrols. We are now six hours from the mouth of the Gironde, where we will pick up the river pilot, then we'll take four hours to move up the river to Bordeaux. I shall have a bit of a cat nap now. Please call me in precisely six hours so that I may be on the bridge to welcome the pilot.' He got up and walked to the hatch then he turned to ask McHenry, 'Did you hear anything about a little boy falling over the side during the transfer operation?'

Bonnette looked across the table at McHenry and shook his head almost imperceptibly.

'No, sir, Cap'n,' McHenry said. 'Everything went as smooth as cream.'

'Good,' the Captain said and headed for the sofa in the radio room.

Henri Fouchet worked very slowly and with easy assurance as he dismantled the old-fashioned Cruse alarms system after he had popped a deck of cocaine. When he was satisfied that the system had been disengaged to his approval he re-set its clock to set the alarm off at eleven thirty-five the following morning when, his instructions said, he would be on a train to Lisbon, and the *Bergquist Laura* would again be back at sea.

He rested for two hours then he took each of the watchmen in turn with a loose, limp sap, dumped them all on a forklift truck and drove them across the warehouse to the rue Lombard truck exit where he bound each man with wide adhesive tape, making them as comfortable as possible, then blindfolded them, making sure that they would be able to hear when they came around. The layout of the Cruse warehouses ran along the Quai des Chartrons from the loading warehouse of current wines at the rue Lombard past rue Pelisson and rue Denise to the

Cours du Medoc. Captain Huntington's main strike area would be in the Aging Cellars under the office building entrance at No. 132 Quai des Chartrons, between and under the surfaces of rue Pelisson and rue Denise. This cellar was two and a half city blocks long and a half a city block wide. It extended in the forward area under the avenue across almost to the river, emerging on a slow rise to come out in the quaiside shed buildings which were directly on the piers.

When Fouchet had all the watchmen trussed up he hit each one lightly with the hypodermic Bonnette had issued to him to keep them in a lightly dazed, disorientated state while the distant sounds of the operation were going on. Then he drove himself across the enormous warehouse area through the Aging Cellars and under the avenue then up the slope to the quaiside warehouse door where he settled down with a cycling magazine just inside the door so that he would be there to open it when the Captain brought the car ferry in to dock directly in front of it and when the truck with the labourers and equipment rolled out along the quai. Excepting a half dozen telephone calls which he was to make from the Bordeaux railway terminal, his work on the operation was over.

As the two-decker freighter *Benito Juarez* headed out into the Atlantic on a south-southwest course carrying the nine hundred and twenty passengers and one hundred and seventeen crew of the *Bergquist Laura*, the car ferry itself manned by four car mechanics, Ford McHenry, Charles Bonnette and Captain Colin Huntington, Royal Navy (ret.), and carrying the cook who had no interest in leaving his galley, Juan Franco-hogar, picked up the Gironde-Dordogne river pilot three miles off the coast of France at La Tremblade, north of Royan. The small pilot's vessel raced along at the side of the huge car ferry moving toward the open sea port where Bonnette and McHenry, in ship's officers' caps, were waiting for him. The pilot stood in the bow of the cutter, as determinedly French as a young Clemenceau. He looked dour but that was a professional pose because he was the youngest pilot in that coastal service. He was curious. It was such an eccentric hour and day for a ship of this size and, although he knew the shipping line which ran it, he had never seen this ship in these waters before.

As the *Bergquist Laura* slowed to its slowest forward speed, the pilot boat speeded to its fastest and the small man leaped aboard with professional agility toward the sea door where he was caught by Bonnette and McHenry.

'Say, that was a real good jump,' McHenry said with his execrable French.

The pilot grunted and dusted his clothes. 'Why is a ship like this going upriver to Bordeaux at this time of a Sunday morning?' the pilot asked.

'You know how Sunday is,' McHenry said. 'Never anything to do on a Sunday.'

'*Comment?*'

'We are going up to Bordeaux so that we may come back, monsieur,' Bonnette said.

'But you will have to pay docking fees for thirty hours before you can unload one box,' the pilot protested as they walked across the vast, empty car deck. 'This is a very unusual ship. It seems like an aircraft carrier on the inside and like a passenger liner on the outside.'

'It's like a crazy, mixed-up ship,' McHenry said.

When they crossed the main promenade lounge the pilot observed that everyone was asleep. 'My God, this is the quietest ship I have ever boarded.' Bonnette put them all into the lift which took them up to the officers' quarters then marched along the silent corridor to the bridge. 'Good morning, sir,' the Captain said. 'I am Captain Huntington.'

'Are you ready to go into the river, Captain?'

'If you please, monsieur.'

'Nice sonar equipment,' the pilot said as he took the con and peered into the radarscope.

'Yes. Well, call me in three hours, thirty minutes, please, Monsieur Bonnette.'

'Aye, aye, sir,' Bonnette answered. Captain Huntington went in to stretch out on the sofa in the radio room and was asleep almost at once. Bonnette and McHenry settled down at the table behind the pilot and began a game of pinochle.

Hector Schraum finished the last touches of the markings for a fire for building number three and set the careful adjustments for his lighting mechanisms because, regretfully, he would not be able to be at three places at once to light the fires himself, so the timer had become necessary. He hated these aloof, scientific jobs where everything was done only for money. A man might just as well work in a bank. He liked to burn down jobs which carried heavy insurance where he was given carte blanche to demolish the building without leaving a trace that the fire had been set purposely. Wonderful fires could result, dangerous fires, artistic fires which called for the personality of an artist, not some machine.

The huge truck, needing thirty-two tyres, moved sedately across the Pont de Pierre in Bordeaux then turned right along Quai Louis XVIII then into the long Quai des Chartrons. When it came to a point just before the rue Denise it began to move out in an arc to the left then in a wide turn to the right to cross through the gateway opposite No. 124 and out to the quai proper. As it reached the river and turned left on the quai under the sheds, the ten-thousand-ton ferry was gliding into a mooring, Captain Huntington in view on the high, open deck beside the bridge, operating the mooring telegraph to the engine room, Ford McHenry on the quai itself with the four mechanics handling the hawsers in the mooring detail.

The Captain turned and scrambled down the ladder to make his way to the promenade deck then to the car deck to open the double ports out upon the quai. On the bridge the pilot said to Charles Bonnette, 'And now that we are moored at the Cruse quaiside at one forty-five on Sunday morning, what do we do now?'

'We rest,' Bonnette said, hitting him behind the ear with a short sap. The pilot collapsed. Bonnette dragged him into the radio room, piled him on the couch and locked the door. Then Bonnette settled down with a pair of naval binoculars to search the left side of the river, in the neighborhood of the warehouse, for the approach of the police patrol car.

The eighteen labourers piled out of the huge truck and opened its unloading mechanisms, fanning out among the slewing crane pillars on the quaiside and pulling on two-fingered leather mittens. Interconnecting endless-belt mechanisms came out of the truck first, then forklifts were piled on the truck's rear lifts which carried the endless belts into place. While these were being connected to operate from far within the Aging Cellars up the ramps into the car deck storage area of the ship, loaders drove the forklifts far to the rear of the storage area as Captain Huntington hitched a ride to the centre of the Aging Cellars and sat down to operate a walkie-talkie radio, and the four car mechanics rolled out two Volkswagen mini-buses and one Chevrolet station wagon from the ship and parked them on the far side of the shed, facing the Quai des Chartrons. Fouchet waved goodbye to Bonnette up on the bridge. The car mechanics got aboard forklift trucks and drove downward into the warehouse. McHenry waited in the shadows of the quaiside warehouse door, watching Bonnette on the bridge for his signal.

Captain Huntington's chair was placed at the centre of three conjoining endless belts and steel *roule* transport avenues. The *roules* moved wine cases by turning pipes and were a permanent installation of the Cruse warehouse. The wine cases were beginning to move out on three levels of *roules*, one level moving directly behind him, one just three feet over his head and one at his right side. As the cases passed him they were taken across the Aging Cellar to a point where the three avenues of permanent *roules* became six avenues of endless belts which the labourers had just installed and which took the cases of wine out of the warehouse, across the quai and into the ship itself where other forklifts distributed them in stacks ranging away from the separating prow of the ship. All along the endless belt mechanisms the four white-jumpered mechanics darted: checking motor parts, adjusting and oiling. Far back in the Aging Cellar nine forklift jockeys raced, wheeled, and turned their mounts picking up sixty case loads which repeated the name CRUSE sixty times and darting forward with them to deposit them smoothly at the beginnings of one of the three avenues of steel *roules*.

As the forklift operators hunted for the areas storing the best wine they would call out the château name and the vintage year into their walkie-talkie mouthpieces to the Captain, sitting at the centre of the complex, and he would accept or reject the marques of wine as they were offered.

'Yes, yes! Load all the Lafite nineteen six you can find – Favour magnums please. Hello, Number nine. No, not that. Pass that. But you will be in a strong area one aisle to your left. You can find me some good Clos du Vougeot there. Roger. Hello, Three. We want that Hospice de Beaune fifty-three. Definitely. All you can load. Roger. No, no. I don't want anything later than sixty-one with the clarets or later than sixty-four with the Burgundies.'

Across the city, Hector Schraum stared at his watch with glazed eyes. He forced himself to lift his head to stare off into a distance across the street from the all-night sidewalk café at which he was sitting.

There was a muffled explosion and a roaring noise. Fire

leaped up behind the windows facing him as though it were frantic to get free. Schraum was enormously excited but he found control of himself and made himself stand. He turned eccentrically and ran like a stiff toy into the café yelling 'Fire!' and pointing behind himself. The *patron* stared, shouted 'Merde!' and ran to the telephone booth, scooping up jetons from the cash drawer as he ran. Schraum scuttered to a car at the curb, parked fifty feet up the street, trying to look backward at the beautiful fire as he ran. He made it to the car and drove away.

Bonnette made out the police patrol car in the night binoculars from the high bridge of the *Bergquist Laura* when the car came around the turn far up at rue Arago into rue Achard. He sounded the ship's horn, looking over the side of the docking deck to the quai. McHenry stepped out from the shadows and made an acknowledging sign. Bonnette ran down the ladder inside the bridge and along the corridor to the elevator, then descended to the car deck.

Bonnette was wearing the dead merchant captain's cap, a dark blue polo neck sweater and a pea jacket. He waited inside the port of the ship, about thirty feet along from the grand port where the endless belts were carrying such enormous endless quantities of wine into the ship, for about seven minutes before the police patrol car actually drove out on the river quai. Then Bonnette came boldly down the plank, his hands in the pockets of his watch jacket.

The patrol car stopped right in front of him. A sergeant of the Bureau de Securité Publique of the Police Judiciaire turned a powerful searchlight on his face. Another *agent de police* slammed out of the rear seat of the car and grabbed Bonnette's arm. The sergeant with the lamp yelled, 'What the hell is going on here?'

'We are loading,' Bonnette said.

'Loading at two o'clock on a Sunday morning? We were not told anything about any special loading.'

'You weren't told?'

'Tell us! Tell us now!' The second *flic* said and banged Bonnette heavily in the ribs.

'It is simple,' Bonnette said. 'We are stealing Cruse's wine.'

The police looked at him blankly. McHenry, with his awful French, stepped around from the shadows and put a gun to the head of the sergeant inside the car. 'Tell that boy to shut his face,' he said, 'or you is dead and messy.'

The policeman standing beside Bonnette bent over slightly to look across the driver at the source of the new voice near the sergeant. He read the scene well. The sergeant had turned to stone. The standing cop turned to Bonnette and said incredulously, 'You are robbing Cruse!' McHenry ordered the two police in the car to get out on the quai then he marched all three up the plank. Bonnette got into the patrol car and drove it aboard the ship far to the rear of the car deck, stopping beside a sea port. Bonnette and McHenry sapped the three policemen swiftly, then they bound their hands and feet with three inch wide adhesive and stowed them in the patrol car, sitting up.

'Good,' Bonnette said. 'Now you go into the shed and see that the Captain stays busy and that they all keep working inside. I have some work to do on those Volkswagen buses.'

Captain Huntington watched the thousands of cases of the finest wine he had ever seen glide rapidly past him like so many toy boats which were floating out toward the river. He knew the police had been stopped because all had gone so smoothly which, he thought, was not quite right. The Cruse family had always been wonderful to him and they surely deserved more protection than this. This group he had gotten together was altogether too professional. He had been counting on their also being altogether human and making some mistakes which could have fouled this operation. If he had only been captured at this stage of the operation, when no one whatever had been hurt he knew it would all work out. Bitsy would be there in the court anxious and tense while Daddy would have secured the service of the finest criminal lawyer money could buy and, through his own long friendship with the Cruse's, his position in the wine industry and Daddy's own place as the owner of the revered Château Ambreaux, it would all have been adjusted somehow and Bitsy would have been sure that he had been desperate to do absolutely anything to discharge his obligation of honour to her and would have written it off. He thought about that for a bit until he remembered the charges of piracy and the tangle of claims and counter-claims which were certain to result because nine-hundred-odd people had been cheated out of their holiday while their precious, anthropo-morphic automobiles had been drowned. No, he supposed it was best that everything had gone so swimmingly. However, as a contest, it was no contest. It did not exist as a game or as a wager. It was a cut and dried business with no feeling and no promise of the dread of terrible punishment which could have made it all worthwhile. As he dreamed, he shouted orders into the walkie-talkie and did intricate case cash-value sums in his head as the forklift operators relayed back the quantities of what they were taking. There was one point of release. His partners, according to the computers, were now about to get ready to murder him to take the entire pot. That would be a contest; an effective game. Things were not as bad as they had seemed. He felt greatly cheered.

Henri Fouchet, the electronics expert, was reading a news-paper in the large waiting room of the railway station. He looked at his watch. He got up, folding the newspaper under his arm and strolled to a booth in the Men's Room where he inhaled one deck of cocaine. Then he walked with a quite considerable amount of poise to a telephone box in the waiting room and closed himself in. He read the top telephone number from a typewritten list Charles Bonnette had given him and dialled. Into the telephone he said, 'Police? This is my only warning. I have been deeply wronged. I am going to burn down the city of Bordeaux.'

He hung up, took out another jeton, and dialled another number, the second on the list on the sheet in his hand. Into the telephone he said, 'Police? This is my only warning. I have been deeply wronged. I am going to burn down the city of Bordeaux.' He repeated the call to the four remaining posts, then left the telephone box.

When he returned to the bench where he had been sitting he looked for the small satchel he had left there. It was gone. His indignation boiled over. He strode angrily to the platform official at the train departures doorway. He was irate. 'I left my satchel for three minutes while I made a telephone call,' he said loudly, 'and some thief has made off with it.'

The official shrugged. 'Go to Lost & Found,' he said wearily after seven hours of being on his feet. 'Perhaps it will turn up in a few weeks.'

'What?' yelled Fouchet, swaying with the injustice of it all.

'I wish you luck.'

Fouchet's hands began to open and close at his side. His right hand dropped into his pocket and came out with a long, barber's razor. His eyes exploded. The guard screamed hoarsely. Fouchet grabbed him tightly by the hair of his head and cut his throat. A gendarme fifteen feet away stared unbelievingly at what was happening and shouting, pulled his gun. Fouchet began to run across the waiting room. The gendarme fired three times. All three bullets hit Fouchet in the back of the head.

*

Hector Schraum leaned against the side of a building wall, weak with spent passion. There was spittle at the edges of his mouth. A raging fire was burning somewhere close by because its dancing light flickered across his face as he stared at it blankly and pulled its heat into himself. Weakly, he forced himself to walk toward his car a few yards away. He stopped to look back again. There was another roaring explosion. He stared at the large shining brass plaque which was fixed to the side of the burning building. The plaque said: HÔPITAL ST JUSTIN.

Schraum could not seem to make himself get away because somewhere deeply inside his memory he knew that this was the perfect fire of all the fires he had pursued throughout his life. This was a fire which not only roared and exploded but contained the forms of many, many, many living people who were now enclosed by it, inside it. He was taken far, far back to when he was a little boy and the beautiful lady was holding him where she held him always when they were alone in his room and she was telling him again the story about the great fire in the waxworks which she had seen when she had been a girl before she had come up to the city to become a nursemaid. She told him again while she held him and rubbed him how she had stood across the street staring at the waxworks through a glass which a nice man had rented for a pfennig and she had been able to see the bodies of the great heroes of all time, formed in wax, as they had twisted and melted until the mighty fire king had destroyed the greatest men who had ever lived: soldiers, emperors, inventors and poets, they were powerless under the might and force of the Fire King.

This was the end of his long journey, the end of the search for the Fire King, he told himself as he stared across at the Hôpital St Justin. He was overcome with lust to absorb the incalculable sensation of the fire. He began to walk toward it then, as people began to shout at him, he began to run. He ran as fast as his short legs would take him, up the few front steps, through the shining doorway, and into the consuming arms of the Fire King.

The nine forklift trucks moved like dancers, swooping, lifting, turning on a button, then charging forward with double stacks of cases of wine, each fourteen feet high, to lower them precisely on the steel *roules*. One wave was always loading, one wave was always depositing its load upon the moving steel pipes and one wave was always moving between the two areas either to get more wine or to bring more wine. From the car deck, McHenry telephoned the bridge to tell Bonnette that they had all the wine they could handle safely. Bonnette called Captain Huntington on a walkie-talkie and told him to terminate the loading then he remained on the bridge, scanning the horizon at the far side of the city where three widely spaced tall fires were clearly visible in the night. Far in the distance he could hear the constantly continuing hooting of the fire trucks. The fire and the frantic sounds were ghastly interlopers into the velvet night. Everything on the left bank of the river seemed to be fast asleep.

Captain Huntington took the bos'n's whistle from his pocket and blew three penetrating blasts. He watched the steel *roules* and the endless belts until they began to run empty. The forklift crews were driving out through the long cellars to the quaiside. The Captain stopped two of them and borrowed one of the machines while the men doubled up to ride out to the exit.

The Captain loaded a tape recorder aboard and drove the forklift to the rue Lombard exit where the four bound watchmen lay in a neat row on the floor. He stopped the forklift fifteen yards away from the watchmen and placed the tape machine on the floor. He pressed the PLAY key of the machine. The sound which came out was the sound of one

231

heavy truck engine turning over, then another, then another after that until there was a bedlam of noise of truck engines racing to warm up. Then a loud, rough voice bellowed out in French with a broad Brooklyn accent, 'What about these here trucks, fahcrissake? Get 'em outta here! All right – you – truck one and truck three, where you going?'

A more distantly placed American voice shouted in French. 'We're ready to roll, boss. We go straight for the Spanish frontier at Irun.'

'Then move them!' the first voice roared out of the cassette.

'And get two, four and six outta here and into Switzerland.'

The Captain watched the four bodies tense as they listened to the playback which was more realistic than perhaps the sounds themselves would have been. There was a building sound of trucks moving away in low gear. The trucks' sound diminished and it died out altogether. Then Captain Huntington knelt beside each watchman and injected each man in the haunch with a carefully measured shot of morphine to keep them asleep until the police came. Then he cut the adhesive tape which bound their legs to improve their circulation.

He turned off the now silent tape recorder, put it aboard the forklift, got on himself, drove rapidly off across the cellars to the riverside quai.

The engines of the two Volkswagen buses and the estate wagon were turning over when he came out and the labourers and the four car mechanics were getting into them. Captain Huntington shook hands with each man, thanking him for their brilliant work.

'You did a fine job. Now it's over and it was completely successful and you can relax,' he told them. 'Some of you will be going to Lisbon by train, some by bus and some by air. Hotel reservations have been made and I know you all have your expense money. We'll all meet in Lisbon in three and a half days and see how it feels trying to walk around with pockets full of money.' The men laughed with delight. 'Good luck and a safe journey,' the Captain said. The four mechanics were casting off the ship's hawsers. The Captain sprinted across the quai and leaped into an open sea door. Then he walked quickly across the car deck to the elevator and made his way up to the bridge.

The big ship began to move out slowly upon the deserted, night river, its engines thrumming lightly. As he stood beside the engine room telegraph on the starboard side of the docking deck he could see the Volkswagen buses and the estate wagon go out through the gate of the Quai des Chartrons and move off in separate directions. The *Bergquist Laura* moved downstream around the gentle bulge of the Garonne river, then past the juncture of the Dordogne into the Gironde and headed out toward the Atlantic under the cover of night.

He had done it. John Bryson was paid. He had repossessed his own buildings and his own wine company to sign over to Bitsy. He would have enough cash to make a sturdy token payment against the cash he owed her as well from earlier annoyances. He was safe and saved. He had done it. He had done it.

'Bring the pilot out of the radio room, please,' he said to Bonnette. Bonnette went in to fetch the man but he returned alone.

'He is dead,' Bonnette said simply.

'Dead?'

'He must have had a paper-thin skull.'

'He must have had a heart attack,' the Captain insisted. 'He must have died in his sleep.'

'Of course. No question.'

'Have you ever struck a man with a blackjack before?'

'Of course. Many times.'

'Have any of them died from that?'

'Never. In fact, I would say it would be impossible to die from that and I have had much experience.'

'This is terrible. We had a perfect record until now. Everything had gone so beautifully until now. It was an accident, of course, but it puts a terrible cloud over everything we've accomplished.'

'Can you get the ship out without the pilot?'

'Yes. I made a careful study of the river before I knew we would have to have a pilot at all. Bring the charts out, please, Monsieur Bonnette. Right there in the library. Clearly marked Gironde River.'

Bonnette returned with the river chart book. 'Thank you,' the Captain said. 'We'll be all right now. I'll have her out in the Atlantic in four hours. Now – if you'll excuse me, please.'

Bonnette went to the promenade deck and sat in the darkened lounge. He was impatient to be told how and where the transfer would be made and how and when the money would be paid so that he could take it away from the rest of them and get back to Paris. For the past two weeks he had been trying to find a market for the wine in the United States and in South America through the Fratellanza. It would all be classical wine and to avoid detection in the future after the alarm had been raised he had toyed with the idea of relabelling every bottle or of dumping the contents of every bottle into common barrels then re-bottling in Canada. He could have had all the cooperation he needed to hijack the *Bergquist Laura* after they had taken the wine from Cruse but the problem of marketing it for maximum returns was impossible to overcome. He sat in the lounge and tried to think like Captain Huntington. Where could he be disposing of such a tremendous quantity of classical French wines which any oenologist could identify as quickly as any art expert could authenticate a painting? He had said they would fence the wine eleven hours after they had stolen it so the transfer would have to be made somewhere out at sea. Bonnette could not figure beyond that. He would have to stay with the original plan: allow the Captain to transfer the wine and to receive the payment, then to kill the Captain, and subsequently McHenry, when the money was aboard the car ferry, then to take the money ashore in the gig and find his way back to Paris. He had had bigger problems in his time.

He looked out at the river bank. The ship was passing a clocktower above a flour mill. The time was two forty-eight on Sunday morning, July 17th.

26

When the Cruse warehouse alarm sounded in the Bordeaux Prefecture of Police, the clock fixed into the alarm system read eleven thirty-five Sunday morning. Police cars swarmed over the Quai des Chartrons, the Cruse cellars and the riverside quai. The great doors leading to the river were securely bolted as they should have been. The river quai itself was as tidy and undisturbed as it had been at the end of the working day on the previous Friday. However, the rear exit from the warehouse, the truck exit which led to the rue Lombard was wide open. Escape by the river and sea was not considered as a line of inquiry because the watchmen lined up on the floor at the rue Lombard exit corroborated that the thieves had left by six trucks through the rue Lombard gate.

'Get the warehouse manager over here,' the police inspector in charge said. 'He's probably out in the country somewhere with his family and we probably won't be able to get anyone who knows anything about the inventory here until tonight. But we have to know how much was stolen so that we'll know how many vehicles to look for on the roads.'

While he talked gloomily, the police surgeon was slapping the watchmen awake.

'How is it going?' the inspector asked. 'What the hell is the matter with them?'

'They've been drugged,' the police surgeon said.

'Why would they be drugged?'

'You figure that out. We've got to do something about their

arms. They've been bound for a long time. This could be serious. They are old fellows.'

'How? What is wrong?'

'It is possible that they could get gangrene,' the police surgeon said. 'Please give me three men. I need help.' He began to massage the arms of the watchman in front of him. The man groaned.

'When will they be able to talk?'

'After we find out about their arms,' the doctor said. 'For Christ's sake, Inspector Grellou, give me three men.'

It was forty-five minutes before the men could talk and then only after the Inspector had insisted that the doctor give them a sharp stimulant to snap them out of the torpor. The four men lay on stretcher beds with their arms stretched outward from their sides while the Inspector talked to them, two at a time.

'How many trucks were here?' Grellou asked.

'Six,' the long, white-haired man said. 'Jesus, I never felt anything like this in my arms.'

'They were big trucks. They sounded like the very big trailer trucks,' the second watchman said. 'We could hear the despatcher send them off.'

'What did you hear?'

'Jesus, I think my arms are going to come off,' the white-haired man said while the police surgeon and an *agent* massaged them slowly and carefully.

'When I heard him yelling at them the loading must have been finished because the truck engines were starting up; it was a terrible racket and this American voice told three trucks to cross to Spain at Irun and he said the other three were going to Switzerland.'

'What else?'

'I – I can't remember anything else.'

Inspector Grellou moved to the two other watchmen, asked

them the same questions and got the same answers excepting that they remembered the sounds of forklift trucks operating in the direction of the Aging Cellars and they remembered voices talking back and forth about chateau names and vintages.

'As if they were talking on the radio to each other?'

'That's it! That's what it sounded like. It was that canned sound like a radio. A bad radio.'

Inspector Grellou went back to the first two watchmen and had them corroborate the voices they had heard and the sound of forklift trucks. Then he asked them to relax their minds and just let the words come out about any sort of sound they had heard until the time the trucks left, the smells, the sound of any movement.

'The *roules* were running all the time, I remember in a vague way, and there was the sound of other machinery going. It was a sound like the endless-belt sound. There were no smells. There was a lot of activity, noise – '

'No smells?' Grellou asked.

'No. What kind of smells anyway?'

'You told me that there were six enormous trailer trucks loaded and ready to go and they all turned over the engines. Did you choke on the smells of carbon monoxide? There must have been smells. There had to be smells.'

'There were no smells. No carbon monoxide. That's funny – eh?'

Grellou checked the smells or lack of them out with all the watchmen. A police ambulance rolled up to the rue Lombard exit.

'What's that for?' Grellou said.

'We have to get this one to hospital,' the police surgeon said. 'His arms are bad.' Grellou grunted. The surgeon signalled to two policemen to lift the stretcher into the ambulance.

'Why would these men be so drugged that you had to stimulate them with a counter-injection to wake them yet they have a clear memory of what was going on here?' Grellou asked the surgeon.

'Obviously, they were injected just as the thieves were leaving,' the doctor said.

'But the alarms went off at eleven thirty-five,' Grellou insisted. 'We were in this warehouse at eleven fifty. How could thieves load six enormous trailer trucks and get out of here in fifteen minutes, hein? But how could they put the four watchmen into that deep a sleep in only fifteen minutes?' Grellou was getting angry. 'There is something entirely fishy about this mess,' he said. 'You!' he yelled at a sergeant of detectives. 'Alert the entire Spanish and Swiss frontiers. Get the Gendarmerie Nationale and the Gendarmerie Mobile on every road in western and southwestern France. Six trailer trucks moving wine on Sunday – an impossible condition. I want every truck stopped and searched. Now! Quickly!'

He stared at the surgeon. 'And we will find nothing,' he said. 'Because that is what they want us to do to waste our time. Get me that goddam warehouse manager!' he roared.

He wheeled on the doctor. 'Listen! You say that guy's arms are so bad that you had to move him out to a hospital. How long do a man's arms have to be bound up like that for that to happen?'

'I would say – and it is just a guess because each of these men responded differently – that it would have to be at least twelve hours.'

'Yeah. That's right,' the second watchman said. 'I don't remember anything after we first came on duty at eight o'clock Saturday night. What day is this, anyway?'

That twenty-five million francs worth of Cruse wine had been stolen was a terrible and serious thing but what made the crime so particularly heinous was that French wine had left a French warehouse without any taxes being paid to the State, making it a crime of crimes. Everyone of the seventeen Services Régionaux headquarters of the Police Judiciaire in all police districts of Metropolitan France were alerted. Four hundred and fifty-three borough police forces, all seventy-four Central Commissariats, two hundred and fifty-three Constituency Commissariats and one hundred and twenty-six local Postes de Police were flashed to be ready to join the manhunt. In all the rural areas of France and up and down the highways traffic police, patrol cars and motorcycle police stopped every truck they saw on the sleepy Sunday morning. All four sections of the Sûreté went out like hunting tigers to stop the men who had removed French wine from a French warehouse without payment of taxes: the Bureau of Sécurité Publique, the Renseignments Généraux, the Direction de la Surveillance du Territoire and the Corps Républicain de Sécurité.

Inspector Grellou found the warehouse manager at four fifty-five that afternoon at Arcachon. He was flown in to Bordeaux by police helicopter. When he estimated that the thieves had made off with a possible maximum of twenty-five thousand cases, on his first spot check, and a minimum of twenty thousand cases, Grellou telephoned the river pilot's base at La Tremblade.

He identified himself then he said, 'Have you taken any heavy tonnage up the Gironde since last night?'

'I'll check.'

The man came back on the phone. 'Yes,' he told Grellou, 'the *Bergquist Laura* of the Bergquist Lines requested a pilot to pick her up at eight twenty last night to go up to Bordeaux.'

'How big is that ship?'

'I'll check the registry.'

The man came back on the phone. 'Ten thousand tons,' he said.

'Has she made the run often before?'

'Never. Because I see a very funny thing here in the registry.'

'What?'

'The *Bergquist Laura* is a car ferry. Say, isn't that the ferry on the Bilbao-Southampton run?'

Grellou hung up. He looked dourly at the Commissioner of Police and a circle of more police brass than had ever crowded into that Bordeaux police building.

'They took the wine out by ship,' he said. 'Somehow, they got the ten-thousand-ton car ferry, the *Bergquist Laura*, Swedish registry, which probably has car deck space like a small aircraft carrier and the river pilot brought her up the river between nine and one o'clock last night. They were so highly organized that they not only loaded the ship with wine but they set those fires in the three government buildings and the Hôpital St Justin as a diversion, last night, causing the deaths of forty-seven people. They have either murdered or kidnapped one of our police patrol cars which keeps the Cruse warehouse under surveillance. They re-set the alarm system to go off approximately nine or ten hours after they had left the scene of the crime, which was sixteen or seventeen hours ago. By now they are far out of French territorial waters somewhere in the Atlantic. For the present, I would say this is no longer entirely a police matter. Among other things, the thieves have committed piracy. Our own Navy and airforce, and the navies of Spain and Portugal to the south, and the navies of Britain and Sweden to the north must comb the seas until they are located. It is only a matter of time now.'

While the orders and requests for cooperation went out the total manhunt inside France continued because it could not be abandoned in case Grellou's conjectures were wrong. The dragnet closed from every frontier of the country into the heart of the sack in Bordeaux where garages and storage warehouses were ransacked for traces of the wine. The police went on working by helicopter, radio, motorcycle and squad car, by foot patrol, telegraph, archives and trucks. They covered buildings, communications, highways, airports, docks, rail terminals, and bus stations. They scoured the four million five hundred thousand personal dossiers and finger prints in the central records. The Brigade Criminelle worked hollow-eyed, without stop. Tempers were frayed and men were busted because they were unable to find six gigantic lorries on the highways of France. Six gigantic trucks filled with twenty-five million francs worth of wine on which the tax due to the State had not been paid, had disappeared from the face of France. Worse, when the thieves were found, the police might have to share the credit with the goddam navy. There would be hell to pay.

27

Captain Huntington set the automatic pilot and took his last nap before the transfer of the wine, on the couch in the radio room where the river pilot had undoubtedly succumbed to a heart attack. Bonnette had thoughtfully removed the body for the Captain's greater comfort.

As he dropped off to sleep, Bonnette and McHenry strolled across the car deck to the port afterside of the ship where the police patrol car was parked with the three officers inside it. McHenry opened the main sea port with some effort. The ship was moving at about fifteen knots. The sea was as flat as a board. No land was in sight, nor any other ship.

Bonnette looked in at the six eyes of the bound and gagged policemen. He opened the door of the car and sat behind the driver's wheel beside the sergeant of the patrol detail. He turned the ignition key and started the engine. He released the brake and got out of the car. McHenry began to push on the left side of the car, Bonnette on the right. As the policemen's eyes bulged and they made strangled sounds behind their gags, Bonnette and McHenry pushed the patrol car over the edge of the ship and down into the sea.

Juan Francohogar, in the galley, was preparing for the Captain's dinner. He would serve cream of broccoli soup, then golden capon with potato mounds and asparagus with lemon crumbs, then a salad of spinach and field greens with a lemon and shallot dressing, topped off with an almond and chocolate torte. The cook's wine cellar was so limited that he had had to build the dinner around the available wine. He had rummaged and had found a good Margaux '59 which would do nicely, and a magnum of acceptable demi-sec champagne to go down with the gateau. A magnum was an impossible amount, of course, but the Messieurs Bonnette and McHenry would also do their part to tuck it all away. Captain Huntington was absolutely mad about golden capon and asparagus with lemon crumbs.

The ship's clock in Commander Schute's cabin said the time was four thirty-five Sunday afternoon. He was seated with his feet up, legs in Donegal plus fours, the tweed Norfolk jacket neatly buttoned and the matching tweed fedora on his head. He vowed to travel with the Bergquist Line again and again because the food which Captain Huntington had brought to him was simply the finest he had ever eaten. He had had no idea that Swedes were that gifted around stoves. He sighed, always regretful at closing 'Animal Dispersion in Relation to Social Behavior', then he stood up and smoothed out his long, gray woollen sockings. He slid his satchel out from under the berth and took out the two Luger pistols which accepted the 9mm bullets which hit the target at six hundred and fifty miles an hour. He sprayed some *Eau Sauvage* from an aerosol bottle to his plump cheeks and golden moustache and left the cabin.

On the bridge, the Captain, Charles Bonnette and Ford McHenry looked out over calm seas. The Captain was at the wheel whistling 'Oh, What A Lovely War'. Bonnette said, 'I think you will agree that the time has come to tell us how you are going to dispose of the wine?'

'Oh, yes,' the Captain said. 'Very soon now.'

Commander Schute ascended the ladder to the sun deck then strolled across the open deck to the bridge ladder.

'We don't want to wait. We want to know now,' Bonnette said to the Captain. The two men bracketed the ship's wheel.

Schute climbed the bridge ladder unhurriedly. He knocked respectfully on the door of the bridge house.

'What the hell is that?' Bonnette asked.

'Probably a seagull,' the Captain said.

'Pretty polite seagull,' McHenry said.

'Yes, as a matter of actual, factual fact,' the Captain replied, 'it sounded much more like the sort of knock my partner would make. Come in, Gash.' The Captain watched the sea ahead. Schute entered the bridge, all geniality. The Captain activated the automatic pilot, then turned for greetings. 'Good afternoon, Gash.'

'Good afternoon, Colin.'

Schute's hands were deep in his jacket pockets and both Bonnette and McHenry noticed that the pockets' hem seemed to come to a sudden point.

'Gentlemen, this is my partner, Commander Schute. Gash, may I present Monsieur Bonnette and Mr Ford McHenry.'

'How do you do?' Commander Schute said affably but he did not offer to shake hands.

'It was Commander Schute who developed the wizard plan we have just executed,' the Captain explained.

'And jolly well did you do it,' Schute said generously. 'An awfully good show.'

'Now,' the Captain said. 'You were asking about the disposal of the wine, Monsieur Bonnette. And well you should.'

Commander Schute moved to the bulkhead of the bridge house behind Bonnette, facing McHenry.

'We will rendezvous at sea with the heavy freighter *Taka Maru*, in twenty-seven minutes,' the Captain continued.

'The *Taka Maru*?' Bonnette asked stupidly. His mind was whirling, trying to adjust to these unexpected developments.

'The buyer is Japanese, Monsieur Bonnette. The Japanese have become the most avid drinkers of French wines in the world.'

245

'Japanese.' His large head was nodding fullest agreement with that piece of the puzzle.

'The *Taka Maru* is equipped with six large lighters and three deck elevator systems. Their crews will off-load the wine from this ship as we lay off the quite small Portuguese village of Arias del Jaime where cars are waiting to drive us to the small airport twelve miles away where the charter plane will fly us into Lisbon to meet the others to divide the proceeds as per agreement.'

'We won't need to divide any proceeds with them,' McHenry said. Bonnette's face coloured with rage. He started forward toward McHenry as though he could jam the sentence back down his throat and have it forgotten, but he got control of himself, keeping his face bland and expressionless.

'Why not?' the Captain asked.

'Because we put time bombs in the three cars and the bombs went off long ago.'

'You killed them?'

'Maybe they died of heart attacks, Captain,' Bonnette said grimly.

'How could you do such a thing?' the Captain said with utter horror.

'We saved us an awful big piece of money there,' McHenry said.

'Pure textbook stuff, Colin,' Commander Schute said. 'It is exactly as set down in the Richard Gallagher book the computer read to us.'

The Captain rushed away from the bridge and they could hear him retching in the head behind the radio room.

'He must think he is playing some kind of game,' Bonnette said.

'That was precisely what he had been thinking,' Schute said.

'He ain't thinking that way any more,' McHenry added as the Captain, pale and shattered-looking, returned to the bridge.

246

'All right,' Bonnette said. 'That is ancient history now. Let's sell the wine. Will this Jap have the cash with him?'

'There were twenty-two men in those three cars,' the Captain said. 'I shook hands with every one of them.'

'The Jap will have the cash,' Schute said.

'How much?' Bonnette asked.

'One million pounds in francs, pounds, deutschmarks, Swiss francs and dollars.'

'And you are saying that he trusts us to give his crew some boxes which we say are filled with classic wines – on the high seas – and he will hand over one million pounds?'

'What we are saying, Monsieur Bonnette, is that he trusts Captain Huntington to do just that,' Gash Schute said. 'They are old friends. And we are all navy, you see, Bonnette. Not your sort of thing at all.'

'Does the buyer bring the money to us?' Bonnette demanded.

'Naturally not. He would see little advantage to have you able to identify him.'

'They all look alike to me,' McHenry said.

'I will go to his ship and bring back the money,' Captain Huntington said with a cold and vicious edge to his voice. 'Commander Schute will keep you company here. And when I return I hope I shall be able to make you regret what you have done to the men who trusted us.' He crossed the bridge house and held open the door. 'For the moment you will get off this bridge.'

Bonnette shrugged and turned away. McHenry tripped over the large, heavy suitcase he had with him since the hijacking.

'And what is in that, may I ask?' Commander Schute inquired.

McHenry flashed his cheesy teeth in a disgusting smile. 'That's sixty-eight thousand pounds from the Purser's safe and the Captain's safe and the roulette room and all the bars plus more cash and a lotta stones I went and dug outta everybody's cabin.' He swaggered to the door. As he went through he turned. 'Hey, Cap'n,' he said, 'you know what?'

They stared at him with all distaste.

'I found a guy in a john down there who had the toppa his head chopped off.' He began to yok-yok. He giggled all the way down the ladder after Bonnette to the sun deck.

28

Two Breguet 1050 Alizé anti-submarine aircraft took off from the French carrier *Foch* carrying one torpedo each and two air-to-surface missiles under each wing, each carrying enough fuel for three and a half hours of low-altitude patrols and well-equipped for general anti-shipping strike tasks. Their orders were to comb the Bay of Biscay and the seas immediately southward from the Bay of Biscay to locate the *Bergquist Laura* which had been identified by telephoto received from the Swedish naval headquarters. Supplementing the search from the carrier, *Clemenceau*, an 1150 Atlantic, a long-range reconnaissance bomber carrying a crew of twelve, with a weapons bay carrying both homing and electric acoustic torpedos began a search northward from Moroccan waters toward a northern range limit of the Bay of Biscay. All planes had been ordered to halt the *Bergquist Laura* by any means without damaging her and to fix her position so that destroyers could go out from the Spanish naval base at La Coruna to arrest those aboard her.

The Japanese loading lighters moved away from the long high freighter which had hoved to at about one hundred yards off the port bow of the car ferry. Captain Huntington released the mechanism which opened the upper jaw of the loading prow and dropped anchor. The two ships lay at about one mile off the Portuguese coast.

Captain Huntington had directed Bonnette and McHenry in

lowering the ship's motor launch. Suddenly the Captain turned upon Bonnette. 'This is the gig. What is it doing here?'

'What do you mean?'

'I ordered you to send the ship's captain, the first officer, the radio officer and the quartermaster to the *Benito Juarez* in this gig.'

'They tried to shoot us when we went to take them to the gig,' Bonnette said. 'They resisted and we had to defend ourselves.'

'In what way?'

'We shot them down.'

'You *killed* them?'

'We were forced to kill them.'

With blanked eyes, Captain Huntington threw a rope ladder over the side then climbed down it to get into the gig.

He started the motor of the launch, then sent it roaring across the sea, gripping the wheel with cold rage and outrage and a blind desire to avenge all of the people whom Bonnette and McHenry had killed to get money. He was trembling at their callousness in murdering twenty-two men who had been their essential crew and killing the three ship's officers and quartermaster in cold blood. He was not aware of the deaths of one old Spanish gentleman, one small boy, one fat lady, one snarling husband, one river pilot, one electronic alarms expert, one station guard, one pyromaniac and forty-seven patients of St Justin's Hospital, all of whom having died in addition to the other twenty-six, because he, Captain Huntington, had to have more money. Because he had wanted to bring his wife's fortune down to a less awesome, less threatening, more reasonable size and because he had agreed to a game of backgammon with John Bryson, seventy-six people had died in the past thirty-six hours but that was not how Captain Huntington recognized it. He only knew what Bonnette and McHenry had done. He tried to think of how he would make them pay. He decided that, on his return from the *Taka Maru* he would share out the money with them, tell them he would not tolerate what they had done, then shoot them down – raising the bag to seventy-eight.

As the launch sped toward the Japanese ship, Commander Schute leaned casually against a samson post of the ship's loading crane system watching Bonnette and McHenry who were at the rail staring at the launch, the *Taka Maru*, as intently as if they could see and count the money within her. They watched two Japanese seamen make the gig fast to the boarding ladder as Captain Huntington scrambled up the ship's ladder.

The Japanese lighter crews were already at work on the car deck of the *Bergquist Laura*, working from operating diagrams which Commander Schute's computers had prepared and by which the wine had been stowed. The endless belt mechanisms moved the hundreds upon hundreds of cases of wine forward to the opened prow to the jury-rigged elevators which took the wine down to the lighters which rose and fell with the rolling seas.

The first lighter began its return to the *Taka Maru*, loaded to the gunwales with two thousand cases of wine.

29

Captain Huntington and Commander Fujikawa faced each other with much pleasure across the broad, polished table in the owner's cabin.

'How delightful to see you again after so short a time!' Commander Fujikawa beamed.

'Particularly after not meeting for so many long years before,' the Captain said.

'And now we must complete this mundane exercise so that we may more quickly return to our places at the tactical board – for I, too, have now provided myself with one of these – to undertake what is our true expression.'

'To that end,' Captain Huntington said, 'I am happy to report that the wine we were able to secure is of an even higher quality than I had anticipated.' He took a list of the wines from his pocket and extended it to the Commander. 'These are the case quantities and vintages of the wines they are unloading now.'

The Commander studied the list with great interest. 'Outstanding,' he said. 'Simply outstanding. I, personally, look forward to the long maturing of the Pape Clement, Sixty-One. There are others on the list which are certainly more meritorious but let us examine the issue again in ten years' time.'

'You are unquestionably on the track of something there,' the Captain said diplomatically. 'In the meantime, do not ignore that Lafite, Twenty-Nine.'

'Well, then,' Commander Fujikawa said, 'while they are off-loading, we must begin counting.'

The Japanese commander lifted a large case to the smaller table at his side. He opened it and reached in to lift out bound stacks of banknotes of different national currencies. He counted bills of Swiss five hundred franc denominations in the first stack, made a note on a pad beside him, then passed the stack to Captain Huntington. The Captain counted that stack, noted the amount on a pocket-sized looseleaf note book and they worked on to count through all the stacks with deep concentration, counting very carefully.

Commander Schute called across the deck to Bonnette and McHenry.

'Gentlemen?'

They turned away from the ship's rail to face him.

'My plan did not stop with getting the wine,' he said. He motioned for them to come closer, as if he were fearful that they be overheard, but when they had taken nine steps he stopped them. 'Far enough,' he said, 'no need to get too close until we are in agreement.'

'In agreement about what?' Bonnette asked.

'About whether we agree that the three of us deserve a larger share of all this than we are getting.'

'How do we get a larger share?'

'We kill Captain Huntington when he returns with the money and split his share,' Schute said coolly.

McHenry answered for them softly. 'We don't need you to kill Captain Huntington.'

'That is precisely what I thought you were thinking,' Schute said. He pulled down heavily on the rigging lever which was part of the samson post. Two five hundredweight crane hooks were released from the foremast behind the two men to come swinging downward in a wide arc at enormous speed. Bonnette reacted reflexively when Schute pulled the lever. He drew a gun and took a step and a half to his right in Schute's general direction.

'What are you doing?' he demanded, still unaware that the step and a half had caused the tremendous swinging weight to miss him, as the twin crane hook slammed into the back of McHenry's head, decapitating him, spattering him over the deck, and sending the rest of his body crashing forward. The terrible sound, and sensing what had happened, turned Bonnette involuntarily to look for McHenry, and took him the pace and a half backward to where he had been, staring at the deck at where McHenry had been standing. As he turned to see where McHenry had gone, his face took the full force of the returning pendulum swing of the quarter ton crane hook moving at eighty-seven miles an hour.

Schute watched all of it with disdain. With delicate care he walked to the far, non-slippery side of the deck to avoid the still swinging hooks and the debris they had caused, and mounted the ladder to the bridge.

Captain Huntington stared at the bank notes with dismay. 'I make it two thousand pounds short of one million pounds,' he said.

'That is correct,' Commander Fujikawa said without hesitation.

'But – how? It was understood that we were to be paid one million pounds.'

Fujikawa was puzzled. 'But, surely, as a wine dealer,' he said gently, 'you knew it was the custom that you should defray a token amount of our carriage costs?'

'No provision was made for any deduction. What was specified was that you would pay one million pounds.'

'The number one million is only a romantic figure,' the Commander chided. 'It is just a phrase, really, isn't it?'

'The wine is worth two million pounds which is to say perhaps two and a half million pounds in Japan. Which is even a more romantic figure.'

'This is a most unhappy moment.'

'It is. It most certainly is,' the Captain agreed.

'It is insupportable that we should haggle like this.'

'No doubt. But nonetheless – '

'It is not only the money. For my people, custom must be observed.'

'Face?'

'It is a delicate matter. It would assume much significance to my colleagues.'

'I also have associates. And I could not begin to tell you how significant two thousand pounds is to them.'

'I see. Well, then – ' They fell into a silence. After a time, Commander Fujikawa cleared his throat. 'If you agree – the only honourable way for us to settle this is to have each of us take an equal chance on getting or not getting the two thousand pounds in a manner which will be understandable and acceptable to our colleagues.' He was extremely uncomfortable that the issue had reached these proportions and, if possible, more uncomfortable for his friend than for himself.

'How do you propose to do that?' the Captain said swiftly.

'We must cut cards for it – unless you have moral compunctions against gambling.'

'Cut cards?'

'Yes. It is easy, simple and quick.'

'Yes.'

'Are you all right, Captain Huntington?'

'What? Oh. Yes. I am all right.' He had grown very pale. His voice was constricted. 'I agree that cutting cards would be the best way.'

Commander Fujikawa summoned a messboy and ordered a pack of cards. Then he opened the seal, took out the cards, then shuffled them elaborately. He set the deck down punctiliously in front of the Captain who spread the deck out in a quick, professional gesture, into a fan shape, faces down.

The Captain's face was the colour of porridge. His eyes were ghastly. His face was drawn in fright. He was seated with four, neat stacks of tall quantities of four national currencies in front of him, spread in an arc on the table. The numbers were in high amounts on the bills and some of the stacks of money were as high as his seated head.

'If you will, Captain,' Fujikawa said because it was to the advantage of whoever cut first because there would be one more card to choose from. Captain Huntington pulled a card out of the fan and turned it. It was the King of Spades.

'Oh, I am cross,' Fujikawa said, pretending to be chagrined. 'But at least we have settled the bloody thing in an acceptable way.'

As though to preserve form, Fujikawa drew a card carelessly and flipped it over. It was the Ace of Diamonds.

'Damn it!' the Commander snapped reflexively. 'That is most awkward!'

'Commander Fujikawa?'

'Yes, Captain. I tell you I hate to have won at this nonsensical thing.'

'Would you consider – that is may I have the satisfaction of doubling the bet to four thousand pounds and having another go?'

'But, of course.'

He scooped up the cards, shuffled them thoroughly then spread them fanwise across the table. Captain Huntington counted out banknotes, then pushed them to the middle foreground. Commander Fujikawa bowed. 'Your turn,' the Captain said.

Fujikawa drew to the four of spades. 'Splendid,' he said, 'You will beat that easily.'

The Captain cut to the two of hearts. He stared at the card expressionlessly. 'May I bet six thousand more?'

Fujikawa was openly uneasy. 'I have no objection, of course, but – I say – isn't possible that you might make things much worse for yourself?'

'Only if I lose,' the Captain said.

30

Commander Schute stared at the *Taka Maru* through binoculars. He heard a shrill whistle below him. The Japanese cargo master held his arms over his head and wig-wagged that their work was finished. Schute removed a white handkerchief from his left sleeve and waved back languidly to signify his understanding. The cargo master climbed down a rope ladder and got into the last remaining lighter which chugged away on its last trip to the mother ship, running low in the water. Everything was trim and shipshape on the car deck. The temporary elevators had been taken away. The car deck was as totally empty as if the *Bergquist Laura* had just come from the shipyards.

Schute stared out at the last of the wine leaving the ship. He lost his aplomb. He snatched up an electric bull horn and bellowed out to the other ship with it. 'What the hell is going on over there?' the bull horn roared.

Juan Francohogar was mashing two pounds of cooked potatoes, beating in a half cup of melted butter and six egg yolks. He formed the mashed potatoes into egg shapes using two tablespoons and coated them with melted butter.

The stacks of banknotes which had once towered above the Captain and all around him, had dwindled to very few. He was sweating heavily but he had attained the saintly look of an ascetic or, more precisely, of a flagellant; burnt-out ecstasy, endlessly on fire, endlessly purifying and beatifying.

'I think perhaps I understand something about you now,' Commander Fujikawa said. 'You want to lose.'

'What?' The Captain felt numb. He could not stop thinking of the twenty-six dead men which Bonnette and McHenry had made.

'You are paying with mere money for the punishment which always seems to be withheld from you,' the Commander continued with a sombre face. 'Has your life been something like the flight of an aluminium bomber flying into the sun, always flying into the safety of a hundred miles ahead of the explosions of the bombs it drops so that, after flight upon flight, you come to believe that you had wronged the bombs to make them explode and you must seek punishment for that by trying to crash your plane each time you land?'

'What?' In his mind he was reliving the ritual of shaking hands with the twenty-two men who had loaded the ship with wine.

'Have you gambled a lot in your life?'

'Too much.'

'Do you lose?'

'Most of the time.'

'Very well, then, dear friend.' Commander Fujikawa reached out and raked in great stacks of banknotes and swept them into the large case. 'Arigato. Arigato.'

'What does that mean?' the Captain asked.

'Arigato means thank you in Japanese. I thank you very much.'

The Captain pushed the last of the banknotes around him to the centre of the table.

'What a magnificent gambler you are,' Commander Fujikawa exclaimed.

The Captain's face seemed to fall apart into shame, pain, regret and hopelessness. 'Magnificent?' he said hoarsely. His voice broke. 'Magnificent? In twenty years of hell I have gambled away my wife, my career, my property, my honour – and even my cook.'

They could hear the bull horn booming out Commander Schute's voice from the car ferry. Captain Huntington glanced briefly toward the sound. 'And now, at last,' he said, 'I may have gambled away my life. Please cut, Commander Fujikawa.'

Fujikawa cut. He held the card face downward as though he could not bear to turn it over. The Captain turned the Knave of Clubs. Fujikawa showed his card. It was the Queen of Diamonds.

'Arigato, Captain,' he said sadly.

The bellowing outside the cabin increased.

'Your friend appears to be afraid that you will sail with us and the money.'

Captain Huntington did not answer.

'You must sail with us,' the Commander said, 'or he will surely kill you. It is in his voice.'

'The only sporting thing to do,' the Captain said, 'is to let him have that chance.'

'Captain Huntington, I beg of you. If you will not sail with us let me have the launch to the offside of this ship so that you may use it as your screen for a few miles or so.'

'Thank you. But that wouldn't do, would it?' He stood up. He stared at the open case holding the dozens of packets of money he had lost – one million pounds he had lost – the only hope he had left; waste paper for which Bonnette and McHenry had murdered twenty-six men. Horror of himself filled his face.

Captain Huntington descended into the launch. The two seamen cast him off. The launch moved out across eighty yards of calm sea on which the two ships had drifted closer together.

Schute stared at the launch and bellowed through the bull horn. 'I don't see the money. Where is the money?'

The Captain stared up at him. 'Where are Bonnette and McHenry?' he shouted.

'They are dead,' Schute bellowed. 'I killed them.'

The Captain hadn't expected Gash to care about what Bonnette and McHenry had done. He had automatically considered that Gash would have written it all off as being none of his business. He was glad Gash had done it. He was glad they were dead.

'Damn you! Where is the money?' Schute yelled.

The Captain cut the launch's engine. He yelled at Schute, fifty feet over his head, 'I regret very much having to tell you this, Gash. But the fact is – you see, Gash – I have lost all the money gambling.'

'Gambling?' Schute could not comprehend what the Captain meant. The computers had mentioned nothing about gambling. 'What do you mean?' he said. 'How? Where?'

'It's no use, Gash. The money is gone, Gash. I lost all the money.'

'A million pounds?' the voice which boomed out of the bull horn was as crashing as the voice of Imamiah, the avenging angel in the cabala; the fallen angel who destroys and humiliates enemies. 'You lost a million pounds?' Slowly, tiny notes of realization spotted his voice and comprehension. 'You gambled with my money?' There was an excruciating pause. 'Are you saying you gambled with my money?'

'Regretfully, yes, Gash.'

Schute went berserk. He flung the bull horn away and sprang to find an arms locker. It wasn't there. This wasn't a naval vessel. His pistols! He raced back to the bridgehouse rail drawing a pistol from his pocket and aiming it.

The Captain held up his hand calmly. 'Not yet, Gash,' he shouted. 'You deserve more of a sporting chance than that.'

Schute hesitated.

'I gambled your money so it is only fair that I gamble whatever I have left – with you.'

'What the hell are you talking about?' Schute screamed down at him. 'What do you have left?'

The launch was close in to the side of the ship. The Captain stared up at the bridge. 'Only my life,' he said. 'This is how we will play the game.' His voice had regained full bounce. 'I will make two full turns in this launch around this ship, standing up behind this wheel. If you can kill me you will have won the bet. But – if you cannot hit me in two full turns I shall consider that we are even – more or less – and take this launch to shore.'

'You bastard!' Schute shrieked into the bull horn. 'You filthy bastard.'

He began to fire the Luger wildly. The Captain gunned the launch to make the first run around the ship. Schute raced across the ship to the port rail and fired downward steadily, not aiming carefully at all because he was in such a frenzy. He changed pistols then the launch raced around the stern of the ship and disappeared. Schute ran back to the starboard side, inserting fresh clips of bullets into the pistols. As he looked downward, sighting much more carefully he saw that from his vantage point the launch was running too close to the side of the *Bergquist Laura* to get a full shot at the Captain.

As the Captain swung the gig wide and turned it at the bow of the ferry, Schute ran down the interior ladder to the officers' quarters and sprinted along the corridor to the elevator. He punched the car deck level. The lift dropped rapidly. He came out of the elevator car running toward the prow of the ship. There he waited at the opened bow, breathing heavily with his pistol at ready, fifteen feet above the waterline, concealed from the Captain behind a bulkhead from which he would spring and fire as the gig made its run directly past him.

The sound of the approaching launch grew louder. The Captain was as rigid as marble as he stood behind the wheel in fright but he stood erect and steered the gig at an equitable distance away from the ship on a course which would put him ten feet away, with his head eight feet below the best marksman ever with the Pacific squadron of the Royal Navy.

As the gig came abreast of him Schute showed himself. With a terrible gasp, the Captain looked squarely into the muzzle of the Luger. He had been certain that he wanted to die for what he had caused and done but he discovered that he had been mistaken. He heard the deadly click of the pistol. Then a shot was fired from somewhere – a shot which had not come from the pistol which had been there pointing at him but which now was gone as Gash himself was suddenly gone – gone as if he had been made of paper and had blown away.

The Captain scrambled to grasp the rope ladder which the Japanese cargo master had left hanging from the prow, then the Captain climbed with the agility of a desperate, old sailor up the ladder to the car deck.

To his astonishment he found Gash dead with a large hole in his chest. Unable to understand how that had happened he looked around himself and the ship. Far off, one hundred and ten yards away he saw Commander Fujikawa standing on the bridge of the *Taka Maru*, holding a rifle with both hands over his head and grinning broadly. He thought of what Gash had told Bonnette, 'We are all navy here, you see. Not your sort of thing at all.' But at least Gash's death had had meaning. He had died for all that he had lived for; money.

'Arigato!' Captain Huntington shouted across the water to Commander Fujikawa. 'Arigato!' Fujikawa grinned, waved with both arms, then turned away. Almost immediately, the *Taka Maru* began to steam away building to full steam, and Captain Huntington was alone.

He had failed again but this time he knew he had failed so

far down at the bottom of human endeavour that there was no perilous path downward and no apparent way to climb back. Everyone else except the engine-room men he had brought along with him on this last voyage of failure seemed to be dead. He saw it almost as a matter of duty that he should now die.

He dislodged the Luger from Schute's fingers. He faced the fact that he could never have merited becoming Lord Glandore and he saw that he had never really possessed the courage or the honour to be called Captain Colin Huntington, Royal Navy.

He walked to the lift to be able to die on the bridge of a ship, the bridge of a car ferry for summer trippers. As he entered the bridge from the officers' quarters companionway he stumbled against the case which McHenry had been carrying around. He lifted it upon the chart table and opened it. It was piled with untidy stacks of used money, counted and marked, an unwholesome assortment of many kinds of jewelry and one rather stunning sapphire necklace which could have looked so marvellous on Yvonne. Sixty thousand pounds' worth, McHenry had said. A pity it wasn't his to give, he thought. He could have bought Rossenarra back from Bryson for sixty thousand pounds. Perhaps Daddy would buy it back, he thought bitterly and walked slowly to the desk in the radio room to kill himself.

He sat in the chair and examined the Luger with experienced eyes. He released the safety and cocked the pistol. He put the barrel into his mouth facing upward into his brains then he decided he would not want to be found in that messy way so he removed the barrel and jammed it emphatically into his temple when Francohogar came into the room, carrying an enormous tray and looking backward for the moment to see where he might have tripped and, greatly embarrassed to have been caught (almost caught) in such an act by a man who admired him as much as Francohogar did, Captain Huntington quickly dropped the Luger into the top drawer of the desk and shut the drawer.

'You refused lunch today,' Francohogar sang, 'so you must dine early tonight. I not only have a very, very good Margaux but – I am very, very happy to tell you – the ship's stores were kind enough to contain one plump, juicy capon so that I have been able to make for you tonight one of your favorites – the golden capon with potato mounds, and asparagus with lemon crumbs and I swear to you I think that this is authentic, genuine asparagus from Argenteuil, in the Seine-et-Oise, of which there is no better in the world.' While he described the dinner, Francohogar laid out the service on the desk in front of the Captain: silver, linen, glassware and condiments. 'But, to begin – aha! – the cream of broccoli soup, eh? And to follow the golden capon? Think of the salad you would most like to have. Yes, field greens and spinach with a lemon and shallot dressing then I have made a little almond and chocolate torte so that you may enjoy this rather less than distinguished demi-sec champagne and better.' He set a soup plate down in front of the Captain and slowly filled it with the thick soup. The Captain began to eat. He beamed at Francohogar. 'It may be, of course, that it tastes this especially good because I have eaten so little today,' he said, 'but I hardly think so. It is, I think, that you have the sort of greatness which urges you to grow and improve every day.'

'Thank you, sir. Thank you, Captain Huntington.'

The golden capon was a triumph, as was everything else and the Margaux was everything Francohogar had hinted it would be while the champagne was far, far better than he had mourned. When the meal was over and the desk was cleared and Francohogar had departed, the Captain felt marvellously fit – at the tip-top of his form. What a boob's idea suicide was, he thought. He opened the drawer, uncocked the pistol, withdrew the clip and dropped them both into the waste basket.

Francohogar popped his head back in. 'At what time do you think Monsieur Bonnette and Mr McHenry would like to dine, sir?' he said.

'Oh! I should have told you, Juan. They will not be dining with us tonight. They have departed.' Francohogar left for the kitchens.

He felt so marvellous that he decided to call Yvonne. He picked up the ready radio telephone and the call was moved through Portugal, across Spain, into France, thence to Charles Street in London. Yvonne answered immediately.

'Is that Yvonne?'

'Colin! You are all right?'

'Oh, splendid.' He poured champagne from the magnum in the ice bucket into his glass.

'Where are you?'

'I am aboard a deserted ship off the Portuguese coast. Everything was a total loss. I am done in. It is all over.'

'What are you talking about?'

'It all turned out so badly that I was thinking of killing myself.'

'Colin! Why? For money? Do you value your life less than money? Don't talk to me like this! Get out of there wherever you are and come home.'

'I can't really. You see, it isn't only the money I owe, darling, although that is a vastly forbidding scene. I – well, I've caused other things. The fact is – something very terrible has happened to your father.'

'My father? What has happened to my father?'

'He is dead. He was murdered by my friend, Gash Schute – and he deserved to be murdered.' The Captain's voice broke.

'Of course he deserved to be murdered. But this is wonderful. If he is dead, everything is solved! Everything is solved!' Her voice became almost hysterical.

'What?'

'If my father is dead I get one half of the money he has in two safe deposit vaults in Genève. It will be automatic. The police will find him and they will take his fingerprints and they will certify that he is dead and I will take that certification to the bank in Genève and we will take out two hundred thousand pounds so that you may pay back Bryson and your wonderful loving wife and stay out of prison.'

'Yvonne! Yvonne, darling!'

'When will you be here?'

'In the morning at latest. Before noon.'

'Hurry. Oh, please, hurry.'

Warmth and life filled him. He could return to London! How super! Why – he could even show his appreciation for what Yvonne was going to do for him by bringing her that adorable sapphire necklace in McHenry's case out there. Good heavens, there was enough money in that case to give them a marvellous holiday if there was going to be any delay in getting Bonnette's money. He had had an absolutely terrible run of bad luck but that was all over now – the law of averages proved that it was all over. Life was beginning.

His eyes filled with tears. He took up the radio telephone and called London again. It rang three times before she answered.

'Bitsy? Colin, here. Bitsy, darling everything has worked out just as I promised it would. My business arrangements have been wonderfully successful and I am going to be able to repay everything.' He laughed joyously. 'I'm coming home to you now, my darling. I am coming home.'

Francohogar and Chief Kullers had a certain amount of difficulty in negotiating the rope ladder from the prow into the launch but they made it satisfactorily and Captain Huntington had them ashore in twenty minutes where the hired cars were waiting to take them to the airfield.

As the chartered four seater jet headed north with Captain Huntington, his cook and his erstwhile chief engineer, toward Spain, the Breguet 1150 Atlantic flying out from the carrier *Clemenceau* off Morocco, sighted the *Bergquist Laura* and circled her at low altitude to confirm her identity. The radio officer of the plane notified the Spanish naval base at La Coruna.

Captain Huntington was simply a naturally lucky man.

More about Penguins and Pelicans

Penguinews, which appears every month, contains details of all the new books issued by Penguins as they are published. From time to time it is supplemented by *Penguins in Print*, which is a complete list of all titles available. (There are some five thousand of these.)

A specimen copy of *Penguinews* will be sent to you free on request. For a year's issues (including the complete lists) please send 30p if you live in the United Kingdom, or 60p if you live elsewhere. Just write to Dept EP, Penguin Books Ltd, Harmondsworth, Middlesex, enclosing a cheque or postal order, and your name will be added to the mailing list.

In the U.S.A.: For a complete list of books available from Penguin in the United States write to Dept CS, Penguin Books Inc., 7110 Ambassador Road, Baltimore, Maryland 21207.

In Canada: For a complete list of books available from Penguin in Canada write to Penguin Books Canada Ltd, 41 Steelcase Road West, Markham, Ontario L3R 1B4.

Richard Condon in Penguins

Mile High

Edward West could do anything.

Owned a string of whore-houses in which he entertained U.S. Senators.

Forced prohibition through Congress, giving himself the chance to make billions in bootlegging.

A friend of the head of the Mafia, invited to dinner by the Pope. Married a sweet-tempered girl of American-Irish aristocracy. Sadistically murdered a black mistress and had it covered up.

He could do anything except that thing he wanted to do most . . .

Mile High is not only a savage novel, it is a savage indictment of America.

Not for sale in the U.S.A. or Canada

Richard Condon in Penguins

The Oldest Confession

In *The Oldest Confession* the death of a supreme
bullfighter and the theft of a great Goya are themes
painted with dabs of cosmopolitan wit on
nightmare insights streaking through a wealth of
variations: an American senator with a taste for
pictures and palate for politics; Dr Munoz, vain,
proud, destructive, atavistic; Jack Tense, a London
gangster working as hard on his legend as at his
profession; a beautiful Duquesa ['By the time she
had found out about Bourne being a criminal he
could do nothing wrong']; and Jean Marie, a
genuine forger with a 'fantast's side'.

Richard Condon steals away disbelief with a precise
sense of what he can give back in a different
currency of verbal sophistication and excitement.

Not for Sale in the U.S.A. or Canada